take a chance of ever letting that happen again. With danger surrounding them, the men set out to give Storm a magical Halloween where nightmares are replaced with I dos, and Happy Ever Afters are real!

Imagine the Worlds of Magic, New Mexico... A series that brings together outstanding paranormal and science fiction authors to expand a town where witches, aliens, vampires, werewolves, goblins, sorceresses, pirates, time travelers, and paranormal live in harmony—when they aren't joining forces to defeat the bad guys. A magical town where being abnormal is the norm!

I'm S.E. Smith, the creator of Magic, New Mexico, and I invite you to curl up with each book now and discover all the action, the magic, and the love that makes Magic, New Mexico the ultimate go-to series for Paranormal/Science Fiction Romance readers.

For all the stories, go to MagicNewMexico.com/books/. Grab your copy today!

Loving Phoenix

Nava Torres' life was one of turmoil and danger. Considered a freak of nature by her peers and hunted by the government, she never expected to find a place where she could feel safe—until she heard about a town called Magic. For the first time since her parents' deaths, she felt awe, hope, and something even stranger—attraction to a man who could heat her blood with one look!

Special Ops Marine, Saxon Wehurst, had sworn off women—at least until he met a fiery redhead with black streaks that made him want to run his hands through the colorful tresses. There was nothing in the world that could fire up his protective instincts faster than a woman with trouble nipping at her heels and fire in her hair.

When outside forces threaten Nava and the town, Saxon and his men are more than ready to gear up to protect them both. For Saxon, it is personal—nothing stands between a Bull Dog and his mate—not even the government. Will Saxon and his men be able to protect the woman he loves and save the town, or will she be taken from him forever? Whatever happens, it is time to feel the burn...

Magic in His Touch

Imprisoned.

Elf's life was confined to the four walls of her prison. Nothing changed the dark horrors of her life. Her one attempt at freedom had nearly killed her. So, she existed—imprisoned within the only walls she had ever known.

Kayden Dresco knew since he was a teen what he wanted to do with his life. What he had not expected was to find Elf. Scarred, frightened, but defiant, this beautiful woman quickly became his world. Now, his biggest fear was if he could keep her safe.

Elf and Kayden had to find a way to escape before the Gifted Special Project claimed another victim. Can Elf find a way past the nightmares that hold her as much a prisoner as the four walls did, or will her fears destroy not only her, but Kayden as well?

Storm's Magic Halloween

Can they give her a magical Halloween?

Storm Lope is half pixie/half human and is known for her hot temper and her ability to hold a grudge. Storm learned to use both as self-defense to protect her fragile heart. Those defenses had worked well for her until she met two irritating men who refuse to be scared off.

Nolan Moree and Matty Draco vow to break through Storm's fiery walls. They almost lost her once. They weren't going to

Contents

Loving Phoenix
Little Angel Rescue, Book 1

Chapter One

Home, this is where Nava belonged. The tightness in her stomach and shoulders were gone. Ever since her parents were murdered, she had lived by the day. Always looking over her shoulder, scanning her surroundings when approaching anywhere new. Never believing in any tomorrows, but for some strange reason, this day was different as she walked through her first apartment. This city of Magic, the only place recently she felt safe enough to put down some solid roots. But then again, Nava was tired of running. This town would be her last stand.

She took a deep breath and smiled, looking out the sliding glass door of her balcony in her one-bedroom apartment. It was one of the main reasons Nava had taken the place. The view over the city was breathtaking; she couldn't wait to see it at night all lit up. She twirled around, feeling free for the first time in a long time. But first, she needed furniture, and Nava had spotted a thrift store right down the street. Grabbing her purse, Nava pulled out cash she had left after opening a checking account. With ten thousand in her new account, she had over two thousand in her purse and another ten thousand hidden in the bottom of her suitcase in case she needed to leave suddenly, all thanks to her parents.

With the special government group still searching for her, Nava had learned quickly how to survive. She didn't know if she would be safe here in this new place, but she sure hoped so. Because there was no way she was going back with them alive. One year with them, in their so-called dorm of gifted people, was enough for her. The first month there, she had it, but her parents hadn't been able to get her out until a year later. Something about a contract they had signed with the government, a mistake on their part. Then, they had changed their names and moved, but their sense of safe had come to an end ten years later when the GSP (Gifted Special Project) team appeared in their lives again.

Nava snorted. "Looking my ass, more like controlling." Nava reached into her purse, feeling the hard edge of the pistol she carried wherever she went. A cold chill ran up her spine thinking of the last time they had tried to take her back to the compound. If it hadn't been for the group of bikers hearing her screams, Nava would be locked up for good. Hence, the gun Flask had given her, showing her how to use it. Tears came to her eyes as she thought of Flask. He had saved her, and because of this, the GSP had killed him. Just as they had done to her parents but only when he had been alone.

A month later, she had finally made it there, to Magic. Buses and fake routes to throw them off her trail just in case some of them had discovered she had left the biker group. Nava only hoped the Knockers full assault on the GSP that wanted her would keep them busy for a long time to come. She was also lucky that the bikers' group didn't blame her for Flask's death. Instead, they had shown her how to cover her tracks and paid for her bus tickets, helping her escape. If she weren't safe here, she'd die because there was no way she ever going with them alive. A tool and a breeding woman for the children with gifts they hoped to breed with their idea of superior individuals. Nope, there was no way in hell anyone would take her.

"Thrift store, lunch and then the department store," she mumbled, closing and locking her door before heading down the stairs to the outside door to her apartment building. Nava would walk to the Mom's Things thrift store and to the diner Krazy Kettle. Nava smiled going down the stairs, loving the name of the diner. But, first, she needed to find a bed, furniture as soon as possible; she was tired of sleeping on the floor or ground.

Peeking through the door, Nava scanned outside. She didn't see any Blazers or Crown Victorias around, the two cars she normal saw the GSP in. Nava stepped outside and took a deep breath of the fall air. The weather was warm but not too hot, and there was a cool breeze that danced over her skin as she made her way down the street toward her first stop. In a pair of jeans and tank top, Nava took in the town of Magic, New Mexico. The streets were lined with flowering hanging baskets under the old fashion streetlights one would see in pictures in the fifties. The main road was done in old fashion red brick, not cement or blacktop like most streets. Storefronts were unique and drew you in every time you turned your attention to it, almost as it was casting a spell on you. Who knew, maybe there were spells on them, especially since this town was filled with others like her yet different. The town was called Magic, after all.

Not paying attention to where she was going, Nava ran straight into what she thought was a wall and would have fallen back onto the sidewalk, but a strong arm wrapped around her waist, stopping her fall. "Sorry about that," Nava said as her gaze traveled up and up to a man built like a tank truck but had a face like that of a Greek god. Never had she thought a shaved head would be hot, but on this man, it was deadly, literally.

Nava took a deep breath, moaning at the cologne the man was wearing and knew she was in deep trouble. The tingling started in her fingers and traveled up as she jumped out the man's arms, putting at least a foot between them, afraid she would hurt him. She could have fried the man, and that was not a great way to have the people of this town meet her. Her reaction to the man alone was confusing and freighting.

The fire inside her slowly simmered as she returned her gaze to the man in question. "Again, sorry; I should have been paying attention to where I was going. If you'll excuse me." She started to move around him, but he reached out and touched her arm, only to quickly snatch it back.

"Damn, you're hot? Are you okay? Do you need to see a doctor?" he asked and moaned, realizing his words. "I didn't mean it that way. I mean you're hot, but... Shit, shoot me now." He shook his head, his friends behind him smirking, and Nava couldn't help but smile.

"I understood what you meant but not to worry." She

looked down at the ground. "I know I'm not hot looking like your classic beauties." She rubbed her hands down her thighs, which were thicker than the norm. No, her body was not the perfect thing men seemed to want. "I should really get going if I want something to sleep on tonight." She once more tried to pivot around the hot group of men, groaning inside at her last comment. "something to sleep on." Jeez. Nava stopped and glanced next to her. Sure enough, the man was beside her, watching, his friends a few feet behind them.

"You are following me because?"

"It's not every day I run into a beautiful lady on the street. Plus, I am really worried about you." He bowed to her. "My name is Saxon, my friend to on the left behind is Kaylen. The one next to him, Prem and the other Tadi. We have lived here a few years and haven't seen you around."

"That's because you didn't." Nava tilted her head to the side and studied the man. She could see he was worried about her, but he also happened to be one of the most handsome men she had seen. Nada knew he was different when his eyes seemed to burn bright when he had touched her earlier, but what he was Nava had no idea.

She sighed. "Nava Torres," she said, looking down the road that she had walked coming into town. "I'm hoping to make this town my home, but we'll have to see." She looked back at him. "But either way, you don't want to get to know me, Saxon. The last person who tried was killed. Please, just stay away for your own sake and your friends'. At least 'til I know it's okay. Excuse me, I must really go." Nava once more continued walking down the street, almost sad the man still hadn't followed her, but she knew it was best. It was the only reason she had opened her mouth warning him.

Saxon stood there trying to control the inner demon in him as he watched his little fire walk away from him.

His military brothers moved to his side. "I'll call in the team, and we'll set up recon on her and her place. Congrats, Saxon. You are the first to find his light. No pun intended either."

"Find out about this threat. If you will excuse me, I have a mate to get to know," he told his friends while following behind the little bombshell. Now, all he had to do was come up with a reason why he was stalking her without scaring her off. Oh, he'd known she was armed; the scent of a firearm and the hard object connecting with his belly had alerted him.

Nava stopped in front of Mom's Things, looking up at the sign before glancing back at him, seeing him coming toward her. Saxon was pretty sure he just saw a puff of smoke come out of her mouth. *Is she a Dragon?* He knew for a fact that she wasn't a demon. They would have recognized each other if that was the case.

"You really want to be scorched? Because if you keep following me, I can't promise keeping you from getting burned. I mean harmed," she said as the local twins came running around the corner. It seemed that day was the day for everyone to run into each other, because as soon as his mate had said that, she was sitting on the sidewalk laughing. Both the boys not paying attention to where they were going had run right into her.

The boys stared at her then looked up at him as he reached down helping her up. "Boys, you know better than running on Main Street," he said, facing the town's little hel-

6

lions.

"Sorry, Saxon, lady, but he wanted to turn Elma into a mouse. I stopped him, and he's mad at me," one of the brothers said, and since Saxon always had a hard time remembering who was who, he shook his head. "No one should be turning anyone into anything. What have your folks told you? Didn't you just get ungrounded?" he asked, hearing about the last prank they had pulled on their teacher.

"How is Calamity Jane doing?" he asked the boys who looked down at the ground.

"Don't know; she won't talk to us. She's a little miffed. We said sorry, and Aunt Lacey has offered to help..."

"But she won't say anything to anyone," the other troublemaker said, finishing his brother's words.

"Wait, you brought back Calamity Jane, the one in the history books?" Nava asked, sounding really impressed.

"The teacher kept going on how bad she was, but we told her that she was a hero. I mean, you should see how she handles that gun, fast." Both boys nodded their head.

"Oh my," Nava said, giggling. "I bet your teacher was surprised."

Saxon leaned over and whispered. "She was thankful they weren't talking about Hitler at the time."

Nava's eyes got big, and she glanced back at the boys then at him. "They could do that?"

The boys giggled. "We could try..."

"NO!" Saxon yelled, making the boys jump. "Sorry, I didn't mean to yell, but remember what you were taught about that man?" Saxon tried to reason with the boys.

"Yes, please don't do that. The thought of that sick man running around..." She shivered running her hands up her arms.

Both boys shook their heads, promising they wouldn't, as they ran off as their mother yelled at them down Main Street from in front of their diner.

Nava shook her head as the door to the store opened up, and Ringo stepped out onto the sidewalk.

"Everything okay," he asked and looked down the street seeing the boys, moaning. "Please tell me they didn't do another spell."

Nava giggled next to him, and he smiled. "No, at least I hope not. But I think I'll have a talk with their father, just to make sure they don't try to bring Hitler back."

"What?" Ringo glared toward the boys in question. "I swear those boys are worse than any of us were when we were their age," he grumbled.

"Ha, that's what you say. Did you forget about the time you and your brother wanted to see the whale in Moby Dick?" his mother said, coming outside to join them. "Matter of fact, I think I still have the harpoon the two of you bought for it," she said, winking at them. "Hi, I'm Darla, 'Mom' of this establishment. Were you coming in to do some shopping?" she asked Nava, holding out her hand to Nava.

Nava placed her tiny hand on Darla's, smiling. "I love the story, and yes. I just rented an apartment here and have nothing in the means of furniture. I was hoping you might have at least a bed or something."

"So, you're new to town, how interesting," Ringo said, taking her hand next, raising it up and placing a kiss on her wrist.

"Watch it, Ringo?" Saxon growled, reaching up and pulling her hand away from him.

Ringo's smile grew. "The Bull Dog has found someone that interests him, oh what fun we are going to have."

"Stop it, Ringo, now." His mother pushed her son out of the way, wrapping her arm around Nava. "Don't you mind those two; they've been teasing each other for the past fifty years, I swear. If I'm not mistaken, I have this Dresden King in the back. I saw it and knew I had to have it for my store. Now, I know it was meant for you."

"Wait a minute, your son and Saxon are over fifty years old?" She looked at him then at Ringo. "Okay, what are you? Vampire, Fae?" she asked.

"Dear, that is a little rude, sort of asking your age thing," Ringo's mother said, patting her arm.

"Oh," Nava frowned. "Sorry, but it became a habit at the dorm when they put us all together..." She glanced up at him. "Sorry, didn't mean to be rude."

Saxon stepped forward and cupped her cheek. "I'm a demon, and I'm over five hundred years old. There is nothing for you to be sorry about. What are you?"

She looked down at the ground. "Nothing that exciting." She looked up, smiling, but it didn't reach her eyes. "I just, well, fire is my element. When I said you'd get burned, I meant it literally." She held out her hand, and a ball of fire hovered above it and then disappeared.

"Impressive and you are something, dear. Come, let me show you what I have. Saxon, I would have a word with you later, please," Darla said, escorting Nava toward the back of the warehouse.

"Okay, why has your mother become attached to my female?" Saxon asked Ringo as soon as they were out of ear range.

"Easy there, Bull Dog, and I have no idea," Ringo frowned. "Right now, I'm worried about Mother. She's holding on, smiling, but inside, I can feel rage and nervousness coming from her... Hell, Dad's here and so is Matty." Ringo turned as both moved into the store, searching. "She's with a customer right now," Ringo called out.

"Who?" was all his father asked, sending a shiver over him. Ringo's father, Darla's mate, was none other than the original vampire all the movies were made from, Dracula, and no one wanted him pissed off.

Ringo pointed to him. "Bull Dog's mate, it would seem. Even though I don't think she knows it?"

Saxon shook his head as Nava and Darla moved back toward the front.

"Ringo, have that bed and that adorable little table and chairs taken to Morris's old apartment. And for Pete sakes, make sure the boys set it up for her. She does not need to be up all night trying to set up the bed, especially since I know for a fact she wouldn't be able to lift one part of that bed." Her gaze turned to her mate. "I'm fine; we'll talk later."

"Yes, we will. Are you going to introduce me to this lovely lady?" Dracula asked, moving toward Saxon's mate, which made him nervous, and a small growl slipped out.

Without even turning around, the master said. "Relax,

Saxon, your little lady is safe with us. It would seem my woman has taken a personal interest in her. She is now family as far as I'm concerned." Dracula turned his head, smiling, his fangs showing. "Welcome to the family, son."

"You mean I have to have that ugly mug as a family member?" Matty frowned, but Saxon new he was teasing.

"Wait, what are you all talking about? I just met him, and why would you consider me family?" She shook her head and went to step away from Darla, but Darla was not about to let her slip away.

"GSP," Darla whispered, and at once, all the blood seemed to drain from Nava's face as she started to shake.

Saxon was at her side before Nava could form any thought, holding her in his arms. At first, she just stood there then Nava was shaking her head. "This can't be happening, how?" she asked, looking at Darla, who growled.

"I thought we took care of them," Darla looked to her mate who wrapped his arm around her, kissing the side of her face.

"It's obvious we didn't get them all. But now that we know they have started back up, we can finish this." He hugged Darla who was as truly upset, as was Nava.

Dracula turned to Nava, still holding on tight to Darla. "Tell me, Nava, where were you kept? Oh, and you can call me Drake, dear. I know why my mate has claimed you as her daughter. You see, she, too, was held by this group a while ago. They are not a government group though, Nava, as they have claimed. They are run by an extreme group of nutcases wanting to breed with us, creating a so-called superior race. It's where I found my Darla so many years ago."

"Really? You were held by them, too? Did they kill your parents?" Nava asked as a tear rolled down her cheek.

"Oh, child, I'm so sorry," Darla said and reached out, pulling her back into her arms, hugging her tight. "I was already an orphan when they found me. So that was a good thing." Darla pulled back and looked down at Nava. "How long have they been after you?"

"My parents got me out a year after they found out what this place was all about. We went into hiding for at least ten years, but then, six months ago, they found us. My parents didn't make it. I ran and made it to the next city, where they found me. But I was lucky the biker group Knockers heard me, but they weren't so lucky. One of theirs, Flash, was killed in the process of trying to protect me. They helped me finally come here. My mom had heard of this town and thought it would be safe for us here. I'm just sorry that we didn't make it here instead of settling somewhere else." Nava frowned and glanced at Darla. "Okay, what kind of spell did you put on me? Why am I telling you all of this?"

Saxon snorted. "Nava, they're vampires. When they ask a question, it's like you can't help but answer them, even I have trouble ignoring them," Saxon said, reaching out and taking her hand, needing to connect again with his woman.

"And when have you tried to resist us?" Drake asked him, giving him one of those looks.

"There are some things that shouldn't be shared," Saxon mumbled, feeling like a child in the presence of Drake, even though he was over five hundred years old, which was nothing to Drake. To this day, no one knew for certain hold old Drake was, not even his sons. "What do I need to know about this group?" Saxon asked.

Drake glanced down at his wife, and she nodded. "You know they'll put in an appearance since it's obvious they are chasing his mate." Darla cocked her head to the side. "There must be something else we are missing, too. Usually, they gave up after a year or two. You must be very special to them, Nava."

"Mate? Whose mate, and I have no idea why they are interested in me. As I said, the only thing I can do is the fire thing; well, and I can usually tell if someone is something else or other species, too." Nava glanced at him then at Darla.

"You're mine. I knew it when you ran into me back there on the street," Saxon said, waiting for her to freak out or deny it.

*N*ava stood there stunned, letting all that had been said sink into her head. Her world just flipped itself upside down. The only thing she could do right then was leave. She needed time to think, and what better way to do that than over a plate of hot food. Her stomach seemed to agree with her as it chose that time to make an embarrassing growl.

Reminding her she hadn't eaten since the afternoon the day before. "If you'll excuse me. Darla, I'll be home in the next two hours. I still need to hit a few places." She looked up at the woman. "Give me time to take this all in. We'll talk, I promise, but right now, all I want to do is settle in my own space." She glanced down at Saxon's hand twined with hers. It felt right inside, but could she allow him close to her knowing what the GSP would do to him if they got their hands on him. "You really shouldn't be close to me. As I said before, you'll get hurt." Nava met his gaze, and she knew. "You're not going to let go, are you?" she asked, raising their conjoined hands.

"Nope. Already have my team coming in; we'll be ready for this threat. What's the next stop?"

She shook her head and sighed, remembering what her mother had told her a long time ago. "Once you find the right one, you'll know. It's like your insides burn, your stomach will knot and thought of not seeing him again will bring tears to your eyes." Not bothering to look up at him, knowing he'd see the pain there, she muttered. "Fine, but if you get hurt…"

Behind her, the brothers snorted. "You don't know who you are dealing with, little sister. Trust your mate."

"He's not my mate yet," she grumbled but still holding onto his hand.

"Nava, why don't you and Saxon join us for dinner tomorrow night? I'm also going to invite the sheriff. He needs to know what to expect, to warn the others since this town is filled with people this crazy group would love to get hold of. Could you imagine them getting hold of the twins?"

Darla sucked in her breath, her hand going to her neck, but then, a slow smile formed on her lips. "But then again, think of all the damage they could do to the group."

Saxon snorted, and Drake shook his head. "No, with our luck, they would unleash the Crackling, and no one would be safe."

"Shhh, they'll hear you. I already need to speak with their parents. They heard me talking about Hitler earlier," Saxon grumbled.

"Oh, that would be bad. Has Calamity Jane shown herself yet?" Darla asked, walking them to the door.

"No, and that has all of us worried. She was furious at the twins when they brought her back, but seeing their faces and realizing how old they were, well, she didn't have the heart to kill the twins," Drake said, reaching out and touching Nava's arm. "I meant what I said. You need anything, you call us. You are family now, Nava, and we protect our family."

"Thank you. It's so weird. Since I stepped into this town, it was as if I was coming home. You want to know something else that is weird?" she asked, looking up at the man who was Darla's husband. "Mom used to tell me stories about Calamity Jane. Mom was heavy into genealogy, trying to find out where my so-called gifts come from, and she swore there was a link between us." Nava shrugged. "It was fun believing it. When I was locked up in that place, I'd dream Jane would come shooting her way in to free me, and Mom would be right behind her. A little déjà vu, no?"

Darla glanced at her husband. "Do you think?" she asked.

"I'm sure we'll find out soon enough when Jane decides to show herself again, but if what you say is true, be expecting a visit from her. Now, go take your mate to the dinner before she falls over with hunger. I'll have the boys take over the furniture and install it, and don't worry we know the owner, he'll help set it up for you," Drake said, opening the door for them.

Once outside, Nava took a deep breath and again scanned her surrounding, making sure there was nothing around when she noticed Saxon's friends coming down the street with a few other men. She shook her head. "You talk with your friends; I'm going to the diner." She went to step forward when Saxon wrapped his arm around her, stopping her.

"We'll go there in a minute. Let me just give them some orders; it won't take me long, okay?" he asked, kind of.

"Five minutes, I have plans for this day all lined up."

"Why do I get the feeling you are one of those planner people who have her life scheduled by the minute," he teased her.

She laughed. "Because I do. If you are lucky, I'll show you my planner," she told him as his friend move around them.

"Report," he said, smiling down at her.

"The rest of the team will be here by tonight. Her place has been secured; we've added extra protection to the doors and windows, and the Adams sisters will be over tonight and cover the whole apartment building, also," Kaylen reported, looking from Saxon to Nava.

"Good. It would also appear that Darla has formed a bond with Nava. I have added protection from her new family," Saxon announced, earning whistles from all of his friends.

"Damn, even we know not to mess with the master. Kind of feel sorry for those that might show up," Tadi said. "So, we heading to the diner?"

"We are, you aren't. Kaylen, will you bring my car around and park it in the front. I have a feeling my mate needs to go somewhere else after I feed her?" he asked, and she nodded her head.

"But I can take a cab just as I planned to do. I have major shopping to do there." She smiled and pulled out a long list. "I even made a nice list, so I wouldn't forget all the things I need."

She laughed hearing Saxon groan.

"And she likes lists. I'm doomed." He groaned again.

"But you like lists," Jonah said, as he and his twin squeezed into the middle of the circle of his friends with his brother.

"You, little wolf, shouldn't be butting into other's business." He went to grab to the little boy, and the boy squealed, ducking away from Saxon, laughing and teasing him.

The boys giggled, running around the group of them teasing Saxon, which only made his mate laugh. "Okay, you two, off with you. I need to take my woman to eat before she falls over. Her stomach is yelling at everyone here, saying feed me." He once more wrapped his arm around Nava and escorted her across the street toward the diner.

Joseph moved up to Nava's side, staring at her. "You'll be a good addition to our town." Joseph's eyes got big. "Oh my, you're family to Jane!" the boy said, looking from Saxon to her.

Nava stopped in the middle of the street, frowning. "Okay, now, how does he know this?"

Saxon moved them to the other side of the street and gave the boys a look. "Go and make sure your aunts are meeting us later at Nava's apartment." Saxon gave them a job just to give them something to do. Turning Nava to face him, Saxon stared down at the beauty in his arms. "You aren't protesting my claims, and for a human, you are taking all of this very well."

"I'm not accepting the mate thing, we'll see on that. But I've heard of mates and others from my mother and father. Now, if you are coming with me, let's get moving. I'm behind schedule," Nava said, smiling up at him. "And if I'm correct, you hate to be behind on things."

He couldn't help it, Saxon threw his head back, laughing. People stopped and smiled at them as his men dispersed, except for two of them following, watching their backs. "Then, by all means, my woman, let's get some food and move on." Saxon opened the door to the Krazy Kettle, and at once, Susanna looked up, meeting his gaze, smiling as if she already knew he'd found his mate. Still to this day, Saxon couldn't figure out what the woman was, but one thing he did know, she could cook up a storm. Her homemade food was a highlight of his evening.

"You're going to love the food here. Susanna is one of the

best cooks around, and her empathic ability to know what you are craving before you do is amazing," he told Nava as they were ushered to a corner table looking outside by one of the many pixies that floated around along with carts carrying food. Pulling out Nava's chair, Saxon could see the diner had Nava's full attention by the expressions on her face.

"My god, this place is amazing. It's right out of a fantasy book." She leaned over as he sat down next to her. "I wonder what food we will be sent?" she teased and he smiled.

"Wait and see, but I'm afraid they can't give me what I want." He held her gaze; the color of her skin turned a slight pink color, and she looked down.

"Saxon, we just met, slow down, please," she said, looking up at him quickly before two glasses of water, coffee and cream were placed on their table.

"I take it you wanted coffee and cream?" Saxon asked.

She smiled, reaching over and fixing her coffee. "Yep, haven't had any all day." She moaned, taking a drink of the nasty stuff.

"Never understood how anyone can drink that stuff; it's nasty," he said and took a drink of his water as two dishes of appetizers were laid down on their table. "Excellent, I think you will love these. My team and I come in here for lunch just for these. The cheese balls and potato skins are top notch, along with the stuffed mushrooms. Eat some," he said, popping a mushroom into his mouth and pushing the plate between them.

Nava stared at the plate, sighing. "I wish I could, but I'm allergic to mushrooms." She grinned. "Guess that means you won't be kissing me for a while." Nava teased, taking one of the cheese balls and popping it in her mouth.

At once, the mushrooms disappeared, and Saxon downed her water and his. "I'll brush my teeth and mouth. You're not getting away from me that quick," he grumbled as another two glasses of water with lemon showed up as if the owner of the establishment knew what had happened.

Chapter Four

ever had she seen so much going on in a small place. Even at the so-called school, she had been held captive, nothing could compare to this. Pixies, who knew there were actual pixies, not to mention other beings all around her. Yes, Nava was finally at a place she could relax. She peeked back at the muscular, more solid man sitting next to her and smiled as he drank down the water.

The man was tall, muscular but not to a point it was gross. His skin had a reddish tone to it. When in the sun, you could hardly notice, and his eyes were black as the night, which was very unusual but cool. Nava swore that when he turned his gaze on her, flames danced in his eyes. Nava was told hers did the same when she was furious.

"You're staring at me," Saxon said, lifting up a cheese ball to her lips.

She took the cheese ball from his fingers, finding it sexy that he was trying to feed her. "Do you really believe that I'm your chosen one? I don't know anything about your kind. How does this work? Do I have to become one of you?" she asked, taking a bite of the potato skin, he held it up to her.

He popped the other half of it into his mouth. "There are some signs of our kind that let us know our chosen one is close. For example, just your scent alone lets me know you are mine. Never has anything affected me the way you do." He leaned down and whispered, "The things I want to do to you right now... Your scent is like catnip to me. My cock has been hard since you bumped into me earlier." He kissed her cheek and smiled as their main course meals arrived, floating to them.

With her face now pink, embracement was her new thing

she'd have to get used to in this town. Nava smiled down at the ribeye steak in front of her. With twice-baked potatoes and green bean casserole, she was a very happy woman. "I think I may never cook again," she moaned. Taking a bite of her steak, she glanced at Saxon who just stared at her. "What? Do I have something on me?"

She grabbed her napkin and wiped at her mouth as he shook his head. "You, my pretty fire ball, are trouble," he grumbled.

"What did I do?" she asked again, frowning but digging into her potatoes when Saxon's hand covered her mouth as he leaned over. "If you moan again, I'm going to drag your cute ass out of here and give you something to moan about."

"Oh, please. I'm just enjoying my food..." Nava pushed his hand away and stared at the two brown Crown Victorias that rolled down Main Street slowly, searching. Her heart, now in her stomach, tears filled her eyes as her fork dropped against the plate. Her worst fears had followed her. She hadn't even unpacked yet, and they were here looking for her. It would seem the Knockers hadn't stopped them after all.

"What?" Saxon grabbed onto her hand, scaring the shit out of her. She jumped up; her chair went crashing to the floor. "Easy, Nava." Saxon instantly moved to her and pulled her into his arms. "No one is going to hurt you," he told her, following her gaze, now seeing what she did.

Nava slowly glanced around the little diner, noticing that everyone had stopped doing what they were doing, watching her when the door opened with a thud as it flew against the wall, drawing everyone's attention away from her.

Darla and Drake, with two of their sons, stood there looking around the room until they spotted them. Drake followed Darla across the room as she rushed to her side. Behind them, the sheriff came in followed by what had to be some kind of old western posse, one you would see in an old western movie, but there was one problem. They were all ghosts. She looked up at Saxon, and he smiled.

"Part of the cavalry has arrived. That is the first sheriff of Magic so long ago and his posse. They can go anywhere. Plus, our town sheriff now, Theo. Think Dragon," he pointed out to her, easing some of her worries as Saxon pulled up her chair. "Come on, sit. There is no sense in you missing your dinner. We can speak to them to figure out our next move while you eat," Saxon said as their table grew larger and chairs were added automatically.

"I knew they'd be on your tail, but do not worry; it will end here," Darla said, taking a seat next to her after giving her a hug. "Nava, this is Sheriff Theo, who's sitting next to Drake, and Sheriff Buchanan and his men are the ones moving around us. They like to help when things get a little difficult. Plus, your man there has at least five, maybe six men in here?" she asked, eyeing him.

"They have already set up watches. We'll know when they move, and your apartment is safe."

Darla frowned and looked around. "Topper, where are you?" Darla asked.

Nava would have jumped if she wasn't staring at the woman with the rainbow-colored hair, an older lady, that appeared next to them.

"Sorry, I'm late. I keep telling my family to watch those two little troublemakers. Mrs. Fitzpatrick wants to kill them personally. I have no idea what is going on, but she has been causing all sorts of commotion for the last two nights." Topper sat down on a seat that appeared out of nowhere.

"I'll go out and talk to her after this mess is taken care of. Did you happen to find out how big of a group we are dealing with?" Darla asked.

Nava squirmed in her seat as Topper stared at her. "You know your hair would look great with more red in it, and yes. It's not good. Over the years, this group has grown. We're looking at, at least, three hundred staff alone in the buildings they own, and it's heavily secured. We're talking about over three acres of property alone, not to mention the idiots they have following your lady here. They have to have some trackers on her because they knew right where she was going."

"What? I got rid of everything I owned a long time ago." Nava frowned.

"Sweetie, did they ever knock you out or did you have any kind of surgery?" Drake asked.

"What? Well, shit." Nava thought she was going to be sick. All this time they had known where she was. "But why did they wait ten years to come after me?" She said. "And kill my parents?" Nava stared down at her arm where the small scar was.

"Most likely your gifts didn't develop fully 'til you were older. Plus, they can't breed you if you aren't old enough," Drake said, coming around to her seat and knelt before her. "Do you mind if I remove this?" he asked.

"But what if there are more, somewhere I don't know about?" Nava asked as a cold chill settled over her. She didn't move. Something or someone was inside her. Nava shivered as the chill disappeared.

"My granddaughter has two metal things in her. The one you will not go near. You are not her mate, and even him," Calamity Jane herself appeared near Saxon. "I will be watching to make sure he doesn't do anything funny until they are married or mated." The woman held what looked like a shotgun pointed at Saxon.

"I really wish you wouldn't point that thing at him," she snapped at the woman, knowing her eyes and hair had changed as tiny bits of smoke came out of her mouth.

The lady standing next to Saxon laughed. "You are my granddaughter, that is for sure. You have the same fiery temper my father had, god rest his soul. Not to worry, granddaughter, I won't harm your man if he behaves. I mean, I can't have a man take advantage of you since you're still a virgin," the woman said as all eyes turned toward her.

"Okay, let the ground open up and take me away," she muttered, stuffing a bit of potato in her mouth before pointing her fork at the ghost lady. "You didn't have to announce that to everyone here," she grumbled. "That's kind of private, you know?"

"Why are you embarrassed; that is a good thing. I'm proud to call you family. In my day, I had no choice giving away something so special, raising my brothers and sisters," Jane looked off to the side.

"Um, can we get back to the issue at hand?" Saxon said, all the while his gaze never left Nava's. Nava swore he was breathing heavier, too. "Where is said—" he stopped what he was going to say, frowning and looking at her distant relative. "Show me how we remove these devices, Drake," he said, standing over Drake.

"I'm sorry, little fire, this is going to hurt," Drake said as his fingernail grew long, but Topper reached over and grabbed his hand. "That is totally barbaric, and there is no reason for her to suffer." Topper opened her other hand, and there in her hand were two small transmitters. "Now, if we are going to free those children, we need to do something with those idiots out there, so they don't hinder our mission and know we are planning an attack." Topper reached over and popped one of the cheese balls into her mouth. "Love these things."

"You are not doing anything." A man moved into the diner, scanning the room before he moved toward them. He was different, but Nava couldn't figure out what it was. His ice blue eyes were stunning, and the tan skin, well if Saxon wasn't her mate and he hadn't been taken...

"He's alien and nephew to Topper," Saxon whispered in her ear for her before placing a kiss on the side of her neck. "Stop drooling over him," Saxon growled.

Frost's lip curled up a little as if he heard Saxon and nodded to him and Drake before turning to Topper. "Your family is all furious. Do you know how risky it was for you to go to that place and alone?"

Nava glanced at Saxon and Drake, noticing the smiles on their faces, while Frost glared at the small woman who waved her hand. "Please, do you really think those peons could hurt us? But tell my family I'll be there soon. Now, go back to your cold world while I show these men what I learned," Topper said as she started pointing out things, as space was made available for a map that appeared on it.

Nava leaned over, staring at the map. "They've added a lot, too, since I've been there. Here and here are all new buildings. Our dorm was here, the boys here," Nava pointed out before leaning over and giving the crazy old lady a kiss on her cheek. "He's right. You shouldn't underestimate these men. Look, they slipped right through the Knockers."

Nava stopped, tilting her head to the side listening before turning her smile on Saxon. "Guess we've got more backup coming. The Knockers are here." Nava got up and moved toward the door, but Drake and Saxon blocked her path.

"You are staying right here while we make sure these men leave our town, young lady," Drake said.

"I am old enough here to decide what I do with my own life. These men helped me get here. I have to let them know I'm okay," she said and tried to step around the men, but they didn't budge. "Damn it, move," she said, stomping her foot.

"Not to worry, granddaughter," Calamity Jane said, floating up next to her. "I'll inform them you are here. Go eat your dinner before it goes to waste." Her grandmother disappeared through the wall before she could stop her. "That might be a problem, folks. I don't know if the Knockers know about others." She looked behind her at the sheriff and then at Saxon.

"Well then, they are in for a rude awaking because it looks like the twins are following this group of yours, too." Topper moaned and disappeared from the room.

"I so need to learn to do that," Nava muttered.

"No," Drake and Saxon said together.

She turned her full attention on the men in front of her, going to give them a piece of her mind.

Chapter Five

Saxon watched the fire enter her eyes, and he smiled. His woman was furious, but he wasn't about to let her go walking outside with the threat out there, and it would seem he wasn't the only one. Drake seemed to be taking the father role very seriously as he scooped up a shocked Nava and carried her back to her seat.

"Sit and eat. Your friends will be here in few minutes, but you need to feed that grumbly stomach of yours," Drake ordered.

Nava opened her mouth then shut it. "Stubborn men," she grumbled and put a bite of steak in her mouth. "I just don't want to start trouble. You have no right to tell me what to do."

Drake leaned down, and Saxon swore his nose was touching hers. "Actually, I do. You see that woman sitting next to you?" he asked, pointing to his wife, but didn't wait for an answer. "She's already marked you; you're part of our family, my daughter."

"What exactly does this entail? Why would you do this?" She leaned over and stared at Darla, who sighed.

"You reminded me so much of myself when we were going through the warehouse looking at the furniture, and then I saw..." Darla looked down at her hands. "I'm sorry. I usually don't pry, but when I saw that group in your head and what they did to you, it brought up such bad memories, I couldn't let you face it alone." She lifted her head, a single blood tear rolled down her cheek. "I knew you were meant to be part of our family. I kind of, well I..."

"What my wife is saying, she took a little bit of your blood and gave you hers." Drake reached over and cupped his

23

wife's cheek. "My wife has wanted a daughter to share every-thing with, but with six boys, well you are her choice and mine."

"You gave me blood? Am I going to turn?" she squeaked, and Saxon laughed.

"No, sweetie. The only way you can turn is if they suck you dry and replace your blood with theirs, but they don't have to do that. You will live my life. My kind is immortal, but that wouldn't even matter since we will live here in town where anyone who lives here is immortal."

"Immortal? Why do I get the feeling I fell down a well or something? So back to this bonding thing. I'm really con-nected to you?" she asked.

"*Yes, you are our daughter,*" Drake said in her head.

She twisted in her chair and looked up at Drake. "How did you do that? I had a friend who could talk in my head, but we... She did it, too?"

"What are you talking about," Darla asked. "Someone else took your blood?" She sounded worried, and even Saxon didn't like that.

"Who?" Saxon asked, taking his seat next to her.

"Why are you so worried? If it weren't for Elf, I wouldn't be here." She waved her fork in the air. "I tried to escape one night; they caught me," she shivered. "They have what you would consider at a prison, the hole, but with this hole..."

"It's surrounded by your worst fears. Mine was snakes," Darla said.

"Mine was spiders, but what they didn't count on was the fact there were a few that had actually bit me, and I hap-pened to be allergic or had a bad reaction. If it weren't for our bond, Elf's and mine, well I would have been dead. She knew I was dying and got some of the staff we could trust to help get me out of the hole." Nava looked down at her arm. "Maybe that is when they put the things in me, I was so out of it."

"Where is this Elf now? Did she escape with you?" Drake asked.

Nava looked up at Drake, and Saxon knew at that minute it wasn't good. Tears were in her eyes as she shook her head.

"No, they caught her, shot her. I don't know what happened to her. It's the one thing I regret the most. She's been with them all her life. Born there."

Needing to hold his mate, Saxon pushed Drake aside and lifted Nava, sitting in her seat with her on his lap. "I'm sorry for your friend, but maybe, she's okay. If she is like Drake and Darla, a bullet won't do too much damage. Have you tried to contact her through your link?" he asked, looking around the diner and noticed a number of the families had left, knowing something was going to happen. He would have to make sure Susanna was compensated for this disturbance in her business.

He rubbed his chin on the top of her head when Nava tilted her head to the side. "How do I do that? She was the one that always contacted me?"

Darla reached over, placing her hand on Nava's arm. "Close your eyes, take a deep breath, and go back, search for that old link that you had with your friend. It's there; all you have to do is find it. If she is living, you'll be able to contact her if she is like us," Darla said. "But, Nava, I'm not going to lie, I'm going to be listening. I want to make sure this woman is true to you and won't hurt you."

Saxon felt Nava's body tense up before she spoke. "But she wouldn't do that?"

"Little fire, sometimes under dire circumstances, people do things that they shouldn't. As far as we see now, she saved you by your words, but if she survived, where do you think she's been all these years? Remember their purpose, this group," Saxon told her, rubbing her arms.

Not saying a word, Saxon watched as Nava closed her eyes, taking a deep breath. Darla nodded to him, letting him know she was with Nava as his little fire ball searched for her friend. For several minutes, there was nothing, but then, Nava gasped, tears started to roll down her cheeks.

"I didn't know, Elf," Nava whispered, opening her eyes. "We have to help her. She's still there. Three children, they took from her, they..."

Drake growled and stood up, starting to pace when he stopped, turning to the door, where several of the bikers pushed open the door to the diner, stepping inside. "It seems you were wrong, Nava. Your friends are indeed like us." Drake said, moving around the table as Saxon stood to put Nava back in her seat, going to join Drake and the sheriff, but Nava beat him to the door, running to one of the men.

The guy in question caught Saxon's mate, lifting her up, hugging her. "You are okay? They didn't hurt you?" he asked, his gaze never leaving Drake's.

Saxon reached out and grabbed onto Nava, pulling her back into his arms, not liking the hold this man had on his mate.

"Nava, are you okay?" the stranger asked, finally breaking his gaze to stare at Saxon's woman.

"I'm fine. Knock it off, Saxon. I told you they were friends. If it weren't for them, I wouldn't be here, remember? You wouldn't be holding your mate thing," she said, rolling her eyes.

He leaned down and nipped her nose. "Your friends are like us, little fire. If I'm not mistaken, this one here is like Drake?"

Drake nodded but never took his eyes off the man in question. The man turned to glance at Drake, hissing. "I'm sorry, sir. I didn't know." The biker dude bowed his head to Drake.

"Better, now introduce yourselves, please, quickly. We need to get this situation under control here before we can rescue my daughter's friends," Drake said, looking down at Nava.

"Your daughter, well hell. I'm Landon Comey, President of Knockers. We had heard of this city but really didn't believe in it 'til Nava shared her knowledge with us. We had planned to come here, but when these people attacked our friend, killing him... He'd sworn to protect Nava and made us promise to keep her safe. He had seen her life and knew she needed to be here. Matter of fact, if I'm not mistaken, Flask should be here."

"What? Really? Grandma?" Nava called out, and Jane appeared next to them.

"Yes, your friend is here," Calamity Jane leaned down and whispered. "I have to admit this Flask is impressive. Him and the sheriff, but too bad the sheriff is taken by the widow. Didn't know he was taken really," Jane said.

"Grandmother, what did you do?" Nava moaned.

"Your grandmother is Calamity Jane?" Landon asked, distracting her.

Nava smiled. "Seems so, I just found out about an hour ago." Nava looked up at Drake. "I think we know why that woman was so mad. And, Flask, you better be nice to my grandma," she said, earning snorts from Landon and his men.

"We need to discuss this situation now. We have company coming," Saxon said, lifting Nava up and moving to the back of the diner where Susanna and a few other females were. "I want you to stay here with Susanna and Darla," Saxon said as Drake set Darla down next to his woman.

Two men of Drake's moved into the room, going to the outside door where the deliveries came in. "All of you stay here, and you two make sure no one gets through that door," Drake ordered, earning a wave of her hand.

"Go do all your warrior stuff while I speak with my daughter. But you might want to watch Jane, she's itching to hurt some of those men, and we need at least one of them alive if we are going to get into that place." Darla hooked her arm into Nava's. "And yes, I'm going. The women are going to need us, so don't think about cutting me out of this."

"Behave," was all Drake said as he turned, leaving the room.

One more quick look at his woman, Saxon turned, but her small hand on his back had him stopping and looking back at her.

"Be safe, Saxon. If this mate stuff is true, I can't lose you."

"I'm going to have to show you how true it is later. You take care, little fire," he said, leaning down and placing a quick kiss on her lips.

With a few quick steps, he was back in the main room filled with men. His, the bikers, and others from the town, including the posse who floated around taking everything in. All eyes turned to him. "Kaylen, tell us where they're at, and Ms. Jane, be careful," he said, earning a snort from her.

"Don't worry about me, boy, I'll be fine," Jane rubbed her hand over her shotgun.

"Yes, she'll be fine," a man appeared behind her, slapping what appeared to be handcuffs to her wrist. "Because she's not going to do anything," he growled, binding her arms. Members of the posse watched, smiling and nodding. It seemed his mate's grandma had been busy after all.

"Let me go. Just wait 'til I get free, you overstuffed deputy," she yelled, trying to get free as another man, who appeared to be wearing the vest of the Knockers, grabbed her shotgun.

"Relax, little lady, we'll take care of you when we're done protecting your granddaughter. Take her to her room; we'll deal with her later." The man turned and stared at Saxon. "You will be good for our girl. I suggest we get moving. They've figured out Nava is in here; don't ask me how. I have a feeling there is someone in this town that has contact with this group. Maybe even been here a while scooping out the town itself."

"Never!" Theo snarled, a small puff of smoke rising out of his nose. "I want everyone on alert. Keep their children close to home 'til we find out what is going on," the new sheriff ordered.

"We'll figure it out later," Saxon said and moved to the map where Kaylen pointed out the men's positions and what they had for weapons. Are they all human?" he asked, and Kaylen shook his head.

"Most are human, but some of them are other, and they also have gifts, so be careful," Kaylen announced.

A bright flash filled the room along with the sound of thunder that shook the walls of the establishment. Saxon hit the floor with everyone else expecting an attack, but as he turned toward the back of the diner, his heart seemed to stop beating at the damage he could see. Immense heat rushed over him as he jumped up, moving toward the back of what used to be the back of the diner, where he had just left his woman. Dread filled him as he and the others rushed toward the back. Not caring what or who was back there, Saxon released the beast inside, shifting. His skin was now red and tough for the battle that was about to come.

Drake's scream filled the air, as all of his sons burst into the room running with him. Darla had been hurt, his mate...

Chapter Six

One minute Nava had been taking to Darla, the next, every nerve and muscle in her was doing the funky chicken inside her. Pushing Susanna and the help next to the freezer, Nava stepped in front of Darla, since she refused to hide. The stupid, stubborn woman was bound and determined to try and protect her. It was weird how quickly this woman and her husband had a place in her heart, and she sure wasn't about to let anything happen to her, but even Nava couldn't stop over thirty darts flying at them through the windows.

The burn was on. How dare they attack these innocent people, hurting them? But then go further by shooting their stupid dart guns at Darla, and that was the last straw. Her skin heated, her vision changed as fireballs formed in her hands as she started throwing them at the men that had broken into the back room. Nothing mattered but giving the men time to get back there to help them. Already the two men that Drake had left were dead, gunshots to the head it would appear to the small holes in their heads as they lay on the ground.

She would not let them take her new family. Nava fought the drug that was now going through her system, trying to give them time, knowing the men were coming. With a thud, Darla fell beside her. Susanna and three of her workers hid in the walk-in freezer as Nava placed herself in front of a sleeping Darla. They wouldn't touch the woman as far as she was concerned.

But the question in her head was forefront. Who the hell knew they were in the back and had squealed on her? *"I really can't hold on here, Saxon, if you can hear me..."* Nava yelled in her head, hoping there was a chance that through

30

the mate thing he would be able to hear her. "But hell, you would think the back of the diner burning..." The door behind her came flying off its hinges as it flew toward the three men that had stormed into the hole that had been created by her first fiery blast. "Saxon?" she questioned, not wanting to take her eyes off the enemy.

"I'm here, little fire," he said, wrapping his thick, red arms around her as others stormed into the tiny room from the hole in the wall behind them.

"I'm tired, Saxon. Make sure, Darla..."

"I've got you, little fire," she heard before the lights went dark.

* * * *

Saxon swung his woman up in his arms as Drake did the same. "I want one of them alive," Drake ordered as Saxon moved into the main part of the diner.

"We need a doctor. We have no idea what they put in those darts," Saxon growled.

"He's on the way," Kaylen said, coming in with one of the men hogtied, dragging him behind him as the doctor for their kind appeared in the room.

"What do we have?" Doc Lope said as he shifted from his wolf form, moving right to Darla, pulling out the dart and sniffing it. "Fuck, Thiopental. Your mate will be out for the rest of the day by the number of the darts in her body. She'll be very hungry, and well, you will be busy for a while. Think of the mating heat of a demon." The doc turned his gaze on Saxon and moved to Nava next.

"I see at least three darts, and she was the one standing?" the doctor asked, removing her darts, throwing them on the table next to her. "Something isn't right. She should have hit the floor first if she is human. Saxon, I'm going to shift. I want you to bring her down to me. I need to scent her to find out what is going on," he said, and Saxon nodded.

Carefully lowering Nava down, Doc Lope shifted and walked around them, sniffing. After a few minutes, bones popped, and the doctor shook his head. "We have a problem here," he looked at the sheriff. "I scent two different forms, a Golem, which would explain why it took three darts, but her other form has me worried. It also explains the fire; we have a Phoenix here. I only heard of one family long ago, but the rumors were they'd been killed off." The doctor looked over at Drake, who sighed.

"By my kind. I had just gone down for my deep sleep when this went down. Believe me, the men who did this were dealt with." Drake glanced at him. "It's good she is my daughter now. But guard her well." Drake glanced at the sheriff. "You might want to inform the town. This could also bring more people here once they hear about her. It's most likely the reason why they haven't given up on her after all these years. After all, a true Phoenix has amazing gifts and love to give to all around her. It's no wonder my woman was drawn to her."

Saxon hugged his woman tight. "How long on the drugs for her?" he asked.

"She should wake in a couple of hours, I think. The drug won't affect her like Darla here, but she'll be confused when she awakes. I'd like to be called when she starts to wake, so I can make sure everything is okay. Now, I'm off, Ms. Merk is about to deliver her triplets. Looks like the boys will have some company," the wolf said as he shifted, taking off.

Kaylen moved up to Saxon's side. "All the men have been taken care of. The posse has rounded up the last of the men, and they are in the jailhouse now. Three of them are dead; no one was hurt but them. Are you taking her to her place?" Kaylen asked.

"No, I want her moved to my home, and yes, you are welcome there, too, Saxon. But if we have a traitor here in the city, my home will be the best to defend than your home or hers," Drake said, moving to the door with his wife in his arms as his sons followed. "Ringo, make sure the west wing is ready for your sister. Matty, go gather her belongings and bring them to the house. Until this is over, Saxon and your sister will be staying with us." Drake gave him a stare, waiting to see if he would object.

"I'm right behind you. Kaylen, go to my apartment and pack a bag for me. A team bag will be fine for now," Saxon said, knowing Kaylen knew he wanted his weapons now, too. He stopped at the door to the diner and looked around him. "Sheriff, all the repairs are on me. Make sure only the best supplies are used."

"Don't worry about it. We'll take care of Susanna," Topper said, appearing with Lacey and her sisters. "Also, you should bring her by Lacey's, there is a special pup there that is waiting for her."

Saxon nodded, following Drake out the door to the waiting limo. His little fire ball wasn't going to be happy about moving into Drake's, but Drake was right. His home was like a fortress and well protected. She'd be able to move around the home, not having to worry about who was after her.

"So, you have any idea who the traitor is?" Saxon asked as they pulled away from the curb.

"No, and that has me worried. The only thing I can think of is someone followed Darla here, which was a while ago. But it still does not make sense since why risk yourself now after so many years?" Drake said, brushing his mate's hair out of her face.

"I think we need a more personal approach to this. To dig deeper into those that came here to extract our women. Because it's obvious they were not only going to take Nava..." Saxon looked up at Drake. "But Darla, too. Otherwise, they would have just shot her and killed her as they did the guards." Saxon watched as Drake's eyes flashed red and black.

"Agreed, and as soon as I get this one home safe in her bed, I will personally be visiting those we have captured. It's time to get to know their plans for Nava and our town since it's obvious they know all about it. They have attacked the wrong family," Drake said and glanced out the window.

"Dad, really?" Ringo yelled from the front of the limo. "Do you know the frenzy this will bring?" Ringo met Saxon's gaze. "He's called all our people on this one, from everywhere."

"What? You think this is wise?" Saxon asked, knowing it would cause a stir around the world.

"Not only have they attacked my family, but if they capture your woman and, most likely, the last Phoenix, it would be bad. You do realize the importance of making sure she lives?" Drake asked.

"Other than a species being destroyed, no?" Saxon said, rubbing his cheek on the top of her head.

"Yes, a Phoenix is born again when she dies, but what others do not realize is that she is the hope for those who are lucky to know her. Not only does her kind bring peace to her surroundings and hope for new life, but births are also increased and new romance blossoms around her. With her death in our city, darkness would settle over us, and I don't think we could survive it. She's already chosen us, honored us," Drake informed him, staring at Nava.

"Don't you think that is a lot to put on one woman? She doesn't even know what she is, let alone about this story or rumor, and she doesn't need to be pressured about this either." Saxon raised his gaze to Drake. "If all this is true, don't you think it would be wrong to allow your people near her after everything that happened to the others of her kind?"

"No, they saw firsthand what happened to their city and their lives. Believe me, she will be protected at all cost. But you are right, it is much to know, but she also has a right to know about herself if she asks." Drake glanced at his son. "The south wing, have it ready, for the others will be arriving in the next few days."

Chapter Seven

Her head was throbbing, wishing the little trolls in her
brain would stop their pounding, Nava tried to remember what the hell she had to drink when everything came
back to her. "Darla!" Nava screamed, lifting up in bed, looking around, frowning.

"Easy there, you're both safe. If I'm right, Darla and Drake
have been very busy for the last day," Saxon said, coming
over with a glass of ice water. "Drink," he said, sitting down
on the bed next to her.

"How long was I out this time?" she asked and sighed as
the cold water soothed the burning pipes inside her.

"Thirty-six hours, which is longer than I thought you'd be
out, young lady," a strange, older gentleman said, coming up
to stand behind Saxon.

"This is Doc Lope. He's been checking on the both of you
but was thrown out of Drake's room six hours ago." Saxon
smiled, and the doctor snorted.

"I should have seen it coming, but I didn't expect her to
start stripping the minute she opened her damn eyes," the
doctor said. "It would seem the dose they used was stronger
than I had expected. How are you feeling?" he asked Nava.

"I feel as if I have a hangover times three. It's a normal reaction for their concoction. It's not just one sedative they mix
but two when they come after you. And what's going on with
Darla?"

"I'll let you explain that to your woman. I'm off to see if
we're any closer to delivering those triplets yet. You take it
easy, young lady, you're going to be tired for the next day as
you know." The doctor moved toward the door, stopping to
look at Saxon. "I'll be going with you when you go rescue

35

those at that place. God knows the kind of damage these idiots have done to those children."

Nava frowned and glanced down at the blanket covering her. She was naked under said blanket. "Did you remove my clothes?" She peeked up at Saxon.

"I did, and I also gave you a bath. You were covered in smoke, ashes, and such. I sure didn't want to put you to bed like that. It's my job to take care of you, little fire, and I take my responsibilities seriously. I do have several questions about the scarring on your back, but that is for another time." He leaned down and nipped her lip then ran his tongue over it. "No one has the right to touch you and hurt you. I 'don't give a damn if it was in the past."

Nava smiled and couldn't help herself, reaching up and cupping the side of his face. "Saxon, I rather not even see the person who did this. I'm hoping he is dead. It's what I had to believe trying to heal myself when I got to my parents." She started to pull her hand away, but he covered her hand with his, holding it there.

"My little fire ball, you have nothing to worry about. This person won't get close to you. I should warn you now." He turned his head and placed a kiss on her palm. "My world has changed, the center of my universe, my heart, and soul is the fire ball I have trapped here on this bed. When we were alone and I was giving you a bath," he took her hand and put it against his chest, "it felt as if my heart was swelling inside. Never have I experienced such emotion, except for the death of my grandfather long ago. It might be too soon for you to feel this way, but know I'm not going anywhere. Wherever you go, I will follow, you will never be alone again, little fire."

"No one has ever said such words to me. Do I feel something for you? Yes. Otherwise, you'd be fried right now for giving me a bath. But there is something you are not telling me?" she asked, tilting her head to the side, studying him.

"Do you know anything about your past, heritage, and not including Calamity Jane?" Saxon asked.

"Not much, Mom was always interested in our genealogy but was afraid to dig after what happened to me. Why?" she asked.

"The doctor is very good at what he does, and you are not just human. It's one of the reasons why you were still standing when Darla had fallen to the drugs. It would seem you are part Phoenix and Golem. Your Golem helped fight off the effects of the drug, which saved you both from being dragged away. Do you know anything about them? What they are?" Saxon asked.

"I mean, I've heard rumors about the Phoenix but nothing on the other. Is this important? Is it why they keep coming for me?" Nava pulled the cover up and tried to scoot around without being exposed.

"I don't know if it's the reason they keep coming after you, but most likely. Drake told me there are not many Phoenixes left in the world; as a matter of fact, you could be the last of your line." Saxon reached over and lifted her up under her arms; the blanket slipped loose, exposing her breast.

She tried to pull the blanket back up, but Saxon grabbed onto her hand, holding her still as he lowered his head, sucking her exposed nipple into his mouth. "Saxon," she whispered. His touch was like fire, sending heated tingles throughout her body. Nava rubbed her legs together as moisture gathered below. "Please, you have to stop," she begged.

"Never," he growled, releasing her breast. "Every single inch of your body is mine to worship, love, and touch." His gaze met hers. "And I plan on touching you whenever I can, but since it's obvious you are not ready for our joining yet..." He tucked the cover around her. "What do you think about doing some exploring? Did you know, Drake's home is built in the caverns? There are hidden natural treasures all around us. I thought we could pack a picnic and go explore." He placed a kiss on her nose and stood. "It would give us time to get to know each other."

"I take it all my belongings have been moved here," she said, sliding her feet over the edge of the bed and standing up, taking the sheet with her. She scanned the room, searching for the duffle bag with her emergency funds and clothes if Nava had to leave.

"The bag is in the closet, but you won't need it anymore. I'm afraid once Drake considers you family, he is very protective. He and Darla have given you the west wing of their home. You even have your own kitchen and living quarters in this wing, not to mention three separate bedrooms, plus this master and two bathrooms. As you can see, the bedroom set you liked has been placed in here along with the other furniture you have chosen. Plus, there is the fact you're not going anywhere without me," Saxon informed her.

She shook her head, looking around for clothes. She glanced up at Saxon. "I will always have a bag packed. Never will they catch me unprepared like they did my parents," she told him with a lump in her throat scanning each inch of her new place. "I have no idea why they would do this. It's too much. Hell, I just met them. Aren't their sons going to be furious they are doing this?"

"Your clothes are over here. I understand the need for the bag, but it will be my job to prove to you that you are safe with me." Saxon moved to her, wrapping his arm around her waist. "You have a walk-in closet that could be a room in itself. As for your new brothers, they are having a blast. Even a pain in the ass telling me what I can and can't do with you, please," he grumbled, and she couldn't help but giggle.

"I always wanted older brothers, how cool is that," she teased, earning another growl, but didn't say a word about her duffle bag, seeing it in the corner of the closet. She moved to it, opening it up to make sure everything was in it, including her... "My gun, purse?" she asked, looking up over her shoulder as Nava stood.

"Don't encourage them, little fire, I might have to physically make that butt red." He leaned over, nipping her bare shoulder. "Your purse is behind you, but your weapon has been locked up. Drake hates guns in his house, not that he needs any," Saxon grumbled.

"Ouch," she tried to jerk away, but he dipped, lowering her in front of him, once more exposing her breast to his view. He just held her there, his gaze traveling down her body as Nava held onto him. "I'd prefer to have you naked, but with so many new faces showing up around here, I'll be damned if I allow others to stare at what is mine," he grumbled and lifted her back up. "Get dressed, baby, before we both burn up here." He set her on her feet and spun, moving out of the closet.

Nava knew he wasn't kidding. The room had gotten warmer, that was for sure, and she didn't know if it was because of her hormones or her gift. "A summer dress is in order." She looked around and sighed, seeing more clothes than Nava had in her wardrobe. Yep, someone had done some shopping while she had been knocked out.

"Hey, Saxon, whose clothes are these? Because they sure are not mine. Nice taste though," she said, going through the dresses, shirts, skirts, and pants.

Saxon snorted behind her. "That would be Storm. She's a pixy who loves New York fashions. So anytime anyone new comes into town, she likes to experiment, and it's her welcome to our town. Do you like the clothes?" he asked.

"Oh my god, who wouldn't. She really made these for me?" Nava looked back at him, and he smiled.

"Yes, but be warned, once you put it on, if she thinks it needs to be adjusted, Storm will do so while you have it on." Saxon shook his head. "She made me a pair of jeans once. They turned out to be one of my favorite ones now, but what I didn't expect was that Storm has a thing for butts. Needless to say, my jeans are now skin tight, showing everything. Mind you, they are still comfortable to wear, but yeah."

Nava glanced down Saxon's body, smiling. "I have to agree, you'd look hot in some tight jeans." She laughed out loud as his pants changed right in front of her. Laughing so hard, she twirled her finger. "Turn around."

Saxon growled but turned around for her.

"Well damn... Yep, Storm, you are so right," she said, watching a little pixy flying around Saxon. She was the cutest thing Nava had seen as she moved her head back and forth studying Saxon. Nava could have stared all day at his ass, but she heard a knock on her outer door. "Storm, I know I don't know you, but could you, really quick, since you have great taste?" she dared ventured as Saxon spun around at the same time the summer dress she wanted appeared on her body. But this time, Storm moved around her, muttering under her breath as she worked on the dress while it was on her.

Changing little things, how it fit, the design, and such.

Nava turned to the mirror in her closet. The dress was a red color, and the material was like that of cotton on the skin but clung like that of silk. The dress hugged her body, showing off her ample breasts and curves. "Wow, Storm, you're amazing." She looked up at the top of the mirror to see the purple-haired pixy cocking her head to the side studying her. Her hair weaved in a braid down her back as she flew around her.

"Thank you, but you are missing something. Oh, I know," Storm said when in front. In between her boobs, the dress gathered to that of a diamond broach of some kind of bird.

"It's beautiful, Storm, but I don't think it's wise to advertise to others what she is," Saxon said, coming up behind her in the mirror, his gaze meeting hers.

"You're right, sorry. How about this?" An orange-red flame belt made out of some sort of weave appeared around her waist as the broach disappeared.

"I still like the bird, but the belt is amazing. Will I need shoes?" Red slip-on sandals appeared in front of her. "Perfect touch! Thank you so much," she said as Matty appeared behind them.

"Storm is amazing, isn't' she? I came to give you a heads up. Half of my father's closest men have shown up already, and they have requested to meet you, little sister. Needless to say, my father is furious that they should even ask for a meeting," Matty informed them, as said man leaned in the doorway to the closet, watching the tiny woman dash around Nava's head.

Nava could have sworn that flames were flying around the small room as her new brother stared at the little pixy who flew around ignoring the man.

"Why don't we take this out of the closet?" she laughed, a little nervous.

Matty glanced at Saxon, laughing. "I see Storm got a hold of..." he stopped laughing and groaned. "Storm, come on. How am I to meet these men in these tight things," he grumbled, his pants now a nice pair of tight black leather pants.

"You don't need to be looking at him," Saxon growled in

Nava's ear as he wrapped his arm around her waist.

"Please," Nava shook her head, watching Storm fly around, blowing a raspberry at Matty before she disappeared.

"Watch it, little pixy, you can only hide so long?" Matty growled, moving out of the closet, earning a look from his father as he appeared behind him.

"Don't start," Matty grumbled. "I made a mistake, I know." Matty moved out of the room before his father could say anything.

Drake sighed and watched his son leave. "It seems even my son can make mistakes about his chosen one." Drake turned his gaze on Nava. "I want to personally say I'm sorry, dear, for this, and believe me, they will all feel my wrath demanding this, but since you are new to our family, they have a right to meet you. But I do have to say, my soon-to-be daughter has outdone herself. You are breathtaking." Drake moved to Nava, taking her hands into his.

"I hope you don't mind me taking the liberty of having you move in here. It is safer, and you'll have more room. Plus, it will give you more time for this gentleman to court you properly. He's very lucky I happen to be fond of him, or I wouldn't have allowed him to take care of you." Drake gave Saxon a look that actually had the big man fidgeting next to her.

Chapter Eight

Saxon escorted Nava down the long hall of carved stone toward what he knew to be the banquet room. He had only been in the room once when Darla and Drake had held a party for Halloween one year for the town. It had been massive as with everything they did. Saxon glanced over at Drake talking to Nava, explaining how long it took to carve out the tunnels for his home. Yes, the man was impressive and scary even for his kind. No one knew the powers this man had, but what he had seen over the years, Saxon knew not to challenge the man, especially when it came to his personal family.

The only room large enough to hold the number of people they had invited, the Dracula family seemed to be always prepared for any last-minute change, including hosting a large number of his people Saxon had seen coming in while Nava had been out of it for a day and a half. He hated the idea of her being paraded around like some showpiece, but they did need the support of Drake's people if they were going to get rid of this threat against all of their kind, not just his woman.

He glanced down at Nava and smiled, seeing Storm sitting on Nava's shoulder whispering to her. Even Drake had a grin on his face. It would seem, Storm and Nava would be close friends, which was good since they both would be members of this family along with him.

"Seems my family is growing by leaps and bound," Drake said to the two women then looked at Saxon. "We will make sure they are safe," Drake tried to reassure Saxon, glancing down at his clawed hand, which was fisted, hidden from Nava. Controlling his other side had always been difficult, but now, it was near impossible with the threat of his woman being hunted.

Nava looked up at him then at Drake, smiling. "You know I've taken care of myself for the last year, well had a little help here and there. Anyway, did you know Storm has her own Boutique in town, Storm's Creations? I'm so going to have to check it out. She even asked if I'd like to come help her out. Isn't that exciting; I've never had a job," she said as they stepped into the big room.

"Wow," Nava whispered, staring up at the ceilings, scanning all around the stunning place. Stone walls and the stalagmite's hanging from the ceiling seemed to sparkle in the room, which was always cool or heated when need to be. "This place is amazing. It's all natural but beautiful like it was made for this room." The last word trailed off as his little fire realized that everyone wasn't staring at the room but at her.

She inched closer to him. There had to be close to a hundred men and a few women.

Within seconds, Darla came out of the crowd, as if sensing her nervousness, and moved to Nava, hugging her. "I can't thank you enough for saving us both. Are you okay?" Darla asked, stepping into Drake's arm, scanning Nava from head to toe just to make sure.

"I'm fine. I even met a new friend, Storm. So, I call it a good day today." She leaned forward. "But, please tell me I don't need to meet every single one here. We'll never get to go on our picnic," Nava whispered.

"No, but they can hear you, daughter. Come, let me do the general introductions." Drake held out his hand, and she looked up at Saxon, which, for some reason, gave him a sense of pride that Nava already trusted his judgment.

"Go on, I'll be close," Saxon said, giving her a kiss on the top of her head.

Matty stepped up to him as Saxon watched Drake and Darla take Nava to the middle of the room. "I'm glad Storm has taken a liking to Nava. I think both of them need a good friend, and I have a feeling they will be close."

"You ever going to tell me what you did? Storm is furious.

I've never seen her so pissed. You're lucky you still have your balls."

"I was a fool." Matty ran his hand over his bald head. "Storm and I had one date over a month ago, and well, I didn't see the connection, while she did."

"Wait, weren't you with…" Saxon shook his head and whistled. "Well shit, you'll be lucky if she even looks at you. I mean come on, a human woman?" Saxon watched as Drake introduced his Nava to a few of his men. "And then, I can't believe you were with Tangy after that. I mean come on, there is no comparison when it comes to Storm. What the hell were you thinking?" he said and reached back, smacking Matty on the head. "Storm deserves better than that," Saxon growled, a little protective of the pixy who had chosen his mate as a confidant.

"Damn it, that hurt. Stop it. I wasn't with them physically. A few dates to the movies and that is when I realized my mistake. But Storm and others, including you, saw us together and assumed the worst." Matty glared at Saxon.

"Well, you do have a reputation with the ladies. What is everyone supposed to think?" he said, growling as he watched a man bow to Nava, taking her hand and kissing it. But what shocked him was when the man jumped back, slapping his palm over his lips and one to his balls as his clothes changed too and not for the better.

The man wore pants he had seen Matty fitted with and knew the stranger had done something to offend both of them, which had him and Matty moving forward. "What's wrong?" Saxon growled, staring at the offending man as Saxon wrapped his arm around Nava and pulled her to his side.

Storm flew around his head, cussing at the man. "He told her she was lovely but didn't know a Phoenix could be a little on the heavy side! The fuck head, like anyone would go out with his stupid, snobbish ass." Storm chatted on, flying around so furious, she didn't realize she had landed on Matty's shoulder, subconsciously seeking Matty's reassurance. It would seem the little pixy still needed Matty's closeness like all mates do, even when furious at them.

"Easy there, my little sunshine," Matty said, trying to calm

Storm. "Why don't you and my little sister go ask the chef if the lunch baskets are ready? That is if you will allow me to accompany you today without shocking anyone?" he grumbled.

At once, the little pixy jumped off his shoulder as if she was burned. "I'll think about it. Come, Nava, this crowd is giving me a headache," Storm said as little bits of electricity flew all around her, lighting her small form up. As soon as she and Nava started to move toward the kitchen, magic filled the air once more. Different colors could be seen everywhere. It would seem no one went unscathed by Storm in the room; each had some strange clothes on.

"Storm," Drake growled, having everyone turn to stare at him. "Return them to normal, please. I will deal with those that offended," Drake said, moving toward the man who had started all of this.

Even Saxon stepped away from the man as said man stepped back seeing the full force of Drake's glare was enough to give any man or women nightmares.

"Go with Storm, little fire, and make sure there is plenty of food for us all," Saxon encouraged, but once more, his woman surprised him, stepping in front of Drake.

"I'm sure he didn't mean to say what he did, please. Let's not hurt anyone. I don't need that also on my head," she said, and Saxon watched the play of emotion on Drake's face.

Drake wrapped his arms around Nava and hugged her. "Relax, daughter, he will survive my thrashing. Now, go do as your mate requested. You four need to have some fun for the day. Tomorrow, we plan on getting your friend and the others free from that place, destroying it for good." Drake pushed her toward the kitchen. "Oh, and Storm, take that shock thing off my son, please. I don't like to get shocked touching my boy and certainly don't need help in the other area," Drake said, giving the pixy a stare, and if at all possible, Storm's little face turned a little pink as she nodded to the man, and Saxon so wasn't going to ask what Drake meant either.

Saxon watched as the women moved through the ring of people, all of them stepping out of their way as their clothes turned back to normal. But as soon as the door was closed, Drake was on said man, lifting him up into the air by the neck. "If you ever insult any of my children, I'll personally wipe you and everything you love off the face of this earth." He brought the man close to him and sank his fangs into his neck, feeding.

Darla moved to Drake's side, placing her hand on his arm. "Drake, release Micro, we need him," she said, calming the beast inside the man. Saxon had heard rumors that Drake was miraculous. Killing those that would even look at his family wrong, but it would seem his mate was the calm of the beast as Drake threw the man down. "You are lucky my daughter and wife are forgiving, but I'll be watching." Drake scanned the room. "Anyone else have anything to say?"

Saxon had to hide the grin as every man there bowed his head and stepped back.

"I apologize, my lord." The man who had insulted his mate knelt before Drake, his head bowed to him. "My past pain has once more raised its ugly head. Maybe I woke too early; I don't know, but please, forgive me."

No one said anything while Drake glared at the man. "We each have had tough times, but you are old enough to know better and to watch what comes out of your mouth. Go home, Joby. Right now, I don't want to have to worry about you around my family when we are dealing with a situation here. But you will hear from me soon enough."

Drake looked at Saxon and his son. "Both of you go and have a good day. I plan on visiting those we captured." Drake glanced toward the door behind them and shook his head. "Jane, will you please stop goosing my men?"

Saxon glanced over his shoulder, seeing said man glaring at Jane. "Fine, but if anyone else insults my granddaughter, I will not hesitate to show them the error of their way."

Flask appeared behind Jane, wrapping his arms around her. "I see you haven't had enough. Forgive me, gentlemen, while I take control of this young beauty here," Flask said, lifting his head up and glancing at Saxon. "Take care of our girl, or you'll answer to us," he warned right before they disappeared.

Saxon frowned and spun around. "I swear if one more person warns me..." he grumbled.

"Welcome to the club," Matty said, walking next to him.

Chapter Nine

$\mathcal{N}$ava stared out at what appeared to be a window, but what she saw amazed her. Three different hallways, all carved out in the underground of New Mexico. Every day, hell, every second this town amazed her, but it wasn't only the town, but the people in it. In her twenty-six years, she had only met a few people that had gone out of their way to help them, but here, it seemed it was the norm.

She looked over her shoulder and smiled as Storm flew around the chef's head, talking to him as he put together their basket for their picnic. Nava knew Storm was nervous to be around Matty; hell, they were both nervous. Saxon was a man unto himself. Even when a man like Drake took control of things, Saxon stood his ground when a lesser man would have cringed.

"Storm, do you know if Saxon is still enlisted in the Marines?" Nava asked, moving toward them. "I mean, I can't move again, and I know for a fact when you are in the service, you move all the time." She reached over and popped an olive in her mouth.

Her little pixy frowned and tilted her head to the side. "I believe he did his time or service already and is just a recruiter now. But then, the way the outside world is, who knows when he could be called." Storm shivered. "Just look at the nut case we have in the office now. It must be a requirement for politicians to lie. I swear, if it wouldn't draw attention to our town, I'd give him a Pinocchio."

"Oh my, that would be something, but then, his nose would fall off." Nava laughed.

"Yes, that would be bad. Even I had similar thoughts, but mine was draining the pompous ass, but with my luck, his blood would give me heart burn," Darla said, coming into the kitchen. "As for Saxon, his actual service has been up for the last five years but volunteered to run the office here in town." Darla moved to her side, hugging her. "I'm really sorry about earlier. Micro has been hurt too many times. I've suggested to Drake that maybe it would be wise to have him come back to Magic. He needs to be able to relax and enjoy life for a few years. He keeps hoping to find his mate but looks in the wrong places. Plus, one can't just pick out our mates. Like your man Saxon, we know when we find our chosen one." Darla looked at Strom. "However, even men can be stupid and ignore the signs."

Storm rolled her eyes. "He did more than ignoring the signs, and you know this. I'm sorry, Darla, but it's going to take more time. I can't trust him; he hasn't earned that. Plus, well..." She looked around and moved a little closer. "I kind of have a date in a couple of weeks. My sister's best friend is coming in from London, and I've promised to take him to the dance."

"Oh dear, this is not going to go over—" The kitchen door slammed open, and Matty stood there, and even she stepped back, seeing the blood red in his eyes as his gaze settled on Storm.

"You will break this date!" Matty growled.

Storm flicked her wrist at him, and Nava swore it was as if a bullfighter waving a red flag in front of a bull. Matty growled and stormed into the room. Storm shirked and disappeared.

"Really, son, have you forgotten everything I've taught you?" Darla said, slapping her son upside the head. "What did you think would happen after the way you treated her? Now, you won't even have the picnic, a first time in two months she was willing to do anything with you." Darla looked disgusted at her son, who lowered his head.

"But she's mine," he grumbled as Saxon and Drake now joined them.

"Yes, she's yours, son, but you haven't earned her trust or even courted her. You don't have the right to tell her anything right now. That will take time," Drake said.

Nava gave Drake a look, and he laughed. "Don't give me that look. You'll see soon enough."

Darla nudged her and leaned down, whispering, "Humor them and allow them to think you are obeying them; that is the way to do that. When, in reality, they will always give you what you truly desire. Believe me, I know. It's taken me over a hundred years with this overbearing alpha to finally get him to listen."

Drake reached over and yanked Darla into his arms. "I would say it was the other way around, wouldn't you?" He gave her a look, and Darla seemed to melt against him, patting his chest.

"Of course, my husband," she said, kissing his chest and glanced over her shoulder at Nava, winking.

Nava laughed when Drake slapped Darla's ass. "Don't think I know what you just did. Do I need to pull out your paddle, my dear?" Drake said and nipped her neck. "It has been a while."

"I so don't need to hear this." Matty turned around, scanning. "I'm sorry, Storm. I didn't have any right, but I would like it if you would reconsider canceling it, maybe. Can we still have our picnic? I know Nava would like your company as I would."

Nava couldn't hold it in, she laughed so hard tears were coming down. It seemed Storm was going on the picnic but not before she had her fun giving Matty a psychedelic head color.

He sighed. "I'm sorry, Storm. I really am." He looked up, and Storm appeared in front of him.

"I can't promise you anything. We have a lot to work through, but I was looking forward to this picnic with Nava and you." Storm glanced at her. "I don't know why, but there is a connection to you," Storm said.

"I feel it, too, and I welcome the friendship. I haven't had a true friend in a long time, since... Maybe when we free my friend, you'd help. I know it's going to be hard for her. Plus, things are moving a little fast for me, too." Nava glanced at the man standing next to her, Saxon. He was built like a tank, and god, did he smell good. She shook her head and looked up. Sure enough, he was grinning.

He lowered his head and kissed her lips softly. "It's normal to feel what you do. When true mates meet the heat, need is ten times that of a human relationship. But I promise I'll court you right, my little fire." He wrapped his arm around her and pulled her up against him.

She shook her head but didn't move, feeling safe in his arms.

Storm smiled and landed on her shoulder. "We'll both help your friend. I think being here in this town will help, also. One thing I can say about this city is we stick together and help each other out," Storm said and glanced over at Saxon. "You are not the only one who is having the same problem, but..."

"I know, you have time. You were hurt; take your time, but don't shut him out if what everyone is saying is true." Nava glanced at Matty. "Give him hell, but also allow him to prove to you that he is sincere in his pursuit," Nava said, earning a groan from Matty.

"Hey now, I haven't hurt you? Why do I get thrown in with him?" Saxon asked.

"No, you haven't, but I still want to go on dates, do things before we commit." Nava looked down at the ground, wishing she had painted her toe... "Thank you, Storm." Her toes now were painted a red color to match her dress. "I was going to say I haven't been on a real date. With us being on the run, we never could trust anyone." She looked at Saxon, who looked stunned.

"Nothing? No movies, nothing?" he asked.

She shook her head, and Drake growled. "That settles it. The both of you will get your courting shoes on and show these ladies that men are not all dogs starting today. Go take your picnic. I would suggest the west pond. I think they both will enjoy it."

Darla clapped her hands together, nodding. "Yes, it's perfect. Now, go, all four of you, and have a great time."

Matty grabbed the picnic basket as Drake handed Saxon two blankets. "We'll discuss our problem tonight." Drake leaned over and placed a kiss on Nava's cheek. "We'll get your friend out and treat her right. We have a great shrink here that can help her, too, and any others that wish to come back with us. We already have many individuals here stepping up to offer their homes for any children that don't have a place to go, including us. Darla and I have decided to open our home. With the boys all older and this place is so big…"

Nava stepped up to the man that everyone seemed afraid of and hugged him as Darla stepped aside. "My father was just like you, and I'm proud to be considered part of your family, thank you," she said, looking at Darla at the same time. "The both of you."

Chapter Ten

Saxon had never seen Drake out of words and uncomfortable as his woman hugged the man, thanking him. He would have laughed, but seeing the tears in his woman's eyes even had his stomach in knots.

Drake hugged her tight. "Go on your picnic, little fire, and know you are safe here," Drake whispered to her before she stepped back to his side.

"Storm, won't you shift for me?" Matty asked as Saxon escorted Nava out the kitchen door and down the right tunnel, which led to the west pond.

The little pixy flew around Matty. "Last time I did, it didn't go so well," she said, and even Saxon could hear the insecurity in her voice.

"I, for one, would love to see the real you," Nava said, encouraging Storm, who blew out a breath before appearing next to her.

"Well damn, don't you look fabulous." Nava took Storm's hand, smiling. "No wonder Matty wanted to see the real you, stunning."

Storm bumped her shoulder. "Please, I'm just bigger, that is all." Storm glanced back at Matty. "Happy?"

Matty smiled and nodded. "Very, thank you for my little pixy." For the next twenty minutes, Matty explained the process his father had gone through forming the tunnels to create their home. The two women listened and pointed out little forms on the walls that appeared to be some pictures of ancestors of Matty's family.

But as soon as they turned the corner, his little fire stopped and grabbed onto the wall, grabbing at her stomach. "No," she whispered, tears rolling down her cheeks.

At once, his skin hardened as he stepped up to Nava, scanning the area. "What's wrong?" he asked as Matty pushed Storm closer to Nava, making sure both of them were secure.

Her tearful gaze lifted. "They know about our plans, Elf says they have upped security and are going to start packing them up. Saxon, they took her babies away from her." Nava's lip trembled as Drake came, moving around the corner with Theo, the sheriff.

"The leak has been taken care of. We go now," Drake said, moving to Nava's side. "Inform your friend not to give up, we're coming," Drake said as he turned the girls around and started to head them back toward the main home.

"How are we going to get there in time? They're already getting ready to transfer the little ones," Nava asked.

"We have our ways to get there, and don't worry, they won't be going anywhere," Drake said as Theo snorted.

"Frost is furious, and I don't blame him. Lacey and her sisters could have been hurt," the sheriff growled.

"What did they do," Saxon asked as he pulled out his phone, sending out a message to his team to get ready.

"The Adams sisters and their aunt Topper paid a visit to the home and disabled all their cars, vehicles. I swear, Frost is ready to lock them all up he's so furious," Theo informed them.

Saxon growled. "I'd be furious, too." He glanced at Nava, who looked over her shoulder at him.

"Well, isn't it a good thing we aren't committed yet? Because I would have been right there with the sisters if they would have let me know about their trip," Nava said, lifting her head a little, giving him sass.

"She's not the only one. We're not useless, you know." Storm glared at him then at Matty.

"And your cute butts would be spanked. The thought of you even near that place..." Matty growled.

"I don't think you have any say in this either," Storm said, and once more Matty was dressed in an old knight metal armor. One step and he was falling face first to land on a pillow.

"Ladies, we don't have time for this. Nava, Storm, if we didn't need everyone, you wouldn't be going and either would Darla. But the women and children are going to need you," Drake stated, which only had his little fire stopping and frowning at Drake.

"I can't thank you enough for all that you have done for me and are willing to help me, but I will do what I think is necessary with or without your consent. I'm an adult, sir, and have been on my own now for a few years." Nava lifted her head and started to walk ahead of everyone.

At first, Drake did nothing, almost shocked, and Saxon couldn't help but smile, even though he knew his mate was going to give him hell and he'd have it no other way. Moving toward his mate, Saxon gave Drake a look as he passed him. "Didn't count on that, did you?" he asked. "Little fire, wait up." Saxon ran to her side, winding his fingers with hers.

"He just does not want to see you hurt, little fire," he said.

"I understand that; I really do. But, this has been my battle for years; they killed my parents, Saxon." She stopped and looked up at him than at Drake, who now stood behind her. "I won't be left out of this. These people have taken too much from me. Not you or Drake will stop me. And if any other group comes along starting the same thing, I'll make sure it's shut down. Do you know how many children they hurt?" She shook her head, and a single tear rolled down her cheek. "It can't happen again."

Saxon pulled her into his arms, hating the sadness coming from her. He realized then and there that he'd do anything to keep Nava happy. He glanced up at Drake. "My team is on its way. We'll be ready to leave in the next ten minutes."

"I still don't understand how you are going to get there so quickly," Nava commented as they started to move back toward the main compound.

"You remember Topper? There are many ways to travel from one place to the next, little fire," Saxon explained.

She stopped again. "Wait, you can do that, too? Go anywhere? Poof, like that?" She snapped her fingers, staring at him with her big green eyes.

"I can do a few things as many of us can," he smiled.

"Come, we have to move." Saxon picked her up and threw her over his shoulder, running toward the main house. From what his scout had reported to him a few seconds ago, they didn't have much time. Things were getting hot. Already the posse had arrived at the school and was rounding up those that they could.

"Hey, I can run," she yelled but stopped when they appeared in the kitchen, giving her the first taste of his kind of travel.

"Wow, that was cool. Will I be able to do that?" she asked as he lowered her to the ground, nodding to Kaylen.

"We're ready. Half the team has split, one covering the girls' dorm, the other covering the little ones they are moving. If we are going to do this, we need to leave now," Kaylen informed him.

"Have the rest of the men start transporting Drake's men and the others. Nava, I expect you to listen to everything I say. I will not lose you after just finding you. Storm, can you..." Before he could say anything, Nava was dressed in black pants and shirt with some boots he'd have to make sure she'd wear later. "You going to be able to walk in those?" he asked.

Nava smiled. "Oh, baby, you should have seen my red shoes. If you find my friend and get her out of there, I'll model them for you later with Storm's help, of course."

Storm giggled. "I have a pair of green ones that are my favorite. But I haven't found anyone yet worthy to show them off to." She got her dig into Matty, who groaned.

"All right, ladies, now is not the time to get your men all hot and bothered here," Drake said as his woman came strolling in, dressed in black. "Darla," Drake growled seeing his wife, and he had to admit all three women were dressed for a night out on the town, not for their mission.

"What? You need distractions; well, that is what we are," she winked at Nava, who smiled.

"Never," he growled, and Matty hissed at the same time.

Chapter Eleven

Nava stood behind the building with two of Saxon's men and a few of Drake's men surrounding her, Storm, and Darla. All three men had refused to listen to them about being a distraction. But Nava was kind of glad they had because what she saw at the compound, well to say she was impressed would be an understatement. But it had taken Nava a few minutes to stop shaking when Saxon had brought her back to her nightmare.

They had twice the people and buildings, the place had changed. The one new building was bigger and even scarier if possible. From what she could also tell, there was a twelve-foot wire fence around the compound.

A cold chill ran up her arms and down her back. Nava knew the nightmares were going to come back, but she didn't care. As long as they freed those that were held there. What she hadn't expected was the number of little ones that had been reported.

"*You okay?*" Saxon's voice penetrated her thoughts, shocking her.

"*How and I'm fine?*" Nava questioned. "*You should be concentrating on what you are doing? Stop worrying about me.*"

The man laughed at her. "*Oh, little fire, I will always be worried about you. And do not worry, I will chase those nightmares away.*"

Nava snorted, drawing Darla's attention. "So, the bond is finally forming?" she asked.

"If you mean him talking in my head, yes. Which someone should have warned me. I'm lucky I didn't piss my pants," she grumbled and turned her attention toward the far left.

"No," she growled, moving away from the group and heading toward the small group of women who were being moved at gunpoint toward another building. "Elf," she whispered.

"*Do not. It's a trap,*" Elf said.

"*If you think for one minute I'm going to leave you again, think again,*" Nava said, running toward the back of Building F she knew all too well.

"*What the hell do you think you are doing? Do not move. I'm coming your way.*" Saxon growled, hearing the orders he was issuing his men.

Catching a movement to her side, Nava sighed. "You two need to go back. I can do this. I know what to expect," Nava said to Darla and Storm.

They both shook their head. "Where you go, we go. Now, if you want to get your friend, we better do it now." Darla nodded toward the building. "If they get inside, we won't stand a chance if we are going to do this."

"They won't be able to get in that door," Nava said, sending a ball of fire at said door, melting and sealing the door. What she wasn't expecting was half of Drake's men and Saxon's to come running, surrounding them, refusing to allow them to move.

"We will discuss your need to help later," Saxon growled, appearing in front of her and pulling her into his body. "They know you are here now. You have distracted them enough, time to go home..." Saxon said.

"No!" she yelled, but to realize she, Darla, and Storm now stood in the kitchen of Darla's home. "That stupid jackass! I swear I'm going to set his ass on fire," she screamed furiously. "I need to be able to help Elf, damn it!"

"Not to worry, granddaughter, I'll make sure she is okay, and then, I'll personally kick that posse's ass. Do you know it took nine of them to lock me up, but they didn't realize I know how to get away from them?" Her grandmother cocked her gun. "Time for some fun. You ready, Topper?" Jane asked as Topper appeared next to her grandmother.

"Let's go. We have babies to help." Both Topper and Jane disappeared before Nava could say a word.

"That is not a good combination. Damn, Theo is going to

have a fit. Topper has been giving most of the men a head-ache popping in and out of places, now with Jane at her side, not good." Darla whistled.

"Can you take us back?" she asked Darla, plopping down on a stool around the island in the kitchen.

"No, even Storm can't do anything. Seems the men have learned a thing or two since the last time something has happened. If I'm not mistaken, Storm, your gifts?" Darla asked.

"Gone. Just wait 'til they come back. Matty's little shock thing was nothing when I get my powers back. Who the hell do they think they are doing this to us?" Storm was furious. Even though her power was gone, Nava could see little bits of electricity zapping around her head.

"Easy there; you know this was all Drake. He's been spout-ing about this kind of thing ever since Lacey was taken years ago. Now, I have to find out how he did it, and I will find out, believe me."

Nava stopped and sighed. "Elf is safe. They have her..." Nava turned to see her friend appear in the kitchen with them.

"Elf!" Nava went to her friend, hugging her tight. "Are you hurt? Darla, the doctor?"

"I'm here; we're getting the hall ready for all of those that don't have a place to go. Come here, child, and let's get a look at you," Doc Lope said, coming into the kitchen.

"It would have been nice to know this was going to happen in my own damn house. How are we supposed to help if we're not told any of the plans?" Darla snarled, marching out of the kitchen with Storm behind her, giving Elf and her some privacy with the doctor.

Elf stepped back as the tears rolled down her cheeks. Elf was thin, she had dark circles under her eyes, and a few new scars that hadn't been there before.

"I'll heal, but thank you. I'm just worried about my chil-dren." Elf looked down at the ground. "They might have been forced on me, but they are mine, and I won't give them up." Elf glanced up at her.

"Of course not, we'll find all three of them, I promise, and you will stay with me until you are ready to get your own place," Nava said.

"Young lady, I must insist, you are bleeding," Dr. Lope said just as Elf's legs gave way. Dr. Lope caught her easily. "You want her upstairs?" he asked, and Nava nodded. "Please, put her in my bed."

"There is no reason to put her in your bed. The room across the way from you is perfect for Elf. There is another room attached to it for her children, and it has its own bathroom, too. I've had it all set. Take her there, and I'll have some donors come up when you are ready," Darla said, wrapping the blanket around Elf as they moved out the kitchen toward her wing at their house.

"Thank you, Darla. You don't know what this means to me," Nava said, reaching over and squeezing Darla's hand.

For the next hour, Nava paced the outer bedroom while Doc Lope ran back and forth, helping the others and checking in on her friend. Right then, there were two females in there, donors Darla had said for Elf to feed. Nava growled. "She could have fed from me," she mumbled.

"Yes, she could have, but right now, your friend does not want you to see her this way. You are all she has left, and Elf's afraid if you see her feeding, you will think of her differently," Darla said. "Our men should be coming back here soon. They have found the baby and the three-year-old, but it seems her daughter, the seven-year-old, was moved to another location." Darla plopped down in the chair. "Fifty-five children under the age of ten with no parents and they call us monsters." Darla looked up at her with tears in her eyes. "I've never been prouder to live where I do."

Nava nodded and sat down next to Darla on the floor. "I know. The way that many of them have opened up their homes for these children..." Nava shook her head.

Darla nudged her. "You have a little one in your bed as we speak. Are you going to see about keeping her?"

Nava sighed. "I'd like to. There is just something about her that draws me to her." Nava smiled, remembering the little one coming out into the hallway running into her as she glanced over at Darla. "You took in a set of twin girls. Oh, is

Drake in trouble." She smiled.

"We have plenty of room, plus they need to stay together. Now, our home will have plenty of females in it, and I won't be outnumbered by my sons, that is if we are allowed to keep them. Theo is already working with outside forces to make sure the children can stay here with their kind. We're lucky we have a few high-top officials that are helping us." Darla stiffened and looked up at the door.

Saxon stood there, holding a little girl while Drake held an infant. The bedroom door flew open, and Elf stepped out. At once, the little girl in Saxon's arms squirmed until he put her down. The child ran to Elf's arms. "Mommy," she cried out as Drake moved to Elf.

"We will not rest 'til we find your other child, I promise. I already have my men searching the files and such. You and your children are safe here, Elf. This is your home for however long you need it," Drake said, placing a kiss on Elf's cheek and gently placing the baby in her friend's arms.

"I can't thank you enough, all of you. I never believed we'd be lucky to escape," she said, whispering while staring down at her baby and daughter.

"There is no need to thank us. I have a few men bringing up a crib and a few other things you'll need. The doctor has looked over both children already, and both are healthy. The tags placed in them have been removed. Would you mind if Nava's grandmother removes yours? You won't feel a thing."

Elf looked up, and her eyes were red. "Get them out of me, please," she hissed.

Nava moved up to her friend as her grandmother Jane appeared next to her. "I have so much to tell you, but first, meet my great, great..."

"If you say great one more time, I'm going to have that man paddle your butt... I'm Jane, her grandmother," her grandmother said right before stepping into Elf.

Her friend shivered as Jane excited her body holding four tracking devices, but there were tears in her eyes. "Every single one of those monsters needs to be tortured," Jane growled right before she disappeared.

"Oh, that isn't good," Darla said. "She's libel to start another war."

Drake tilted his head to the side. "Nope, the posse has her tied up, and Nava's friend has taken control of her." Drake turned his eyes on her. "As for you, young lady. What the hell do you think you were doing out there?" he snarled.

"Excuse me? What did I tell you earlier? Don't growl at me," Nava said, and by accident, with all the extra stress she had been under, let a little bit of fire escape her.

Drake jumped out of the way, but his hair took the brunt of her fire.

"I'm so sorry, really," she said, horrified at what she had done. Even now his hair was still smoking, and the smell of burnt hair was everywhere.

"Well, I always did love it when he went bald, but it serves him right getting all mouthy with you. You were doing what you thought was best; he had no right to say a word," Darla said, coming up to her side as Saxon stepped in behind her.

She glanced behind her and hissed. "You come near me, and your ass is going to be burning I am so pissed at you."

"If you will excuse us. Elf, we are right across the hall if you need us, but this one and I are going to have a long chat," Saxon said right before he once more lifted her up over his shoulder, slapping her ass hard.

"What the hell?" she shrieked and tried the get down, but he held her tight right before he appeared in another room and dropped her on the strange bed.

Chapter Twelve

*N*ever had he been more scared or furious. The four men that had been with her were now doing patrol for the next year. To think they didn't stop the three women just pissed him off more. Even Drake had confronted his men, and it hadn't been pretty, but his little firebug was about to get a lesson in not to push a pissed full-on demon.

Already, he was having trouble pulling in the dark side of him as he watched Nava scoot up the bed, staring at him.

"What the hell is your problem?" she dared ask him.

"We have only known each other a few days, so I'm giving you a lot of leeway here, but if you keep giving me sass, I swear, I'll paddle your ass 'til it's pink. Do you know what it was for me to watch you move toward those SOBs? They were waiting for you, and you were going to just hand yourself over without a thought to yourself or the other two women?"

Nava stood on the bed, her hair blowing as if from unseen wind. If he had been smart, he would have been backing up, but right then, his demon was in control as Nava clenched her hands tight. Smoke started to come from her, and he knew she was trying to hold back, and of course, his demon didn't care. "Sit down and quit acting like a child," he snapped. "We need a serious discussion here, and it's time for you to learn a few things," Saxon said just as his demon took control, shifting right there in front of her.

Her gaze scanned over his now seven-foot-tall frame. His skin a dark red, hard. He had a tail that could kill any man or give pleasure to a stubborn female when it was time. Nava gasped as her gaze lowered to his cock, now that he was naked in full form. "What the..." she sputtered. "Damn." Nava shook her head and plopped down on the bed. "We're going to have major problems here, because there is no way that thing... Nope"

If he weren't still pissed, he would have laughed. "It will fit," he said, moving to the side of the bed when something felt strange.

"Well, it sure isn't going to fit with that on it!" Nava giggled, pointing at his manhood.

No one had ever laughed at his cock. He growled and glanced down. "What the hell?" His cock was fully dressed in a tux outfit. "Storm!"

His mate fell backward, laughing so hard she had tears in her eyes as they both heard Matty and Drake yelling. \

Nava lifted her head up. "It would seem she is a little pissed about her gifts being taken away. She wanted to show you appreciation for giving them back," his little fire laughed, rolling around on the bed.

Saxon shook his head, hiding the smile on his face as he turned and tried to remove the dress coat, shirt and bow tie, but every time he removed one piece, another would replace it but in a different color. "Storm!" he growled, earning another laughing fit from his mate.

Shifting to his human form and clothing himself, Saxon stormed toward the door when he heard Nava's statement. "You know she is hiding." Nava got up from the bed and moved to him. "Storm, would you please remove the cute clothes from my man. I think he has been shown his error, haven't you?" his little fire dared ask.

"My mistake was allowing you to step foot near that place. I knew it was a risk, but you just didn't listen." He ran his hand over his buzzed head. "The thought of them capturing you, hurting you..." He closed his eyes, trying to calm the demon once more inside when he felt Nava's hand on his chest.

"Saxon, I'm afraid these people won't stop. If there is going to be anything between us, you'll have to expect this. I can't be wrapped in bubble wrap," she said, as he opened his eyes, seeing her shrug and go to step back, but he reached around her and pulled her into his body. She looked up at him with tears in her eyes. "Maybe that was what I was born to do. Help those that have been taken. Try and free them."

"You were meant to be my mate, my little fire," he grumbled and wiped the tear away from her cheek. "If it is important to you to find these places, we will do this together, but you will have to listen to me, little fire. I've been on many missions, and I can't have you second-guessing me. You could be killed and so could others. I need your promise, little fire," he pleaded with her as he reached up, cupping the side of her cheek. "You have a little girl in your bed. Do you wish her to be part of our lives?"

She tried to look away, but he held her still. "She's like me, Saxon. I was drawn to Ana, well we both were drawn toward each other. I can't let her go."

Saxon sighed and placed a kiss on her forehead. "Then, you must think before you do things. If we bring a child into our lives, she must be protected, and that also means for her not to lose her new mother. Don't you think it would devastate her to lose another parent after she has bonded with you?" Saxon said, grasping at anything to get her to understand how important she was to him and to others.

"I'll try, that is all I can promise. I know Ana needs me as others, but seeing them hurt..." Nava turned her head and placed a kiss on his hand before smiling up at him. "So, we're going to keep Ana?" she asked.

Saxon moaned. "It's a little bit more complicated, little fire. We'll have to be approved first, but if what you say is true, that she is like you, then most likely we will have no problem adopting her. Then, there is the problem that we are not mated yet," he said, lowering his head and covering her mouth with his.

She slid her arms around him, her nails digging into his back as he slid his tongue into her mouth. She tasted of hickory and coffee as he explored every inch of her tongue before breaking the kiss. Her stomach growled, and he smiled. "I'm sorry, little fire, we didn't get our picnic and missed lunch. Come, let's go see if the little girl would like to join us for dinner. I hear her moving around."

Nava laughed. "She most likely heard you and the other

two yelling at Strom. I totally forgot we hadn't eaten. Yes, let's grab Ana. From what she has told me, she's about six. She never knew her parents, but I'd like to make sure. If there is any chance they are alive, she needs to know them. It's really sad. Ana said she never met her mom, that she had been born there," Nava said, moving in the hall.

Saxon stopped and glanced down at his heart. "Nava, do you think they could have taken any of your eggs? Could Ana be your child?" he asked, growling.

Nava placed her hand on her heart, stopping to look up at him. "I don't know, they could have." She grabbed onto his arm. "How do we find out?"

"Drake," Saxon said, looking up as said man came moving toward them.

"You do know this creates a bigger problem if this is true? Darla is a nervous wreck at the thought of her children out there, and I have to agree." Drake glanced down at Nava, holding his hand out to her. Do you mind sharing your blood with me, daughter?" he asked.

"No, take what you need, always," Nava said, as Drake brought up her wrist to his mouth, licking the skin before sinking his fangs into her.

She didn't even flinch, watching him feed from her as Darla moved up to his side. Saxon could see the tears in her eyes as her gaze met his. "Do you know how many children they could have of ours if this is true?" she said as Drake sealed the holes in Nava's wrist, wrapping his arm around Darla, bringing her closer to him. "If it happened, we will find out. I already have my men going through all the computers, files, and such. Let's go see if this little girl is our granddaughter," he grumbled.

Nava smiled. "I could so see you as a big pushover when it comes to little girls," Nava teased, moving to her door, but when they all turned, the little redhead was standing there in the door staring at them all.

"You think I'm your daughter?" she asked, obviously smarter than a normal child her age but looking so small and alone.

Nava at once went to the child, kneeling before her. "That

is what we need to find out." Nava reached up and moved a piece of the child's hair out of the way. "Would that be okay?"

Saxon did have to admit the child did have Nava's nose and eyes, but who would have been the father was a question as Nava explained what would happen.

The tiny girl held out her wrist without batting an eye. "I want to know. I've never had a momma. Would he be my daddy?" The little girl nodded to Saxon.

"Saxon is my mate, so yes, he would be your daddy. Would that be okay?"

Saxon bowed to the little girl, earning a giggle from her. "It would be my honor to have you as my daughter, but I should warn you," he looked up at the little girl. "Anyone who does not listen to me, I eat," he teased.

Nava rolled her eyes. "Not to worry, Ana, he can't eat you; it would give him a tummy ache. Plus, I have it on good authority he's a big teddy bear."

Ana giggled and looked up at Drake who moved up to her. He knelt next to Nava. "You know what I'll do?" he asked.

She nodded. "I saw you feed from Momma," Ana said, looking right at Nava.

A little squeak came from Saxon's little fire, and he moved behind her, placing his hand on her shoulder. "You are a very brave little girl, and I'd be proud to call you my daughter," he told Ana as Drake didn't wait, sinking his fangs into the little girl's wrist. It only lasted a second before he carefully closed the holes and stood. The anger radiating from him even had Ana stepping back away from him.

"Sorry, Ana. I'm not mad at you, little one. I'm mad at those who did this to you and your mother." Drake nodded to Nava, who fell backward on her ass. Tears rolled down her cheeks as she stared at her daughter.

"My baby," she whispered and held out her arms as the little one flew into them, hugging her tight.

"You're really my momma," Ana cried.

Saxon had tears in his eyes and looked up at Drake.

"I need to inform Theo and the others," Drake said, looking at him then at Darla. "We'll find out, I promise," he told his mate, hugging her tight as she cried. "How many of my babies are out there?"

Chapter Thirteen

Nava watched as her man, Saxon, talked with her daughter. She had a daughter and had lost six years of watching her grow. But she was determined to enjoy every second with her little girl.

"So, you see, you'll have two sets of grandparents. Drake and Darla and my folks, which will be here next week." Saxon's gaze swung to hers.

"What? I'm not ready for that. What if they don't like me?" Nava said, lowering her fork of food as the food in her stomach seemed to flip around.

"It's the next step since I intend to make you my mate soon," Saxon said, giving her a heated look. Her body burned, and her nipples hardened under the shirt she wore. Dampness gathered between her legs, and Nava knew her face had turned a pink color.

"Stop that," she whispered and broke his gaze, noticing Doc Lope coming into the kitchen. Nava grabbed her glass of wine and took a sip, knowing that Saxon had asked the doctor to come to make sure everything was okay with Ana.

"Doc Lope, thank you for coming. I know you are very busy this night," Nava said and nodded to the chair. "Please, sit and join us. We have plenty of food."

The doctor pulled out the chair, turning it around, straddling it. "I hear Ana is your natural daughter. We have a mess down there. You are very lucky you found her. The records are scattered all over the place. What can I do for you, Saxon? You know Ana is well; I've already seen to her."

Saxon sighed. "I'd like you to shift and tell us what she is? I want to make sure we know everything, so we can make sure she is exposed to her other half."

To say Nava was surprised was an understatement. She hadn't even thought of that. "Do you think her natural father is someone different, too?" Nava looked from Lope to her daughter, who was stuffing her face with ice cream, which she had chocolate all over her. "Oh my, you like your chocolate, don't you," she teased and dipped her napkin in the water, wiping away some of the big spots on her cheek.

"It's my favorite," she said, keeping her gaze on the doctor. "Am I sick?"

"No, sweetie, your daddy Saxon wants to make sure we know what you are made up of. You know like, bugs, worms, snakes, and such," Nava teased, tapping her nose.

The little girl giggled and watched as Doc Lope stood and shifted right there, turning into the large wolf. Ana squealed with delight and jumped off the chair, going toward the doctor. "Can I pet him?" she asked, looking from Nava to Saxon.

Saxon laughed. "I think he'd like that."

Ana put her hand out, touching the big wolf as he came over, rubbing his head against her tummy, making her laugh. "He's so soft. This is the Mr. Lope? He's a wolf, really? Do you think I could do this?" The questions rolled out of her mouth as she pet the doctor.

"That is what we are trying to figure out. Your daddy Saxon can shift, also, but he's big..." Nava said, making Saxon choke on the sip of his beer, glaring at her.

"That was not nice," he growled.

"Well, you are," she giggled as Ana crawled back on her chair as Doc Lope shifted, frowning as he stared at Ana. "What? Is something wrong?"

The doctor shook his head and glanced at Saxon. "I need a word with you in private." He glanced up and smiled at her. "She's definitely like her momma, but she also has wolf genes in her. When she becomes of age, she'll be able to shift, but already her wolf is there sleeping, which is strange in itself. It might have to do with the fact that you are the Phoenix. I've heard when one mates with another species, their children are early at all that they do."

"Hmm, then, I guess we'll need to find the alpha or whoever is the leader of the wolves here, right?" she asked, looking from Saxon to the doctor.

Saxon smiled. "We already have him standing here. Doc Lop is the alpha here," Saxon stood. "I'll be right back."

"You'll tell me everything," she asked, glancing at Ana and back to him.

"Yes, now, finish your food. Ana is already done with her ice cream while you are still working on your dinner." Saxon pointed to her plate.

Nava smiled. "And if I don't?" she asked, earning a growl from him.

"Woman, you are playing here, and I don't know how long the other half of me can hold off before claiming you," he said, moving toward the doors that led out of the kitchen.

"Maybe I don't want to wait," she whispered, looking down at her food. The man had been by her side for the last three days, and Nava had to admit the thought of him leaving her scared the shit of her. Already, he had a big place in her heart, and she didn't know how, but Nava loved the big ox.

"Momma," Ana placed her hand on her arm. "Do you think we can go exploring?"

"Sure, why not. Even I haven't seen the whole house." She grabbed a roll and stood to take her daughter's hand. "Let's start with the tunnels; we were going to explore them earlier but had to come rescue a cute little girl," Nava told her as the moved out of the kitchen, knowing Saxon would be able to find them when he was done with his so-called chat.

"Wait for me. I don't want you roaming around alone with Drake's men all around," Saxon said.

"We'll be fine until you are done," Nava said, lifting Ana up so she could touch one of the pretty stones in the wall. "It's like a kaleidoscope, don't you think?"

"What's a kaleidoscope?" Ana questioned as they moved down the tunnel.

"It's a whole bunch of colors mixed together. I'll get you a toy that shows you what I'm talking about later. But we're kind of in a tunnel that has its own kaleidoscope," Nava informed her, frowning and scanning around. Something was off; she felt as if someone was watching her. "Ana. I think we need to go back and wait for your daddy. I know he'd love to show us places I've never been to," she said, turning around to head back when two men stepped in front of them.

"*Um, Saxon, right now might be the right time to do the appearance thing,*" Nava sent as the men's gazes sent a shiver down her spine as she pushed Ana behind her. "Can I help you?" Nava asked.

"It seems you've been replaced, my dear. Our leader now has his two daughters, he won't even miss you," the one with pink hair said, stepping forward. "But I'm sure that my brother and I could show you some fine places." He peaked around her, trying to get a look at her daughter, and that is when the fire rose.

"Back off, dick head," Nava growled as fire spark around her.

"Easy, baby," Saxon said, coming around the men with Doc Lope, Drake, Matty, and Ringo. "Why don't we finish that walk?" Saxon growled and bared his teeth at the men. "They are lucky to be Drake's men. Your father can handle this, but if there is a next time..." Saxon growled at them who had the good grace to step back.

"We were going to just have some fun. We meant no harm," the other one said, looking at his brother. "I told you this was a bad idea, dick head." He slapped his brother's pink head.

Drake ignored the men for a second, smiling down at Ana. "I happen to know there is a pool-well ponewith a slide down that tunnel," he said, earning a squeal from Ana.

"Can we go, please?" Ana asked, forgetting everything else.

"I don't see why not." Saxon swung Ana up in his arms and wrapped his arm around her waist. "Doc, we'll talk tomorrow," Saxon said, leading them away from the confrontation that was about to come.

Nava patted Saxon's arm. "I need to say something to Drake." She spun around and walked up to Drake's side. He glanced down at her.

"What's wrong, daughter?" Drake asked.

"The man with the pink hair, he's the one who had the mouth. The other didn't do anything; he actually looked a little terrified, just thought you would like to know. I really didn't like the way the pink prick looked at Ana." A small amount of smoke came out of her mouth. "If they are into children, I'd be looking into their family to see what the hell is going on because they had to learn it somewhere." She glanced at the man in question. "No one looks at my child wrong." She hissed, allowing a little stream of fire to come out at the pink-haired man, who jumped out of the way, falling to the ground.

"Wow, didn't know my sister was a bad ass," Matty said, winking at her. "Go on, little fire, we'll find out what's going one, I promise, because no one messes with my niece." He snapped, stepping toward the man in question.

"Have fun," she said, not caring what happened to the man. Maybe that was wrong, but she was tired of people taking shots at her and her family. No one would hurt her daughter again if she had anything to say about it.

"Our daughter," Saxon said as she joined him. "Let's go swimming, shall we?"

"Yes, let's go swimming, and then, you can tell me what the good doc had to say," she said, earning a snort from him.

"You know we need swimsuits," Saxon's little fire said, drawing his attention back to her and Ana. Right now, the young men that had threatened his woman were dealing with a furious Drake. Their parents now under the scrutiny of Drake and the elders. If it was one thing, any species caught touching or harming a child would be put down immediately. Already the one with the pink hair had sealed his death, the other, Drake was still considering after draining him halfway.

As if on cue, Storm came to the rescue as she stepped from the tunnel into the hidden pond. Ana squealed with delight, Saxon couldn't tell if it was from her new swimsuit or the pond itself. "Ana, do you know how to swim?" he asked the little girl who shook her head.

"I want you to promise to stay by the shore, sweetie," Saxon said, lowering the little girl to the sandy ground as some floaty things appeared around her arms and waist. "It might be shallow, but I want you close." He ruffled her hair and watched her take off toward the water as a blanket appeared at the shore edge for them.

"Thank you, Storm, but you can join us if you would like," Nava said. "I'm sure Ana would love to meet her soon-to-be aunt," Nava said as Storm dressed his woman in the hottest bathing suit he'd seen. "Nice, I like," Nava said and looked over her shoulder at him. "Now, I do believe you need a suit, too."

Saxon knew as soon as Nava said that he needed a swimsuit he was in trouble. Sure enough, hearing Ana's squeal of laughter before he even looked down, he knew she was laughing at him.

"Oh my, please, tell me his, umm, thing isn't in the trunk," Nava whispered to Storm, giggling her head off.

He looked down to see the elephant trunks he had on and moaned. Sure enough, his cock was now encased in the elephant truck. "Really? We have a little one here, Storm." Saxon shook his head as the trunks changed but still had the picture of the elephant.

His little fire smiled and moved to the water with Storm, sitting part in the water and on the sand, watching Ana play. Saxon scanned around the natural pond, it was a small one compared to a few of them in the area. He knew this one was fed by the Haven River. Soon, he'd have to take his mate to the healing pools, hot springs for some alone time.

"Do I need to call in help?" Saxon asked as Matty moved to his side, his gaze on Storm.

"No. Dad and Ringo are handling this. He wants us to concentrate on our mates." Matty snorted. "Mom said she wants lots of grandbabies to keep Ana company. Told to start crawling if I have to."

Saxon smiled as Ana came running over to him, looking from Matty to him. "Are you going to come in?" Her little hand slid into his big one, trying to pull him toward the water. "Who's that?" she asked Saxon.

He leaned down and lifted up his wet little girl into his arms. "That would be your Uncle Matty." He told her, but already, she had turned her attention onto something else, his chest, staring at the picture of his demon tattooed on his chest.

"Is this you?" she asked and shivered.

"It's my other form, but you have nothing to worry about. He or we would never harm you; my other side would protect you as I would your mommy. You are our daughter, Ana." Her gaze lifted to his, and he swore someone had punched him in the gut when he noticed the tears there.

"You promise?" she asked, her voice nothing but a whisper.

Without thinking, Saxon shifted, making sure he was clothed properly, wanting his little girl to meet his other half. "I promise, no, both of us do, my little princess," he said, rubbing his cheek against hers, making her giggled.

She reached up, placing her hands on his cheeks, staring at him, and Saxon swore he could already see the flames in her eyes. "You are pink! My favorite color," Ana said.

"Red, Ana. I'm red," he grumbled as Storm and Nava laughed, coming up to join them.

"I agree with Ana. You're pink, and I think you look pretty," Nava teased, taking Ana out of his arms and making a run for the water.

"I do believe that is a reason to attack, don't you?" Saxon growled to Matty, heading after the woman and Ana, making her squeal and laugh as Matty and he chased the girls in the water. For two hours, the four of them playing with little Ana, until she was falling asleep in Nava's arms.

"I think it's time to put this little one to bed," Nava said, placing a kiss on her cheek.

Saxon stood and stretched before reaching down and taking Ana into his arms. She didn't even wake up as he held her, helping Nava up. Both Storm and Matty moved with them out of the little cove and into the tunnels. "I think our little princess here will always remember this day. It's the first day she could be a child," Saxon said.

"And she'll have many, many more if I have anything to say about it." Nava frowned and looked away but not before he had spotted the tear running down her cheek.

"What's wrong, little fire?" he said, pulling her close to him.

"What if Ana wasn't the only child? There could be others out there that we wouldn't even know about." Nava looked up at him. "Can you really accept me and the possibility that there might be more children out there?" She shook her head. "Hell, it's even too much for me to accept, let alone you."

Saxon stopped and turned fully to his little fire. "Look at me, Nava," he growled and waited. Slowly, she lifted her head, looking up at him. "These past few days have taught me one thing. No matter if there were a hundred children out there, I'm not leaving." He looked around him. "There is no heart, no heat without you in my life. You are the fire, my light; never will anything, anyone stop me from loving you, being at your side."

Nava snorted. "I don't think I could have a hundred babies out there. You don't think I do, do you?" she squeaked.

Matty reached over and squeezed Nava's arm. "Talk to Mom, Nava. I think you and Elf should speak with her because if I'm not mistaken, I think the three of you are in the same position, but with mom, her children could be my age and older."

Nava gasped and put her hand on her heart. "Their damn dicks need to be chopped off and ground up to feed to the damn sharks. Who does this to you would think in this time and age..." she shook her head. "You're right. Maybe the three of us can start to dig deeper into computers and see what we can find. Set up a website or something for others to reach us because you know that this one place isn't the only facility they have."

"You know I have an empty office on the side of my building. You guys could set up an office there away from home," Storm offered. "It happens to be close to the sheriff's office, too."

They all started to walk again. "I like that idea. Thank you, Storm, I'll speak with Darla and Elf about it tomorrow. It might give Elf something to focus on to help. We do need to start looking for our own place though. I can't keep taking from Darla and Drake. They have done enough for us," she said.

"You will be going nowhere right now," Drake growled as Darla and he met them when they stepped into the kitchen a few minutes later. "I mean it, Nava, this is your home now; as you have seen, there is plenty of room, and it's safe. You can even redecorate the west wing. Hell, Darla has a whole shop of furniture."

"Drake, I know that I picked out some, but really. You have other sons and now two little ones. Saxon and I will need our own place eventually anyway if things keep moving along the way Saxon hopes it will," Nava said.

"May I make a suggestion?" Darla asked. "How about the caretaker's old place? It's connected to the house but separate. It would give Nava and Saxon their privacy, but still offer the security of our grounds. I mean, the house has over six bedrooms, and it just needs fixing up."

Drake nodded. "I never thought of that, and it's been just sitting there empty. Why don't we show it to you two tomorrow? Darla had a few things added to the room next to yours for Ana, that way she won't be so scared. Elf and her children are settling in. So, you two, go spend some quiet time, and we'll see you in the morning," Drake ordered, leaning over and placing a kiss on the top of Nava's head. "We have much to discuss, Nava, but it's been a tiring day, night." Drake met Saxon's gaze and nodded to him. "Tomorrow we all need to sit down and talk."

"Why do I get the feeling something has happened?" Saxon said as Ana moved in his arms, a little whimper coming from her had him reaching up and rubbing her back.

"Tomorrow. Matty, Storm, follow us, please, I would have a word with you both before your mother and I turn in," Drake said, turning around, moving toward the north wing of their home as Darla, Storm, and Matty each said good night, following Drake.

Nava looked up at him. "I feel like it's been months, not days. So, what bad news do you think he's going to lay on us tomorrow?" Nava asked, moving toward her wing of rooms.

"Who knows if it's bad news. There is no sense in thinking the worse," Saxon said, but in his gut, he knew something was about to happen that would affect all of them.

Chapter Fifteen

It was late, and Nava was not only physically tired, but also mentally. What was in order was some nice soft jazz music, which so happened to reach her as Nava stepped into her room after putting her little girl down for the night, explaining they were right next door if she needed them.

But what had surprised her and Saxon for Ana's room were what Darla and Drake had done to the room. A small pink canopy bed was in the middle of it surrounded by dolls and stuffed toys for her little girl to explore, but crawling into bed, Ana had latched onto a small wolf with big green eyes. Nava swore those eyes reminded her of Doc Lope.

"You going to tell me what the doc wanted?" she asked, smiling, seeing the candles and bubble bath that awaited her as she stripped out of her clothes, not even caring if Saxon saw her. "Thank you." She moaned, sliding into the warm water. "I don't know if I like you in my head, but right now, I sure am a happy camper here."

"You are not the only one who loves a bath. Scoot up, little fire, I plan to join you in there. After a hard day training, I believe the hot bath will work wonder on the muscles," Saxon said, stripping out of his damp trunks and scooting behind her.

"I don't know why I'm allowing this but too tired to argue," Nava said, leaning back against Saxon's big, muscled chest. "You don't get hair on your chest, do you?"

"No." Saxon wrapped his arms around her just holding her. "What the doc wanted to speak to me about was he thinks our little Ana is his mate."

She would have jumped up and glared at Saxon, but he held her tight, not allowing her to move an inch. "Damn it,

Saxon, she's only six. How the hell does he know?" Now agitated all over again.

He reached out and twined his fingers with hers. "Relax, little fire. Doc knows he can't do anything. If anything, he'll be more added protection for our little girl. Many of our species can tell early on who will be their mate, but even we were confused about this. It's usually not this early. Doc thinks it has something to do with the fact she is like her mother, a Phoenix." He lifted her arm up and started to wash her with a giant soft natural sponge.

"Tell me why my kind, the Phoenix, is so special and sought after? And that does not mean I'm going to allow Doc to claim our daughter right away. She has the right to date and stuff; you can't take that way. Prom, high school dances and things like that," she said, relaxing a little more as he pushed her forward and started to rub her back and neck down.

"You didn't have that, did you, little fire?"

She shook her head. "No, Mom home schooled me. We were too afraid of someone finding us." Nava smiled. "I sort of had a prom. My mom and dad one night put up tons of little Christmas lights in our tiny backyard, decorations Mom had made and called me out back where my father and mother proceeded to teach me every dance they could think of." She peeked over her shoulder at him. "I really miss them."

"I'm so sorry, little fire. If I could bring them back for you, I would."

"Question, if my grandmother can float around here, can't my parents come to Magic too? I mean it wouldn't be the same, but knowing they were around so I could to speak to them," she asked.

"I don't know. Your friend is here that died recently, so I don't see why they shouldn't be able to come here. Maybe we should ask Topper or Drake; they could find out. Even your grandmother might know what happened to them. Because it sounds like your parents loved you very much, and I believe they would be here if they were able to." She felt his breath on her right ear. "But let's hope they don't appear right now," he said, running his teeth against the side of her neck.

Her nipples hardened, and Nava swore her blood started to heat up as Saxon lifted her up and turned her, so she was facing him. He reached up and cupped her face, holding it in his hands, staring in her eyes. "For the last few days I've spent beside you, I've come to realize I can't be separated from you, little fire." He took a deep breath, resting his forehead against hers. "I know—

Nava placed a finger over his mouth, stopping his words. "Time seems of little importance right now, don't you think? Look at what we have been given in the last few days. A new family, brothers, and sisters. A daughter and a warm home, but above all, you, Saxon, have become the center of my life in that short space of time." She leaned in and placed a little kiss on his lips. "My mother always told me I'd know when I'd find the right man. That my heart and body would belong to him and no one else." Nava smiled. "You should have seen Mom's face when I asked what she meant about the body. My dad laughed and explained a few things to me. To say it was embarrassing, well yeah."

"That is one conversation I can wait for with our little girl," Saxon said, nipping her lower lip before bending her backward and sucking one of her nipples into his mouth, staring at her the whole time.

"Saxon," she whispered, holding onto his head as he played with her breasts.

He reached up and twisted her other nipple with his fingers. *"Will you give yourself to me tonight, my little fire? I want to make you burn tonight. Will you allow my claim?"* he asked inside her head, still sucking on her, holding and watching.

"I knew when I bumped into you on the street the other day that you would be the one to take what I had saved for this night. But a girl has to allow her man to chase her a little, no?" she asked, running her hand over his short, stubbled hair.

Saxon released her nipple, placing a kiss on it before placing a trail of kisses up her neck until he got to her mouth. "I'll always chase you, my little fire. No matter where you go, I'll be right beside you, making sure your flame burns deep and bright for me, only me." He growled, covering her mouth in a kiss that lit the burning passions inside her.

He stood, water dripping from him, as he broke the kiss. Saxon didn't say a word as he carried her to the bed and softly placed her at the end of it with her feet dangling off the edge. He reached down, lifting one of her legs, placing kisses all down her leg before placing her foot on the edge of the bed before turning to do the next. The way he had her laid out, open for him to see everything she was, had her drawing her legs together.

"No, little fire. I want you open. I intend to play for just a bit tonight," he said, lowering himself to his knees. "Mine."

She was about to say yes, but nothing came out as he lowered his mouth and pushed his tongue right into her. "Saxon!" She grabbed onto the bed quilt and held on as he made love to her with his mouth. In and out, little nibbles to her thighs, sucking her nub with his fingers rubbing some little spot that had her burning so bad she saw stars. When she finally could put two thoughts together, Nava realized Saxon was standing at the end of bed watching, stroking his cock back and forth with a satisfied smile on his face.

"Welcome back, little fire. Turn around, on your hands and knees. Give yourself to me," his voice dark, deep and a tiny bit of a whip to it.

Nava glanced down at his cock and realized it was time, that he had given her a sample of his loving before his claiming. Nava whimpered as she slowly moved to position herself for him.

She glanced down as he grabbed hold of her hips and brought her back a little, so her knees were on the end of the bed. His gaze met hers. "To claim you in the way of my people, I will be in my natural form. Are you going to be okay with this?" he asked, running his fingers over one of her ass cheeks, sending a slight chill up her spine. "You'll carry my scent as I wear yours now." He lowered his head and ran his tongue over her wet lips, sending a quick orgasm through her when he hit her small nub.

"So ready for me. You will carry my mark, little fire." He

squeezed her ass cheeks as he shifted.

She might have fire running in her blood, but he was the ignition switch that started the actual fire. A small swat to her ass brought her back to the present. "Did you know in this form, my tongue..." he lowered his head and pushed his thick, long tongue into her, reaching that delicate membrane that she had saved for him.

His eyes seemed to dance as he stood, rubbing his cock up and down her pussy lips. "Do you accept my claim, little fire?" he growled.

"I do, but Saxon, I want a wedding when things settle down," she said, smiling as she glanced back at him again. "With dancing and the town of Magic there as our guests since they have been so nice to me."

He moaned but nodded. "It will be done. Hold on, little fire," was the only warning she got as he slid the top of his cock inside her, stretching her he was so thick.

"Look at that pussy taking me in," he said, squeezing her ass. "This is going to hurt for a second, little fire," he growled out and pushed his cock forward, breaking the membrane, claiming her. There was no wait; her breath got stuck in her throat as the pain shocked her for a second before Nava remembered her mother's words. *"When we give our body to a special man, our pain for the first time is more intense than that of a normal person. Not only is that man claiming you, but your body will also claim him, giving him part of you that he'll carry with him always. So, make sure this man is the one for you, Nava, because once you give that gift, there is no going back for us."* Nava remembered her warning just as Saxon's words drew her back.

"What the... Little fire, did you forget to tell me something?" Saxon growled as he pushed all the way into her, leaning down over her small body, covering her.

The pain slowly faded, and Nava could answer his question. "Mother told me about something..." she said, glancing back at him. "Didn't remember it 'til you... well you know." She moved her hips and earned a growl from him.

Chapter Sixteen

*H*is back burned, knowing his little fire had just branded him with her mark as he had with his. But he had a feeling her pain took away the aspect she now wore his family's mark on the left side of her neck and down her shoulder. Yes, she was totally his, and he couldn't be any happier.

But it would seem his mate had surfaced from the pain to needing him as he needed her. He grabbed hold of her hands and squeezed them as he started to move in and out of her pussy. Her body accepting him into her heated tunnel had him gripping her hips tight. "Never will be a part again," he ground out, reaching around, circling her sensitive, swollen nub, building the fire that would only end with the both of them combusting together, sealing their bond.

"I love you, little fire," he said, placing kisses on her shoulder and neck before the demon side of him sank his teeth into her shoulder, holding her steady as he increased his pace and the force of his thrusts. Never had he been so hard, Saxon was afraid he'd come too fast and not give his woman the experience she deserved—a night of passion that lit the room and her eyes as she came, not to mention the little cries that came from her when she exploded from his touch.

Her legs started to shake, her skin clammy against his chest and her breathing came in gasps as Nava cried out as he pressed down on her swollen clit, sending her over at the same time he released his seed inside her, hoping that a child would be born from their love. One, two, three, more thrusts into her and she fell onto the bed, panting. "Not moving," she mumbled into the blanket under her.

He licked the spot where he had buried his teeth into her

shoulder. "Don't. I'll take care of you, little fire," he said, sliding out of her, moaning right along with her. Saxon stood there staring down at his woman all stretched out, his seed running down the inside of her leg, and he couldn't help but feel humble she had given her maidenhead to him, seeing the little blood, too.

"You'll be a little sore tomorrow, and I'm afraid I got a little carried away, for that I'm sorry," Saxon said as he moved to the bathroom, soaping up a cloth to clean her.

"And I'll smile inside each time I move thinking of the way you claimed me," Nava said, lifting her head up and held out her hand. "Here, give me that; I'll clean up. You shouldn't be cleaning up after me."

"No, I will take care of you," Saxon said, kneeling down between her legs, gently cleaning her, not giving her a choice.

"Are your parents really coming here?" she asked as he threw the cloth in the bathroom and scooped her up into his arms.

"There is no sense in worrying about it. We are already mated, their daughter now," he said, pulling back the covers and laying her in the middle of the bed before crawling in next to her. He wrapped his arms around her, pulling her body into his. "Sleep, little fire, it's been a long day, and I have a feeling tomorrow will be just as busy," he told her, placing a kiss on the top of her head.

It didn't take her long before her breathing evened out and Saxon heard little snores coming from her. He looked up and froze. A man and woman stood at the edge of their bed, smiling down at them. Saxon swore the woman looked just like the one in his arms. "Little fire, I think we have company," he whispered into her ear.

"What? Is Ana..." Nava sat up in bed when she let out a cry. "Momma, Papa." Tears rolled down her cheeks.

"Oh, baby, look at you. You're are such a beauty," her mother said, earning a squeak from his mate as she lifted the sheet covering her body. "Relax, I've seen you naked before. I think you should introduce us to your man here."

Nava took his hand and twined her fingers with his. "Mom, Dad, I'd like you to meet Saxon." She glanced back at him. "He's my new world now, along with Ana."

Her mother frowned and looked at her father. "Who is Ana?" he asked.

"My daughter. They took my eggs, Daddy. We don't know how many of my children are out there alone," she whispered, earning a growl from her father. Fur started to cover his skin, shocking her. "You're a wolf?"

Her father's gaze left his for a minute. "Yes, baby, I'm a wolf shifter, and you?" he asked Saxon.

"Demon, and it's a pleasure to meet you. Are you two going to stick around? We have others that have passed that stay here. Matter of fact..." As if on cue, Calamity Jane appeared next to the woman, startling her.

"So, this is my granddaughter. She has my eyes. It's good to have family here. It's been a long time." Jane looked over her shoulder. "But you'll have to excuse me; I have a posse on my tail, and they're not happy," she said, disappearing again, but right after she left, three of the posse showed up, half-dressed, fire burning in their eyes.

"Where is that woman? And don't you try and protect her; she needs to learn her place," the one man said right before he found himself on his ass. "Damn it, Jane."

"Knows her place? Really," Jane's voice rang out as Nava busted out laughing.

"Welcome to our new city, Momma and Papa." Saxon's woman laughed, curling up next to him, yawning.

Both of them shook their head and smiled. "You two, get some sleep. We'll talk in the morning, and relax, we're not going anywhere, pumpkin," her father told them. "We'll help in any way we can to track down our grandbabies if they're out there." Both of them disappeared.

Nava turned in his arms and threw herself at him, hugging him tightly. "I love you," she whispered, placing kisses all over his face.

He rolled her onto her back, looking down at his woman. "And I love you, my little fire. Now, go to sleep before I'm tempted to take you again when I know you are tender." He grumbled and started nibbling her neck down to her breast.

"But what if I want you to make love to me again? You

know I'm kind of wide awake here now," she said and tried to flip him back on his back, but he didn't budge, smiling down at her.

"No, your health comes first. It's been a very long day," he rolled onto his back, pulling her to his side. "Sleep, but tomorrow morning be prepared to be ravished," he told her.

"You don't think my parents were waiting until we got done... you know." She squeaked, looking at him.

"Making love, and no. I would have felt their presence. We'll find out more tomorrow along with Drake's news." Saxon turned his head, looking toward the door. He had a strange feeling it had to deal with Elf, but he wasn't about to say anything until he knew for sure.

His woman curled up against him. "I bet Momma and Papa are checking in on Ana. Just think she takes after Daddy, he'll love it," she whispered just before closing her eyes. His woman, his life would be a challenge loving a Phoenix, but Saxon knew he was up to it.

* * * *

Elf stood in the doorframe of her suite staring at her friend's room. She still couldn't believe she was free and that two of her children were with her. But what had her confused was the fact that she was actually standing her own mother's home. Elf had known the minute Darla had stepped onto the property where she had been held, that there was a connection to this woman. But now, it all made sense. Elf was one of those children born in a lab.

She turned and quietly shut her door, thinking of the man that was Saxon's best friend, Kaylen. Even thinking his name sent a shiver up her spine. But right now, she couldn't think of that as the door to the children's door opened, and her little one stood there with tears in her eyes. "I thought it was all a dream. We're really safe?"

For a three-year-old, Maranda was very smart and had been poked on most of her life. "We are safe," she said, scooping up her daughter and moving back into the room and her child's bed. "Would you like me to sleep with you?"

Her little daughter nodded, popping her thumb into her mouth and laying her head on her shoulder. As she turned to crawl in the bed, a woman with crazy colored hair appeared near her. She reached out and wrapped her arms around her tight. "I could feel your sorrow from so far away. I know I am your mother, and you are now at home, child. Believe in our town, Elf. You're safe," were the last words she heard as her eyes started to close as Elf lay her daughter down, crawling in next to her. "You'll sleep without nightmares, that I promise, all of you." The colorful woman told her as she took a deep breath, feeling safe for the first time in her life. Her new adventure just starting to begin.

Magic in His Touch
Little Angel Rescue, Book 2

Chapter One

$\mathcal{E}$lf took a sip her cup of coffee, wandering down one of the tunnels of the beautiful home her mother had. She smiled; Darla was her natural mother, and her stepfather, the one, and only Dracula, or Drake, had made sure to take her blood, giving her his, also, connecting all of them. Now, he and Darla were watching her little ones, seeing Elf had needed some alone time.

She shook her head, remembering that morning at breakfast three days ago, where everyone had joined her and Nava at the table. Drake, Darla, Saxon, Matty, Ringo, Doc Lope, Storm, and, of course, the children.

Her little boy in her arms, Elf had been feeding him from her breast, while his sister sat next to her eating a bowl of cereal.

"We have found out that this so-called organization, GSP, have been taking the eggs of females from all around the world. Creating children, breeding them with other species. To do what? We are still trying to figure this out. Not only have they taken Nava's eggs producing Ana, but my wife has also found out they have taken some of her eggs as well. We believe Elf is Darla's daughter, correction, our daughter," Drake had said, giving her a look from across the table, waiting to see if she objected, but who was she to object to an already-made family. One she had wished for, for so long.

Elf met his gaze, hearing all the gasps around the room but finally turned to look at her mother. "I knew when I saw her on the compound. Darla is my mother, the blood connection is there," Elf said as Darla came to her side, kneeling in between her and her own daughter.

"How old are you, Elf?" Darla asked, taking her hand,

squeezing it as she hugged her. "I missed everything; they've hurt you so bad." There were tears in Darla's voice, which brought tears to hers.

Elf took a deep breath, trying to swallow the knot in her throat, but it didn't work as she remembered her mother's expression as she told her how old she was. "I'm twenty-nine years. Don't know what day they birthed me," she said.

Her mom, Darla, laid her head on her shoulder. "I would have been gone two years when..." Darla looked down at Malcom in her arms. "He's beautiful, and your little girl stunning," Darla said, glancing at Maranda. You have two brothers here, and of course, the two little girls we have adopted, Elle and Tara. You know Nava, who we have taken in as our daughter, too."

Darla stood up. "She has a daughter Ana. She too was born at the..."

"Prison," Elf said, lifting her son up and starting to burp him after fixing her clothes. "The women weren't the only ones who had children taken from them. My natural father had been held captive there for over fifty years, 'til he died." A tear rolled down her cheek. "He found me when I was five; he was an elf. They killed him when they found out he was trying to get me out." Elf looked up at Darla's husband. "They have little prisons around the US and other countries. Willow could be anywhere."

"All over the world?" both Darla and Nava whispered together.

Elf glanced over at her friend-sister, watching Saxon lift her up and place her on his lap, holding her tight. "We'll find every place, the children, and destroy their little prisons," Saxon growled.

"The first thing we do is find the damn traitor living among us," Drake said. "But Storm's idea about opening up an office is a good one. If there are any children out there that have gotten free, I want to set up a safe place for them to come. I even believe the town folk will help."

"I've been thinking about that. What do you think about the name, Little Angel Rescue?" Nava asked, and Elf smiled.

"You remembered," Elf said.

"Who could forget. I still see her running and hiding from us..." Nava closed her eyes.

Elf had excused herself, heading back to her room when Darla had caught up with her, knowing she had needed time alone to comprehend everything that had happened in the last twenty hours.

Darla reached over, taking her son into her arms, while Drake had knelt down to explain to Maranda who they were.

Elf's laugh echoed in the tunnel she was in, remembering how big her daughter's eyes had gotten, looking at her to see if it were true.

As Elf stepped around a corner, she stopped, noticing a small group of men there talking. What she didn't like was their attention was now on her, and damn it, she'd wanted to see the waterfall Darla had told her of.

She had two choices, go around them, ignoring them, or turn around, but it would seem the idiots choose something totally different, surrounding her before Elf could do anything.

One was so brazen that he ran his finger down her scared back. "Look, the woman likes the whip. Never knew Drake to have such lovely ladies around. Just might have to move here to Magic after all," he said, sending a shiver down her spine and not a good one either.

"And I'd have to kill you," a very pissed-off Ringo, her brother, said behind her, with the one she had heard called Kayden.

Kayden didn't say a word, shoving the offending man away from her and pulling her back to his side. "If I did wanted Drake to kill me, you'd be dead, touching what is mine," he growled, shifting right there.

If Drake hadn't appeared next to her, Elf would have given Kayden a good swift kick to his shins. *His, my ass.*

"Daughter, I believe you wanted to see the waterfall. Ringo, please escort your sister there, and Kayden, we will speak later as to this claim you have just made."

Drake leaned over and whispered to her, "My granddaughter is right now showing my wife how to finger paint. I have to say, our two little girls were having a ball face painting with Maranda."

Elf laughed, she couldn't help it, picturing Darla covered in paints. "I've been there a few times, but she'll have fun getting it out of her hair."

Drake smiled as Ringo pulled Elf around the group of men, heading toward her original destination when she heard the scream. Elf stopped and started to turn back when both Kayden and her brother shook their heads.

"No, little sister, it is my father's right. This is our home, and many of our people are here as guests, but some believe they have free rein while here, and that is not so as they are finding out," Ringo growled.

Elf frowned and jumped in front of both men, turning to glare at both. "You should have let me handle it. I'm not a wimp, and who the hell are you, claiming I'm yours? I don't even know you, and put on some damn clothes," she muttered, waving her hand at his body part that was very impressive, but she'd be damned if he would know what she thought, at least now.

* * * *

Kayden shifted, clothing himself, all the while never taking his gaze from the stunning woman before him. Oh, there was no doubt she was his mate, but was he truly ready for an already-made family?

Elf snorted. "Better," she said, spinning around and moving back down the tunnel.

Ringo reached out and smacked him upside the head. "What the hell is wrong with you? Why didn't you tell her that you're her mate? If you're screwing around with my sister's head, I swear, best friend or not, I'll rip you apart." Ringo started to follow his sister, but Kayden reached out and grabbed his arm.

"She's mine, never doubt it, but do I have the right to claim her so fast when she's been through so much? Plus, I'd like to give her little girl time to get to know me," Kayden said right before he almost knocked Elf over as she stood there staring up at him.

"Mate? Like in real mate thing? Like Nava and Saxon?" her voice squeaked, and he couldn't help but smile at the little beauty before him.

Before he could say anything, Elf was growling. "That's why Saxon told me all of that stuff about demons, isn't it? He knew?"

Kayden frowned. "I don't know. The only one I told was your brother and now you. This is new to me, too, Elf. My father told me what it would be like, but I just ignored him. Boy, was that a mistake. The first time I got close to you… Let's just say yesterday was a rough day, maybe that is why Saxon knew. It took me a few minutes just to be able to move," he grumbled, earning a smile from Elf.

"You really had a hard time and want to get to know my children?" Elf asked as if she didn't believe he'd like to get to know her babies.

Kayden couldn't help but reach up and cup her cheek. "Of course, I would want to be part of your children's lives. They are part of you, Elf." His cock hardened to the point of pain when his hand touched her face, but he ignored it.

He would take his time with this lovely lady, showing her the outside world she never had gotten to see. "Let's go see this waterfall, and maybe, later, we can take your little girl for ice cream?" he asked, running his thumb over her bottom lip, which quivered beneath his touch.

She spun away from him and would have run smack into a wall if he hadn't reached out and pulled her back into his arms. "Easy, little filly, don't need you hurting yourself."

Elf tilted her head back, staring up at him. "You really want to take us out for ice cream? You do know I have three children, not two?" Her eyes filled with tears, and Kayden had to push his other half back, knowing right now his Elf needed gentleness.

"I will promise you this right now, Elf. I will stand beside you every step of the way as we try and find your other daughter. She will be part of our family, and yes, I want to take you out for ice cream this afternoon. It's supposed to be really nice today. A perfect day for your first outing."

"Come here, little sister, let's show you these beautiful falls and give you time to think without his hands all over you," Ringo growled, glaring at him.

"Damn it, Ringo. She's my mate," he said but followed them into the next alcove to stare in awe at the beautiful site. "Wow, impressive. It almost reminds me of the jungles of the rainforest when we were down there."

Ringo nodded. "My father took my mom there for their anniversary, and Mom loved it. So, slowly, my father has been adding to it, turning it into the place they loved."

"It's one of the most beautiful things I've seen," Elf whispered, moving forward, stepping into the jungle. "There are animals here, too." Elf smiled, looking at him. "Hear the birds?" she asked, and he nodded.

"What other animals did you bring?" he asked, walking behind Elf.

"Actually, we didn't bring the animals. They found a way in from outside," Ringo said, but his attention was on Elf as she jumped up on one of the larger boulders.

"What are you doing?" Kayden asked, jumping up, joining her. "Never mind, damn, this is stunning."

A bright-colored rainbow formed over the falls, birds, and trees so large you'd swear they had been there for years, but what impressed him the most was the way the light from the outside sun broke over the massive rock structures of the caverns. "How?" he asked Ringo, who joined them on the rock.

"It's not the sun but lights powered by the sun." Ringo pointed around the rocks, showing them what they had missed.

"Amazing. I think this would be my favorite place, too. I know one place where I need to visit now," Elf whispered, sitting down, hugging her legs, resting her chin on her knee.

Kayden knelt down next to her, brushing a lock of her hair out of her face. "What can I do to help?" he asked, seeing the pain in her eyes.

"There isn't much anyone can do. All the places I used to dream of going as a little girl..." Elf said, just staring.

"We have a lifetime to visit anywhere you want, but first, we find our other daughter. We need our family whole so all of you can start healing," Kayden said, sitting down next to her.

Ringo took the other side of her; he nudged her with his shoulder. "Remember, little sister, we have all the time in the world to visit any place you want."

"True, but you know the two of you don't have to stay here with me; I'll be okay." Elf looked at him then at Ringo.

"Hey now, I just found out I have another baby sister; do you really think I'm going to let you out of my sight." He reached over and took her hand in his. "Where do you think Matty is?" Ringo asked.

Elf laughed and shook her head. "Nava."

"Yep, you get to put up with all of us for the first few years. We need to get to know our sisters and make sure the lug heads treat our sisters right," Ringo said, giving him the eye. "Even if he is my best friend."

Kayden growled and went to reach around Elf, ready to throw his friend off the rock. "You little weasel," he growled.

Elf laughed and pushed him away. "Hey, leave the family alone," she teased. "After all, I have no idea about this mating thing. You could have made it up. I mean, I don't know much of anything," she said, frowning, getting up and jumping off the rock, leaving them. "I have to get back to my kids," he heard her say as she ran out of the cavern back into the tunnels.

Kayden sighed, getting up and following her, giving her the time she needed to sort things out in her head. "I want to find every one of those bastards and kill them," he growled next to Ringo.

"Stand in line. They've destroyed so many lives, but I really think opening this office will help all three of them sort this out and find others that need help. I have a feeling our little town is going to be growing," Ringo said.

"I'm not letting her get away, Ringo. For the first time since my mom was killed, there is... I don't know how to explain it. Already, Elf has left her footprint on my heart. But I was thinking, you know that old mansion out at the end of our city? Why don't we fix that up for those that show up and need a place? We could make it into some little apartments."

Ringo punched his arm. "Now, that is just sappy, jeez. But I like your idea; we'll talk with Dad and Saxon later."

"Wait, my friend, 'til you meet your mate," Kayden growled and shoved Ringo into the stone wall right before they walked into the kitchen to see one pissed-off Dracula.

Chapter Two

Elf had run up the stairs to her suite of rooms, looking for her mother and the children. Dracula was ready to blow, and Elf wondered if her mother would be able to help him.

When she had stepped foot in the kitchen, his bloodshot eyes had met hers, and she froze. The only time Elf had seen someone that furious had been when Tormac...

Drake must have seen her tremble as she remembered the one man that scared the shit out of her the most. The one of a few hundred that Elf had found out that were helping the nut cases, telling them where to find their kind.

Taking a deep breath, Drake tried to smile for her, but it was worse, with his big long fangs hanging out. "Elf, would you find my wife; I'd like to speak with her, please," he had asked, and all she could do was nod, running out of the room fast. Ignoring the other men in the room totally.

Elf stopped at her door, trying to catch her breath and stop the shaking. The thought of Tormac searching for her had never crossed her mind, but now...

"Elf, are you okay?" her mother asked.

She had been so out of it, Elf hadn't heard the door open. "Your husband needs you downstairs. Sorry, ran up here. Guess I'm out of shape." Elf smiled. "Here, I was looking forward to seeing you all painted up, but you're clean already." Elf pouted, and Darla laughed.

"One of the good things about being with Drake, he does have his gifts. The little guy is out cold, and Maranda is coloring in Nava's suite with Ana and your sisters. But, Elf, there is nothing you can't tell me. We're all here to help." Darla squeezed her arm, moving past her, going to find her mate.

"Soon," Elf whispered, knowing she'd have to share this

news if they were ever going to stop this. Closing the door to her room, Elf made her way into the bedroom, when off to the side, the closet door was wide open, and a light was on.

What she saw had her grinning from ear to ear. Nava had told her what her soon-to-be sister-in-law had done for her, and it looked like Elf had gotten the same gift. "Thank you, Storm," she whispered, walking into the closet, staring in disbelief at the beautiful clothes before her.

Tears ran down her cheeks. "I've never had anything new," Elf whispered, running her fingers over the clothes.

"My gift to you. I also have some clothes over here for your little girl." Storm flew by her, pointing to the corner. "I even did a couple of daughter-and-mom outfits if you're into to that." Storm smiled.

"You don't know how much this means to me. I've never had new clothes." Elf smiled. "Maybe you can help me. We're supposed to go out to the ice cream place with my brother and Kayden, who says he's my mate..." Elf waved her hand. "But would love something casual but maybe a little teasing?" she said, looking at Storm, who smiled.

"When are you going? Do you want your daughter to match?" Storm asked, flying around her, and Elf swore she could see steam coming out of her head.

"I knew I'd catch you in here. Isn't she great," Nava said, coming to join her in the closet.

"She's amazing. I've asked her to help me with my first outing. Kayden is taking all of us for ice cream later. I'd like to walk around town, and maybe, we can stop by Storm's shop. I'd like to see the part we'd change into an office. I don't mean to be ungrateful, but it might be wise to have the office somewhere else, because you know they're going to come after us, and I don't want Storm's place ruined in the crossfire."

Storm shifted to her full size, frowning at Elf. "One, our building is protected not only from me, but also from the local witches in town. They were lucky at the dinner, we weren't expecting a full out attack like we got. So, Topper and her sisters all went through the town protecting it. If that isn't enough, do you really think Drake is going to allow anything to happen to the three of us, not to mention our mates."

Elf moaned. "Please, don't say that; I'm certainly not ready yet for Kayden's claim. Plus, some things need to be done before I'd feel safe to, well, you know," Elf said, looking at her friend. "So, where are our little girls?"

Nava reached over and twined her fingers into Elf's. "We're safe here, Elf."

"Not yet, there are others, Nava. Ones you didn't see, traitors, who helped these men. Willow is daughter to one of them. I need to find out if he's the one who took her."

"Is he the one who hurt you?" Nava asked.

"They all hurt me, Nava, but yes, he was one of the ones who raped me. Guess I was his kept prize until he found out that the humans were going to double cross him. Six of their men died, and Tormac disappeared."

The growl behind her had Elf jumping along with Nava and Storm. In the doorway, Drake and Kayden stood, behind them, her brothers and Saxon. "Tormac from the North?"

"I have no idea where he's from." She rubbed her arms, just thinking of the man.

"He was in my home, ate at my table, and he betrayed us? We need names, Elf." Drake demanded.

"Knock it off!" Darla said, pushing through the men—two stepped in front of them—and pointing with her finger. "Get out of here now. You don't come in here and demand a damn thing. I don't know what bug crawled up your butt, but you will not act like a damn idiot," Darla hissed.

"Mother, it's okay. I was going to talk to them anyway," Elf said.

"No, it's not okay. You haven't even had a day to rest. So back the hell out of here, now." Darla growled, shocking her and even her husband, who stepped forward.

"Darla, calm down. No one is going to hurt Elf, I promise." Drake inched closer to her, earning a growl, which had Elf inching up and looking at her mom.

Her eyes were red, fangs long and very close to losing it from what Elf could see. "Mom, did you know Storm was going to help me get ready for my very first date?" Elf said, trying to calm her mother. "I kind of had to ask her with clothes since, well, you know, I never had anything new. Want to help?" she asked, placing her hand on her arm, seeing Darla was trying very hard to pull the control back in.

Darla reached over and covered Elf's hand with hers. "And who is the lucky man that is escorting you out? Don't you think it's a little too soon?" Darla asked, turning her focus to her, and Elf could have sworn everyone released the breath they had been holding, well except for one, Kayden.

She took a peek over her shoulder at him and smiled. "It seems I have a mate, or at least, this is what I've been told. He'd like to take the children and me out for ice cream," Elf said, smiling, looking back at her mother, who was frowning, staring at Kayden.

"I know your kind does not make mistakes about mates, but you'll give my daughter the time she needs," Darla said, giving him the eye.

"He will, or I'll put some buckshot in his ass," Calamity Jane said, appearing next to Nava.

"Wait, I have an idea," Darla said and pulled out her phone.

"Darla, what are you doing?" Drake asked.

"Last-minute party. Hello, Lanny, have a question for you. How would you like to rent out your store for an old fashion Ice Cream Social this afternoon? Drake and I would be glad to pay you." Darla glanced at Drake. "Get your checkbook out, honey, we have money to spend for Ice Cream Social for our residents. We can have the sheriff block off Main Street, maybe even have your friend set up a band."

Elf watched a play of emotions run across his face, but he nodded. "Kayden, Saxon, get your men on security and call the sheriff make sure the posse is out scouting. When you're done with that call, you might want to contact Topper and see if she can get her family on decorating the streets. If you'll excuse me, I have a man to start to track down." Drake stepped up to her, and Darla stopped talking, watching her husband.

"I'm sorry if I scared you." Drake grinned and reached out. pulling her into his arms. "I have a feeling you are bonding with our daughter. You had the same reaction with Ringo and the one nurse." He placed a kiss on her cheek. "Let me know the damage."

"Are we having a party?" Ana asked, pushing her way into the closet with Maranda. "Never been to a party."

Darla knelt down in front of the two girls. "I'm planning one right now for this afternoon, an ice cream one. We can all get dressed up and have some fun."

Maranda looked at Elf. "We going?"

Elf knelt down and brushed Maranda's hair back. "Yep. We're going with that man behind you. His name is Kayden, and he's asked to escort us there." Elf leaned over and whispered, "We even have new dresses, too."

Maranda's eyes got big. "Really?" she asked, all excited. "Do we have hats, too?"

Elf smiled and looked back at Storm. "This is going to be your aunt, Maranda. Her name is Storm, and she has designed all these pretty clothes for us. I'm sure we can get some hats, too?" Elf looked at Storm, who nodded.

"I can even make one for him," Storm said as a big woman's hat appeared on Kayden's head, making everyone laugh and him groan.

"Really, I thought my color was purple?" Kayden said, winking at Maranda, making her giggle.

"Well, I was thinking a nice suit for the men, nothing fancy. I do believe Kayden would look handsome in a dark gray pinstripe suit. What do you think, Storm, Elf? Yes, I think all the men should be in pinstripe suits," Darla said before following her husband out of the closet followed by Ana and Nava but not before Nava stopped in front of Kayden.

"You hurt her, you'll be crispy bacon," Nava said, just as casual as ever, but Elf and Kayden knew she was dead serious.

Elf took her daughter's hand, hearing her son starting to stir in the other room. "Come, Malcom is waking. We'll put you in the tub, while I feed the little guy. Storm, thanks for the clothes; I can't wait to try them all on. I hope you and Matty will be coming to the ice cream party?"

Kayden stepped aside, allowing her and Storm to move into the main living quarters when Elf hear Storm snort. "I haven't spoken with Matty in three days." Storm frowned and looked toward the door. "I don't know what's wrong. One minute we were talking, and now, if he keeps this up, I'm done. I can't keep the rollercoaster ride up much more." Storm turned and smiled down at Maranda. "Even if he is my mate."

"Do you want me to speak with him," Kayden growled. "I can show him his errors."

"No, no more help. I'll be back in two hours to help with your outfits," Storm said, disappearing.

"Okay, remind me to punch my brother," Elf said, earning a laugh from her daughter.

"Not before I do. I better go help with security. Three okay?" he asked her, placing a kiss on her cheek and kneeling down, doing the same to her daughter. "I can't wait to see you in your pretty dress," he told Maranda, who smiled. "Be safe, you two lovely ladies," Kayden said, giving her a heated look before spinning around and heading toward the door.

"Be careful, Kayden, Tormac does not fight fair if he's around," she said, heading to her son.

Chapter Three

*K*ayden moved toward Drake's office, knowing that Saxon would be in there with Drake working on security. But upon stepping into the office, a free target stood there listening to Drake talking.

Not waiting, Kayden tapped Matty on the shoulder, waiting for him to turn around, drawing everyone's attention. Matty had no warning as his fist connected with him in an uppercut, sending him across Drake's desk.

"What the hell?" he growled, getting up and ready to come across the desk at him when Drake slapped his hand on the desk, stopping all movement.

"You want to tell me why you just hit my son?" Drake growled.

"Because I just saw his mate with tears in her eyes. If he doesn't do something, I don't know what Strom will do. She's fed up, Drake, and I mean fed up. I swear I've never seen her so sad," he growled.

Drake turned his glare on his son. "Kayden is right; this has gone on long enough. I thought you two were working it out?"

"Stay out of it, Dad. I had to check something out, and I just got back. I'll let that one slide because I had it coming, but don't interfere, any of you," Matty growled, leaving the room.

Drake sat down in his seat, shaking his head. "He's going to lose that girl, and I have no idea why? Saxon, you're best friends with him; anything?" Drake asked his friend and commander.

Saxon shook his head. "They were doing really good until he got a call two days ago. None of us saw him again. I hate to say it, but Nava's ready to fry his ass. Storm even closed down her store yesterday. She was gone all day. Nava was having a fit she was so worried, and I have to say so was I. I've never known Storm to close her store."

"This is not good at all. Is Storm planning on going to-day?" Drake looked at him.

"I don't know. I know she'll be helping Elf and her daughter get ready in a few hours," Kayden said.

Drake smiled, and it wasn't a good one as he reached over and picked up the phone, covering the one end with his hand as he said, "It's time I took matters into my own hands. Saxon, I've already called the brothers in. And, my general, they will meet you at the square to discuss security. I want this town sealed. These children need to be able to relax and not worry."

"It will be done." Saxon nodded and went to leave. "Come on; let's get our men moving. We still don't know who the damn traitor is, so I want everyone on alert. I hate this not knowing, looking at people I've known all my life wondering if they are the one," Saxon said, glancing at him. "Did Elf tell you any more about the traitors?"

Kayden shook his head. "No, I don't know if she isn't sleeping or if this Tormac has Elf so wound up and careful that she keeps to herself. Today was the first day since her arriving here that she's actually come out of her room, except for meals."

"What's your gut telling you about this Tormac?" Saxon asked as they moved down the tunnels to the middle of town.

"He hurt Elf somehow, and if he's as possessive as I feel right now, he's close, waiting for his chance." Kayden growled, the beast itching to come out and search for the man but had no clue on whom and what this man was. "Would like your permission to have Dagr to run a check on him."

Saxon stopped and looked at him. "You know we're treading on Drake's territory?"

"I know, but I have no choice. I need this information if I'm going to keep her and our babies safe." Kayden clenched his fists, needing to find this threat to his mate and destroy it or rip it apart, which he'd prefer.

"There is no need; I can tell you what you need to know,"

Matty said, coming toward them from behind. "But first, thank you. I didn't realize Storm was so upset."

"You've spoken with her?" Kayden asked.

"I hope she listened. I've asked her to the Ice Cream Social. There's so much I need to share with her..." Matty closed his eyes and took a deep breath.

Kayden reached over and squeezed his shoulder. "From what I could see, she's hurt and scared."

"Scared? Of what?" Matty growled.

"*That* you will have to find out, but be warned, parents sometimes take things into their own hands," Saxon told Matty. "But for now, tell us what we need to know about this Tormac."

"Tormac runs, well, used to run the whole east coast from New York and up. He knows the layout of our home and has been here many times." Matty glanced at Kayden. "He's a nasty SOB. I've seen him rip apart his own general for making one mistake, and it wasn't pretty. Even Father had to get on him about it."

"Great, just what Elf needs after her," Kayden growled. "I want guards at the entrance of her rooms and at the end of the wing. We have children up there, including yours, Saxon."

"It's already done. Dad's asked the Moree brothers to watch your wing. Needless to say, Tormac does not stand a chance. I know I wouldn't want the Moree brothers after me."

Kayden could only nod, agreeing with him, having heard the stories of the brothers long ago. "Wait, does that mean.." Kayden glanced at Saxon, who moaned.

"Please, don't tell me the beasts are coming, too?" Saxon questioned him.

"Afraid so, they go everywhere with Alaster now. It's the only way they could keep people from getting ripped up trying to get to their home. Believe me, Drake laid into Alaster, one of the only men brave enough to, because I sure wouldn't."

"They better not harm one of the children," Kayden growled.

"Relax, Alaster has all of them under control, and even they know better to cross the man, which is totally strange."

All three of them stepped out onto the main road as Matty closed the door behind them, the sheriff there waiting for them, with the posse floating around them.

"So, who are we going to kill," Calamity Jane asked, appearing next to the sheriff.

"Bloodthirsty wench, let the man speak," Flask growled, yanking Jane back up against him as he nodded to them. "We're all here to help."

"Theo, I believe you met Tormac when he paid us a visit the last time?" Matty asked.

"Son of a bitch! How the hell are we supposed to find him? You know damn well he can change his appearance." Theo glared at Matty.

"That's why all of you will have to use your sense of smell," Drake said, coming up behind him as if appearing out of thin air. Drake held a large plastic bag with a shirt in it. "I call him here once a year for this purpose. Everyone, make sure you know this scent because this man raped my daughter and might have my granddaughter hidden somewhere."

"He what?" Kayden released his demon, taking the bag, making sure that the scent was imprinted on his brain. This man was a dead man, his time limited on this planet.

* * * *

The material was the softest thing Elf had ever felt as she stared in the mirror as Storm flew around her, turning her head from side to side. "Yep, I think this color is perfect for you. The pink is perfect. Do you like it?" Storm asked, shifting and standing next to her.

"How can I not. I feel like a queen, the dress is so elegant but sexy, and Maranda's dress... Well, look at her. You even gave Malcom a little suit. Now, tell me what's going on? I see you are all dressed up. Matty taking you?" she asked.

"Nope, I'm being escorted by Nolan Moree. You should see the man, hot..." Storm said.

"You think it's wise with Matty being around?" Elf asked as her daughter came over smiling.

"He thinks I'll just sit here and wait, well I'm not. Twice

he's hurt me; it's going to take a long time if at all. Plus, Nolan makes me feel safe." Storm rubbed her arms and looked around.

"What? Is someone bothering you?" Elf asked, placing her hand on Storm's arm.

"It might not be anything. I have to go. I promised to meet Nolan downstairs." Elf leaned over and place a kiss on her cheek. "Have fun today; you deserve it," she said and disappeared as Kayden knocked on her door and peeked inside.

His gaze roamed up and down her body as he stepped inside, shutting the door behind him. "Beautiful, the both of you are amazing. You sure you want to go? Because I don't think I want to share you just yet," he grumbled, and she laughed.

"Too bad, you promised us," Elf said as Kayden stepped further in.

"Fine, but don't blame me if I rip someone's head off if they get too close. Was Storm here? Matty has been looking all over for her."

Elf moved to the crib, picking up her son, trying to calm her hormones. Not only was Kayden handsome, but in the suit, she could stare at him all night. "Storm went to meet her date. Looks like Matty waited a bit too long. Actually, I'm a little bit worried about her. There's something she's not sharing, it's almost..." Elf looked up into Kayden's gaze. "As if someone is hunting her. I never thought of it, but it could explain why she'd disappear and reappear a few minutes later. Maybe she doesn't want someone tracking her?" Elf pointed to the closet behind Kayden. "Would you pull out the stroller for me?" she asked, reaching down and lifting her son up. Kissing his belly, her little guy laughed. Elf had been very lucky all her children had been happy babies, even when tensions were high they seemed to know when to be good.

A knock on her door had her looking up to see Matty peeking his head in and looking around. "Is Storm here?" he asked.

Elf hated to break the news to her brother, but she wouldn't lie to him. "No, she has a date for the social. She went to meet him." Matty's eyes, turned a red color, and she could hear the growl as her daughter hid behind her, holding onto her leg as she did when frightened, afraid the guards would take her away.

"Get out," Elf ground out. "You're scaring my daughter. Maranda, it's okay, baby, your uncle is just having a bad day," Elf said, placing her son in the stroller, kneeling down to face her. "We're safe here, baby," she whispered, pulling her into her arms, hugging her tight. When she looked up to see Matty there, his eyes were normal.

Kneeling next to them, he sighed. "I'm sorry, princess, I didn't mean to scare you. I was just a little upset and hurt."

Her daughter peeked at him, "You won't hurt Momma? I'll be good," she whispered, bringing tears to her eyes.

"No one is going to hurt you or your momma again, Maranda, that I promise." Matty stood but not before placing a kiss on her daughter's cheek and leaning over, squeezing her arm. "Now, if you excuse me, I need to find a little fairy and apologize again and deck the idiot she's with," he grumbled. "You don't happen to know who she's with, do you?"

Kayden glanced at her, and Elf sighed, pushing the stroller toward the door. "I shouldn't be telling you this, but someone named Nolan Moree." She looked over at Kayden, who was laughing so hard she thought he'd fall over when Matty punched him in the arm.

"It's not that funny," Matty said and moved out of her quarters as Kayden stepped up beside her, lifting Maranda up in his arms.

"Ready?" he asked, placing a kiss on her daughter's cheek, making her giggle.

"Let's go, and you're going to tell me what is so funny?" she asked as Saxon and Nava met them in the hall with Ana.

Maranda squirmed until Kayden put her down so she could walk with Ana. "Ana, you look so pretty in your dress and hat, just like your momma."

"Oh my god, you look amazing. I so love the dresses. Now, do tell me what is going on with our dear brother?" Nava asked.

"He found out Storm had a date," Elf said, looking at Kayden. "And Kayden was going to explain why Storm's date was so funny?"

"Who?" Saxon asked.

"Nolan Moree," Kayden said, smiling as Saxon shook his head.

"Now I kind of feel sorry for the man," Saxon said as both she and Nava looked at each other.

"See, this is what I was talking about," Elf said, glaring at Kayden. "Spill it now, and so help me, if this guy hurts Storm, I'm going to hurt you both, now tell us."

"There is nothing to worry about, Storm is with one of the best hunters around. Matter of fact, Matty was just telling us how good today. That he wouldn't want to come up against him and his brothers."

"Really, interesting. I can't wait to meet this man and his brothers," Elf said, winking at Nava, who nodded.

"Yes, I have to say, I'd like to meet them, too. If they're this good, they must be something," Nava said, and both of them waited. Nava mouthed, *one, two...*

"There is no reason for you two to see these men," Saxon growled.

Elf laughed. "What? It's our duty, as sisters, to make sure this man is good enough for our..." Her words died out as two men stepped in front. Both Ana and Maranda came running back to them, hugging their legs.

"Alaster, Cahir, quit scaring everyone, jeez. I told you three you need to work on your manners. Definitely going to have to find all of you a mate," Darla said, pushing between the two men, followed by Drake and her sisters, Elle and Tara.

"Elf, Nava, these two plus their brother will be guarding this wing for a while. I wanted you all to get to know each other, so they will be escorting all of us to the social. Ana, Maranda, come here, little ones; we have something you need to see," Darla said, holding out her hands.

Her mom looked stunning in her green summer dress with matching hat and shoes. Her long black hair, just like hers, swirled in ringlets down her back.

Slowly, their little girls moved to their grandma, taking her hand. "Ana, Maranda, these are your guards, but they also bring some animals that you shouldn't be afraid of. They won't hurt you when they come out at night. They just go after the bad guys, okay?" her mom said.

"What animals?" Nava asked, frowning.

Drake smiled at the girls as Darla made Alaster and Cahir bend down to meet the girls. "Alaster has been adopted by the beasts of Tuamgraney. I'm afraid they will be here with him at night. So, if you get up at night, do not be afraid of the animals; they will not hurt you. Right?" Drake said, looking at Alaster.

"They will not hurt anyone, but they shouldn't be played with either." Alaster glanced at the two girls, smiling. "These animals are trained to hunt the bad guys. They hunt at night, so we can't bother them when they are working, okay?" he asked.

For a man his size and his scary appearance, Elf had to admit he and his brother both handled the girls as if they had been around children before. Rising, both men bowed to them and stepped aside, allowing them to proceed down the hall.

Nava leaned over. "I have to say, I can't wait to see the other brother. I can see why Storm would feel safe around him if he's like his brothers. I guess we are all lucky to have men who can handle themselves."

"It will be interesting to see how Matty handles himself. I have a feeling if he embarrasses Storm..."

"She's going to fly in the wind. I, too, am afraid of this," her mother said, sliding in between both of them as Ana, Maranda, Elle, and Tara skipped in front of them.

"Let's hope my son uses my advice this time," Darla growled and looked over her shoulder.

Drake smiled. "It's got his attention at least."

Elf glanced at Drake. "You asked him to do this?" Elf questioned, and Nava growled. "Do you know what this will do to Storm's confidence." Elf shook her head. "This is not good at all."

"No, it's not, because last time I talked to Storm, she already doubted herself." Nava glared back at Drake as they rounded the corner to a hall Elf hadn't been down.

"My son needed a push, and believe me, their brother is not being used," Drake said as Alaster snorted behind him.

"Rest assured, ladies, our brother finds all ladies attractive, and he met Storm before, so she knew who he was," Cahir said as he moved to the front of the girls. "Little ones, we are getting close to the door to the outside world, please, go to your mommies right now so we can make sure it's okay?"

All four girls ran toward them, hiding behind them.

Elf sighed. "Great, now they're going to be scared to go outside." She glared at the man.

He shrugged. "It's our job to protect you." With those words, Cahir and his brother both moved ahead of them, opening the door, letting in the sunshine.

Elf stopped and stared at the door. It was the first time in her life Elf was actually going outside without bars, guards, and guns all around her. A knot formed in her throat and tears filled her eyes as she took a deep breath, she was really free.

Chapter Four

Kayden stepped up to Elf, wrapping his arm around her as she stared at the door. A single tear slid down her cheek, breaking his heart. "Elf?" he asked, wiping away the tear.

"We're really free, aren't we?" Elf asked, looking up at him.

"Yea, baby, you're free," he said, placing a kiss on her forehead. "You ready to greet our tiny town?"

Darla reached over and took her hand. "We're all here for you," she said with tears rolling down her cheeks.

Drake stood behind his wife, rubbing her shoulders as Saxon had his arms wrapped around Nava, knowing how much this moment meant for both women.

Little hands pushed in between them as Kayden glanced down to see Maranda. "Momma?" she questioned.

"I'm fine, Maranda, just a little bit nervous," she said, placing her hand on her daughter's head. "Come, let's explore our new home," Elf said, looking at Darla smiling. "I'll be okay, just going to take a while to get used to all of this."

Elf stepped forward, reaching down, taking her daughter's hand and pushing the baby stroller up the ramp to the opening door that Cahir held for them.

She and her daughter stood out there in the sun. Elf took a deep breath, a smile slowly appearing on her beautiful face as she scanned around her.

Kayden stepped outside when Alaster moved to his side. "We will be staying in town to help find these monsters," Alaster growled, his brother nodding his head, agreeing with him.

"Thank you, I have a feeling we're going to need all the help we can get finding the children and others being held. They were too organized, but we hit them hard, and we're still going through the computers and files that we got with the raid."

"Twenty-two," Elf said, glancing back over her shoulder.

"Twenty-two what, baby?" Kayden asked, stepping up to her side.

"Last I heard, they had twenty-two prisons, but that was a year ago. Who knows how many now, but can we forget that for now, please?" Elf asked, looking at him.

"I'm sorry." Kayden reached over and rubbed her back. "So, what do you think of our fair city?" he asked, nodding to the end of Main Street.

"It's stunning. I love the red brick road, the flowers on the old fashion lights, but I didn't realize so many people were coming. And look, everyone has dressed up," she said to her daughter.

"Look at the hats, Momma," Maranda said, smiling up at Kayden.

"They're very pretty, but I like yours and your momma's hats the best," Kayden said, lifting Maranda up into his arms as they moved down the sidewalk. Kayden did have to admit, it seemed the whole town was out and about today, dressed in their finest clothes.

"This is my shop," Darla said, stepping up to Elf's other side, pointing out her store. "When you are ready, we can come here and go through it to see if you would like anything for your suite. I know I have a nice little bedroom set that would be perfect for Maranda."

"I'd love to see your business, and the name of it is perfect, 'Mom's Things Thrift Store' is a catchy name. Maybe we can go there tomorrow. Where is Storm's shop? Do we know how big the offices are that she was talking about?" Elf asked, nodding to the doctor who joined them with her brother Ringo.

"'Storm's Creations' is there across the street. Her business is in the front, the offices we'll be using will be in the back. Anyone see Storm?" Nava asked, looking around as they were getting closer to the center of the park.

"Music?" Elf asked, smiling.

"Of course, a live jazz band just like the old days. We can

dance; there are going to be games for the children, too," Darla said. "We had many helping, but Lanny is a planner like me, so I know she went way over the top."

"Which is why we will pay her nicely for all of this, making up for her losing the business she would have had," Drake said, rubbing her back and kissing her cheek.

"Excuse me, excuse us," Joseph said, pushing through them almost knocking into Elf, followed by his twin, Jonah.

Nava laughed, and Saxon growled. "You two better cool it before you knock someone over. I swear those boys never learn," Saxon growled as a couple showed up next to Nava.

"Momma, papa, I'm so glad you could come with us. Darla, Drake, Elf, Kayden, Doc. these are my parents Janita and Jaguar Torres. They showed up a couple of days ago," Nava said, smiling.

Drake nodded. "It's an honor to meet you both. I hope you like our city. There are a number of other shadows here. Have you met your grandmother, Calamity Jane, yet?"

"Yes, we met, and I really hate the word grandmother." Calamity Jane appeared behind them with Flask by her side.

Elf shook her head. "This is so weird. I mean, I've seen many shifters, but... Wait, who's that?" Elf asked, nodding toward Frost and Lacey, who were walking toward them.

Kayden smiled. "Elf, Maranda, I'd like to introduce you to Lacey Adams and Frost. Frost is a Star Ranger, patrols the space, rounding up alien criminals."

"Again, wow," Elf said, reaching out and shaking both of their hands. "It's a pleasure to meet you both."

"I also run the local animal shelter, and if your little girl would like a puppy, I have a few left," Lacey said.

"Really? Momma?" Maranda asked, and Elf laughed.

"Not right now, Maranda. We live in your grandparents' home, sweetie. Maybe when we get our own place." Elf reached up and squeezed her hand.

"Nonsense, why don't you let me take her tomorrow. I'll take all the girls to the farm she runs. I think the children would love a day on the farm," Darla said.

"Excellent, I'll even have lunch for everyone. You should see all the different animals I have." Lacey looked at Elf.

"Rest assured, my sisters and I have the farm well protected. Not to mention blue man here," Lacey said, and Frost grunted.

"We also want to help with finding any others out there. I have a few friends that will come here to help, just let us know," Frost growled.

"Thank you, both of you. I'm sure the girls would have a ball at the farm..." Elf frowned and turned her head to the left, searching.

"What? Elf?" Kayden asked, looking around.

"I don't know, it feels like..."

"He's here, isn't he?" Maranda buried her face into his neck, wrapping her little arms around his neck tight, her little body shaking.

"Who's here, Maranda, Elf?" Kayden asked, rubbing Maranda's back, trying to calm the small little girl.

"I don't know if he's here or not, Maranda. But I want you to stay with us. Don't go off by yourself at all, okay?" Elf said. "Tormac, he's close, and if he's close..."

Nava finished the sentence whispering. "Then, the others are here, too?" Nava rubbed her arms, scanning around.

Calamity Jane's gun appeared in her hand as she cocked it, growling. "How the hell did he get in the town. I thought the posse was scouting?" she asked Flask.

"Believe me, he can get by anyone. Maybe we should just go back?" Elf said.

"NO! You are going to have your party. Alaster, Cahir, where is your brother? I want them close. Let's move to the square; it will be safer with everyone around," Drake said. "Maybe we can catch this traitor because I have a feeling that is how they got in again without us knowing. Ringo, Doc, I want you two to account for all of those that we rescued that are still here in town."

"Nolan will meet us at the square. Sheriff is already there, and Saxon's men are also waiting," Alaster said as they headed toward the party.

Kayden was furious. Her first outing and it was ruined. This prick would go down today, but for now, he'd make sure his two women and his little son were safe and having a good time, and they were his. He'd be damn if he allowed anyone to take his family away from him.

He glanced over at Saxon, who nodded, giving him the hand gesture that their team was ready. One thing this suit had was the perfect hiding spots for his weapons.

As they turned the corner, Elf stopped moving. "My god, this is beautiful. Maranda, look, sweetie," Elf said, reaching up and rubbing her daughter's arm. "Look at all the pretty flowers, balloons, and they even have a merry-go-round."

Slowly, Maranda peeked, looking around. "Can we go on it?" she asked, her eyes all big as she watched the other children riding it.

"Come here, Maranda. I'll take you over while your mommy and Kayden find us somewhere to sit," Darla said.

"Cahir, you're with us," Drake said as Darla took Maranda out of his arms as Saxon called over two of their men, pointing at the girls and Darla.

"How many men do you two have here?" Elf asked as Nava and Saxon moved beside them, as the sound of motorcycles came roaring down the street.

"I told you not to worry, little lady, I knew they'd show up and help out," Flash said, looking at Calamity Jane before moving to the side of the road as two of the bikers pulled up, Kayden recognizing the president from when Nava had arrived last week.

The president of the Knockers, Landon Comey, was a man that reminded him of Drake. One you really didn't want to get pissed, and this group had already done that killing their member Flask.

"Impressive and kind of hot," Elf whispered to Nava, who was also watching.

Kayden growled and leaned down, nipping Elf's ear. "You don't need to be looking, you're taken, *my* lady."

"Really? I still don't understand this mate thing. Maybe you just say that so I don't scope out the other men," Elf said, giving him a look that not only had his inner beast ready to claim her right there, but it also wanted to go rip off Landon's head.

Kayden slid his hand up through her thick, long hair and

pulled her head back, staring into her gaze. "Mine," he snarled right before covering her mouth, showing his lovely mate they belong together.

He slid his tongue into her mouth, tasting her and the coffee that she had earlier. Her hand slid up and around his neck as her tongue danced with his. But all too soon, Elf jerked back when a balloon popped behind them, scaring her. "Easy, baby, it was a balloon," he told her, placing a quick peck on her lips, releasing her hair.

"If you're done sucking face, let's find a place to spread the blankets," Saxon grumbled.

"Leave them alone. Hell, you do the same thing to me all the time." Nava smacked Saxon in the stomach, earning a laugh from Lacey.

"They all do. My sisters and I have our blankets set up over there if you'd care to join us?" Lacey asked.

"We would love to," Elf said before she leaned over and whispered. "Not to worry, I think Mr. Biker guy has eyes for a little blond." Elf nodded to Lanny, and Kayden shook his head.

"He's in for a big surprise there, Lanny hasn't dated anyone since she arrived last year. She's run off three of our men and a dozen others who had shown some interest in her," Kayden said, spreading their blanket out as Elf took the little guy out of the stroller and sat down, placing him on the blanket next to her as Nava and Lacey joined her.

"Lanny is special, Kayden, plus she's more into a little kink. I know for a fact she visits Club Eros in the next city over. Nice place and fun from what I've heard," Lacey said.

"And you would know this how?" Frost, her mate, asked, standing behind her.

"She said she'd heard," Sam's sister said, coming over to join them. "And who is this handsome little man," Sam said, kneeling down next to Lacey.

"Elf, Nava, meet my sisters, Sam and Joanna," Lacey said as Kayden noticed Storm coming their way with Matty and what had to be the other brother Nolan. Neither of them looked too happy.

Elf half listened as Storm raged on about Nolan and Matty getting into it non-stop since Matty found them. She glanced over where Maranda and the other girls were laughing as they rode the merry-go-round. But... *"I know you're here. Never knew you were a chicken shit."*

"Aww, princess, in time, in time." Tormac's voice answering her back in her head.

"And I will personally be waiting for you, Tormac," Drake's voice joined Tormac's in her head, as Elf glanced up to see Drake staring at her.

"Elf," Kayden growled. "Why provoke him?" Kayden pulled her up and wrapped his arms around her. "Nava, would you guys watch the little guy while I dance with my woman?"

"I'd be happy to sit. Storm, you are not going to allow those two knuckleheads to ruin our day. We have a baby to play with and an office to plan," Nava said, shooing Elf away while yanking Storm down on the blanket, handing her Malcom.

Elf couldn't help but laugh as Storm stared down at her son, not knowing what in the world to do. "Relax, Storm, Malcom is a pretty sturdy little guy," Elf said as Kayden led her out into the crowd in front of the gazebo where the band was playing a nice slow song.

She wrapped her arms around Kayden's neck, starting up at the man. "You do know I don't know how to dance, right?"

Kayden smiled. "I've got you. Put those little feet on mine and just hold on," he whispered in her ear before scrapping his teeth over her neck.

"I can't do that; I'm too heavy," she squeaked as he lifted her up.

"You're not too heavy; if anything, we're going to put a few

119

pounds on you," he said as she placed her feet on his.

Kayden could dance that was for sure as she rested against him. "So, what is it you would ask of me?" Elf questioned, looking up at him.

He sighed. "Our bond is already growing, I can feel it, but I would like to speed up the process by taking your blood and you taking mine."

Elf said nothing at first, letting the fool stew a little before she broke away from him, heading toward her son without a word.

"Elf, wait." Kayden lifted her up into his arms. "Look, I know you're mad, and I'm sorry, but this man scares the living piss out of me, Elf. The thought of him near you or the children..." He closed his eyes and took a deep breath, the demon so close to the surface.

His skin changing to a light-colored pink and, to touch, Elf could tell it was thick, almost leather like. Elf rested her head against his shoulder. "Kayden, you are the first man, and most likely the only one, I'll be out on dates with. I don't want to rush anything, only if we have to will I consider it."

"Drake thinks there is a way..." Kayden said just as Drake stepped up to them.

"There is a way to break the connection you have with him. So he won't hear and see what you are doing. I should have done this before, and I'm sorry I didn't," Drake informed her.

"And you'll never see our daughter again," Tormac hissed, but then, she heard his scream of pain, but Elf could have sworn it was...

Kayden laughed, placing a kiss on her cheek before lowering her feet to the ground. "Let me take you back to the girls while I help Drake find out what this Tormac knows." He placed a kiss on her cheek.

"Wait. what you said... was to get Tormac?" Elf asked, and he nodded.

"The only time I take your blood will be when I claim you while we are making love," Kayden told her.

"My daughter!" Elf swung around. "You have Tormac?"

Drake reached up and cupped her cheek. "We'll find my

granddaughter, I promise you, daughter. Go have some ice cream with the ladies and your daughter." He leaned down and placed a kiss on her forehead.

Elf took a deep breath and made her way back to the ladies. As soon as her daughter saw her, Maranda came running to her, smiling and wrapping her arms around her. "Momma, they have bubble gum ice cream."

"They do. Did you get some?" Elf lifted her little girl up, carrying her back to the blanket where the woman with the long blond hair stood talking to Darla.

"Elf, I'd like you to meet Lanny; she's here to take our ice cream order," her mother introduced them.

"You have a beautiful family; welcome to Magic," Lanny said, reaching out and hugging her, and that is when Elf noticed the biker and Alaster, both staring holes into her back.

"It looks like you have two very interesting men staring at you," Elf whispered as Lanny stepped back, rolling her eyes.

"They're a pain in the ass. I don't need or want a man in my life..." Lanny said, looking back at said men. "Been there, done it and been ripped apart, too. Don't think I'm going to risk my heart again. Now, tell me what flavor of ice cream you would like to try?"

Elf smiled and glanced at Nava, who shook her head. "You know they won't stop if you are their mate, right?"

Lanny lifted her chin. "But I'm human, so none of that is going to work on me," she said, earning a shake of Darla's head.

Darla patted her hand. "Don't worry, Lanny, right now, I think both men are trying to figure out what the hell is going on, and if you have both of them... Well, it will be interesting." Darla leaned over to Lanny, nodding to Storm, who stood off to the side.

"See my son and Nolan speaking. I bet you odds that those two are just figuring out that they share the same woman," Darla said.

"What? Storm?" Nava got up and turned to look at the little fairy. Everyone did as Storm glanced up meeting their looks.

She frowned, going over to them. "Okay, why are you all

staring at me? Do I have ice cream on my face?"

Nava pulled Storm down on the blanket, but Darla's words had Nava pouting. "It's their place to inform her, Nava."

"What are you talking about? Whose place?" Storm asked as Matty and Nolan came up to them.

"Storm, we'd like a word with you, please," Matty said, holding out his hand for her.

She looked at him then at Nolan. "Why?" she asked, looking back at Nava then at Elf. "You guys know something?"

Elf shook her head. "Sweetie, I've been locked up all my life; believe me, this is all new to me."

Storm came over, hugging her tight. "If I could find those assholes, I'd send them to another planet," she grumbled.

"I know you would. Go on. Go so you can tell us the latest gossip when you get back. Oh, I think they caught Tormac. I'm hoping my oldest will be here soon," Elf announced, drawing everyone's gaze.

"Really? Where is the asshole, so I can send him into space?" Storm growled.

"Hey, none of that. I have enough creeps to go after, I don't need more out there," Frost said, coming over with Drake and Kayden.

"Well?" Elf asked moving toward Kayden.

"We have men on their way now to retrieve my granddaughter Willow. She'll be in your arms soon," Drake promised.

Elf closed her eyes, trying to hold back the tears and swallow the lump in her throat. She would have her family all together soon.

Kayden's strong arms wrapped around her and pulled her into an embrace and was about to tell her something when the gazebo behind them blew, knocking her and Kayden to the ground. Her arm hurt like the devil, she had ringing in her ears and a nice bump on her head if the slight pounding in her head was any indication.

"Maranda, Malcom..." she screamed.

"Are you okay?" Kayden growled as he shifted right there on top of her as he lifted up, jumping up. He reached down, helping her, holding her, thank god, or she would have fallen flat on her ass again as her leg gave out.

Swinging her up in his arms, he glanced down at her. Before Elf knew what was going on, she was back in her rooms. Kayden gently laid her down as Drake showed up with her mother and Saxon with Nava.

"I need to go back now," Elf growled just as Alaster came in carrying Malcom and Maranda in his arms. Behind him, her sisters Elle and Tara carried by Cahir, and Anna being carried by Ringo."

"Sorry, Doc wanted to check each of them quickly. They all have scrapes, but little Malcom might be a little sore, Storm dove over him, saving him," Alaster said as he put her son in her arms.

"Storm?" Elf asked as Miranda curled up next her, holding her arm.

"She took a direct hit in the back of the head. It's not good. My brother and Matty are with her as Doc works on her. We called in three other doctors to help. Every single person in the band, gone."

"Alaster, enough," Drake growled as Kayden stepped in front of her.

"What is your problem," Kayden growled.

Alaster moved away from her. "Storm is my brother's mate and Matty's. I'm sorry, his pain is swamping us both." Alaster stopped and looked to the left. "They have to take Storm to the hospital in Farmington. There are physicians there that know our kind."

"Go be with your brother," Drake said, but Alaster shook his head.

"No, we stay here and find the bastards who did this. I've called in the family. My cousins will have their backup. I'm sorry, Drake, I should have run this by you, but she's family now."

"As you are with us now, Alaster. I would have the same," Drake said.

Elf grabbed onto Kayden's arm and pulled herself up, limping toward Alaster. "This shouldn't have happened."

"Don't say it. These people are like the plague, but we know how to wipe it out, and we will do the same to them,"

Alaster said.

"But..." Drake turned, placing his hands on her shoulders. It's not just you, Elf, they are after the whole town now. Placing that bomb there, they've declared war, and we are going to wipe them out. Now, go sit down before you fall. Alaster, I want the sheriff here as soon as we get the mess cleaned up and our folks healed. Ringo, I want you to set up trust funds for every member of that band for their families. Their children, wives will be taken care of."

Elf turned and limped back to the sofa, curling up with her daughter Maranda.

Kayden knelt in front of them, resting his hand on her knee and on Maranda's. "Why don't you guys get cleaned up, all of us, and meet back here. We can have our ice cream here. Hopefully..." He looked back at Drake, who nodded to him. "I'm hoping by the time you get cleaned up, we'll have Willow here." Kayden reached up and cupped her cheek. "You'll have your whole family here tonight, my lady."

Elf couldn't help it, she rubbed her cheek on his hand before turning and kissing his palm. She'd only known the man a few days, but each day that he was around her, it's like her body quivered, hormones started doing the jig inside her. Maybe she was sick, but then, Elf shook that off as Kayden helped her up and he placed a kiss on her cheek.

"I'll be back before you two are cleaned up. I'll even pick up some pizzas for all of us since I know we haven't eaten," Kayden said, turning to leave and that's when Elf noticed that the others had left, too.

"Kayden?" Elf said, stopping his movements toward the door. He glanced over his shoulder at her. His dark blue eyes meeting hers. "Thank you, for everything." Before he could say anything, Elf moved into her bedroom with the children, shutting the door. She really needed to talk to... *"Nava, when you have a free minute, I'd like to ask a few questions, if you don't mind, before Kayden and the others come."*

"I'll be there in thirty minutes. You okay? Do I have to hurt Kayden?" she asked through their link Elf had started years before.

"No, Kayden didn't do anything directly, just a little con-

fused, and with you mating with Saxon, well, I have questions. If it's okay?" Elf started the bath water for her daughter before sitting down to feed her little man as he started to fidget in her arms.

"Anything I can do to help you know I'll help. See you in a few," Nava sent as Elf sat back and watched as her daughter started to rip off her clothes. If it was one thing, her daughters both loved their baths like their mother.

"Your toys are in the basket but not too many today, sweetie, we have to get ready quickly before everyone comes back," she told Maranda, who nodded, picking two toys and getting in the tub. One thing good about her suite, she could see into the bathroom, watching her daughter from where she sat feeding her son.

But what had her really nervous was wondering if her oldest had been hurt. She hadn't seen her in what seemed like forever, and the last time Elf had held her... "I won't cry," she whispered as a tear rolled down her cheek.

Kayden stood in the middle of town staring at what was left of the gazebo. Blood covered parts of the ground where six band members and four people standing next to it were killed. Many more in critical condition from what Doc had told him.

Storm had gone into surgery to remove the piece of the wood but still nothing. His heart heavy, it was the first time in a long time anything had happened like this to their town. The last time... he sighed, remembering the blood and one of the reasons he had joined the service. Humans had murdered his little sister and three other teenagers when they had found out they were different, and that was over forty years ago.

Sure enough, over the years, there had been bloodshed here, after all, the city was over two hundred years old, but this was different. Not only were these monsters aiming for them, but they were also stealing their children. Something no species would do, knowing how special children were.

"I thought I'd find you here," Saxon said, appearing at his side. "How are you?"

"Brings back so many memories in a way. Have we heard anything from the two the Knockers found? Do they need help interrogating them?" Kayden asked.

"No, they are singing just fine. Seems the two we caught had no idea there were shadows here," Saxon laughed. "One of the posse members went right through the man, and he fainted. We'll find out all of the information later, but come, I've come to help you get the pizzas and ice cream. Elf's daughter should be arriving soon," Saxon said as they both moved toward his truck.

"Did you call Nala? Is she open?" Saxon asked.

"Yep, she's going to hold Mystic Pizza open 'til ten tonight.

She knows a lot of town people aren't going to want to cook, so she made sure to have enough for whoever wanted pizza tonight." Kayden smiled. "That little unicorn needs to find a male. I've caught her out in the woods by herself feeding. I hope, with all that is going on, she realizes it's too risky to go out," Kayden growled. "I have to agree with Drake; we need to speak with the sheriff and others. Our women are at risk here, and so are our children. Maybe a patrol."

"The patrol isn't going to do much if we don't find the damn traitor. That's twice these peons have gotten by our men. I almost think there is more than one person here in town," Saxon told him.

"If that is the case, we have more trouble than we thought. Why aren't you with Nava and Ana?" Kayden drove down Main Street, turning onto Incantation Street, where Mystic Pizza and their recruitment center was, along with Doc Lope's office.

"Nava and Elf are having a powwow, and I have a feeling it's about you." Saxon smiled.

"Me? Why? I haven't pressured her or anything. I thought I was taking it slow, and I have to tell you, it's killing me. Especially since the attack. My demon wants to claim her now," Kayden informed him.

"Same thing happened with Nava after they attacked us at the dinner, but you are going to have to watch it with Willow. I'm afraid that little girl is going to be a mess when she returns to Elf. Hell, they are all a mess after what happened," Saxon growled, looking out the window.

"What we need to do is set up a trap for the traitor, but the only way to do that is to use bait, and I know for a fact our women are not going to be used." Kayden hit his steering wheel as he parked the truck in front of Mystic Pizzas.

Kayden and Saxon didn't say much, going into the pizza place where Frost and a few other men were picking up orders.

"How are Lacey and her sisters doing?" Saxon asked.

"Each of them was hurt but not severely. This has to stop. Parents are afraid to allow their children out to play. Even the twins have been hog tied and forbidden to go anywhere without one of us."

Saxon froze, growling. "We have trouble. They have breached Drake's house. Elf is missing, and so is Nava," Saxon disappeared with Kayden following him, appearing in Elf's rooms.

Blood was on the carpet, and Darla held Malcom in her arms with Ana and Maranda each curled up next to her crying. Behind the love seat another little girl, bruises covered her face, but there were no tears on her face, just fear in her eyes—Willow.

With tears running down Darla's face, she looked up at them as Drake paced back and forth. "They have Nava and Elf. They shoved Maranda and Malcom in the bathroom, making sure the door was locked while they fought them off trying to protect the children. Just as we arrived, Willow was brought here. I want my daughters home NOW."

Maranda moved off the couch, coming to stand in front of Kayden as he tried to get control of his demon. Her little hand took his clawed one. "I want my mommy. You can find her?" she cried.

Kayden knelt down as Willow moved behind her sister, resting her hands on her shoulders. "I promise you both I will find your mommy and aunt. We'll be that family you all deserve," he said, promising both of them. "Willow, I'm Kayden. I'm your mommy's mate. I know things are scary right now, but soon, you'll have your mother."

The girl nodded, not saying a word, but Maranda climbed up on his body, wrapping her arms around his neck, she gave him a kiss on his cheek, hugging him tightly. "You'll be our daddy?" she asked.

"If you want me to, I'd be happy and proud to have you girls as my daughters, but I want you two to stay with Darla until I find your momma and bring her back for you." He stood, hugging Maranda and placing a kiss on her cheek. He held out his hand for Willow, waiting.

She stared at her sister then at his hand. Slowly, Willow placed her hand into his.

"Darla, take the children to our wing; you'll all be safe there, but just in case, Alaster and Cahir will be with you and the girls 'til we find that traitor," Drake said as Alaster and Cahir came into the room.

"We'll take the children and be right back," Saxon said, scooping up Ana into his arms as Darla carried Malcom. Moving down the hall, Ringo, his team, sheriff, and the posse moved down the hall toward Elf's rooms.

"Are they going to help you find Momma?" Miranda asked, watching the men move by them.

"Yes, we have many that are going to help get these bad men, your mother, and aunt," he said, rubbing his cheek against the top of her head and squeezing Willow's hand. "Willow, what is your favorite meal?" he asked.

She frowned. "I don't know, we didn't have much food," Willow said, her voice a mere whisper.

"Well then, I think, when we get your mom and aunt back, we have a little food party at home. What do you think, Darla? Maybe samples of many different favorites so everyone can see what they like the best? We could have Chinese, Greek, Italian, and, of course, many American dishes."

Darla looked over her shoulder, smiling. "I think that would be an excellent idea. I know one of my favorites to make is the Sheppard pie. It's comfort food when I feel down. Of course, warm blackberry pie and ice cream is my favorite to eat."

"Okay, my stomach is rumbling," he grumbled, and Maranda giggled as Willow smiled.

"On my way back to the meeting, I'll have someone pick up the pizzas for you girls, so you have some food to munch on with some different snacks and drinks. You can let me know what you think when I come to get you. But until then, you don't leave, understand?" he asked as they moved into Darla and Drake's private suite.

Both girls nodded as he set Maranda on the floor, kneeling down in front of them both. "I know you two don't know me, but I promise, I'm not going to stop 'til we have your mommy here with us." He reached up and brushed Willow's hair out of her face, ignoring when she flinched but held her ground. "I will never, and I mean never, raise a hand to you guys." He ran his finger over her bruised cheek. "Tormac is no more,

Willow. He can't come and hurt you again."

Her eyes got big and watered. "Really?" she whispered.

"Really." He rose, leaning over, kissing the top of Willow's head. "You're safe. No more prisons." He moved to leave, but Willow's little hand on his arm had him stop.

"You really want to be our daddy?" she asked. "And you won't hit us?"

Kayden knelt down and pulled her body into his, surrounding her with his arms, hugging her frail body. "I promise, I will never hit you, and yes, I want to be your daddy. Now, Willow, Maranda, that does not mean I might not get frustrated with something, but when you love someone, that happens. Just means I have to try harder." He kissed her cheek, leaning back and smiling at her.

"I'm not perfect, Willow, no one is. But I will try my hardest to make sure your life is a happy and safe one," he said again and would keep repeating it until she believed him.

Willow stepped back. "Thank you," she whispered as he stood.

"There is no need to thank me. To me, you are already my daughters." He smiled. "Wait 'til you meet your cousins and other grandparents." He laughed and ruffled the girls' hair. "Be good, little ones," he said, following Saxon out, closing the door as Alaster and his brother stepped into the room while two other men that looked like them stood next to the door.

"Their cousins. Seems they also have special abilities," Saxon snorted as they made their way back to Elf's rooms.

Entering the suite, Drake's gaze caught theirs. "They secured?"

"Yes," Saxon said, moving to his side. "So, how do we find them and the traitor, because this isn't going to stop even when we do get the ladies back until the traitor is caught."

Everyone agreeing with him as the posse came in, along with some of the Knockers, Nava's parents, and Calamity Jane.

Drake smiled, and it wasn't a good one. "We have something they don't know about," he said, stepping to the side, revealing three of the scariest creature's Kayden had ever seen and that said something.

One had to be some kind of bear as it stood on its hind legs sniffing and growling, its eyes a blood red. Another, a wolf, Kayden believed, and the last animal, he shivered. This was not any Rudolph he ever saw.

"Gentlemen, may I introduce you to the Tuamgraney Beasts, well three that agreed to help us," Alaster said.

"They are not ordinary animals, and the hunt will go fast, be ready," Drake said. As said animals disappeared from the room, an eerie howl filled the hallway as all filed out, following the animals, his beast out now searching for their mate.

$\mathcal{E}$lf's head was pounding like a bitch, not to mention her arm and thigh were bleeding bad, but she was really worried about Nava behind her. She was still out of it, and who the hell knew what they were going to do to them.

She didn't move an inch as Elf took in the small room they were in. No one was there in the room, but that didn't mean they weren't watching. Elf could hear them yelling, and someone was not happy they were there it appeared.

"Where are we?" Nava asked, still not moving as Elf glanced back really quickly to see her looking at her.

"I think we're in someone's cellar, but where ever we are, they are not happy we were brought here. I think we're in the home of the traitor. Are you going to be able to move when they come in here?

"They hit something in my back. I can't feel my legs, Elf," Nava said calmly.

"Assholes. Do you think they'll find us?" Elf asked, hating the uncertainty in her voice. *"I don't know how long we've been out either."* Elf reached down and ripped the bottom of her shirt and started to wrap her leg to stop the bleeding. She, sure as hell, didn't need to get any weaker if she was going to try and keep the assholes away from them.

"Elf, I know that voice. It seems we have found our traitor, and it's freaking sad. Boy, is Drake going to be furious," Nava said.

"Who?" she asked out loud, forgetting. Her captors went quiet right before Elf could hear them coming their way.

"I told you to keep them knocked out!" The voice yelled as the locked door flew open, hitting the concrete wall.

Four men came into the room, staring at them as Elf jumped up, ready to take on any of them if she had to. But what Elf wasn't expecting were the three animals that appeared in front of them. If one could call them animals.

"Alaster," Elf whispered as one turned its red eyes on her for a second before it turned to stare once more at the men in front of them. Elf risked a look back at Nava, who smiled.

A growl so fierce and loud had Elf jumping and crouching, ready to attack anyone or thing that came her way.

Her eardrums rang as if they had bells in them, covering her ears, afraid they were going to erupt. She turned and watched as one of the stupid men started to move toward them, dumbest thing he could have done as the big animal chose that time to attack him.

The bear-like creature was massive and quick as the blood of said man now covered the wall and floor. His scream died the second the animal ripped out his throat at the same time their men appeared in the room with help.

Nava's grandmother, Calamity Jane, moved to Nava's side and cocked her gun. But her man, Flask, appeared next to her, grabbing the gun away from her. "No, we need them alive for now," he told her. "See what is wrong with Nava," Flask said, moving toward the other men, as Elf plopped down beside her sister of the heart, Nava, taking her hand into hers.

"I really hate being hurt," Elf grumbled, and Nava laughed.

Both Saxon and Kayden knelt down next to them, both men in full beast looking each of them over, growling. Elf did have to admit Kayden was hot even in his demon form. His pants ready to rip at the seams kneeling next to her.

The intensity of his gaze had her blood warming and her heart rate increasing like that of a drum. Elf never believed she'd be one to give her heart to any man let alone her body, but it would seem both were now craving him like someone would dark chocolate.

"Three stab wounds," Kayden growled and reached up, cupping her cheek. "And she's going to have a nice shiner, too." He leaned down and whispered, "You keep giving me that look, and I swear, I'll claim what is mine."

Saxon's words broke the intense feeling moving through her as Elf glanced down at Nava, seeing her smiling up at her. "Some kind of dart in the spine. Nava, can you move your legs?" Saxon asked, and she shook her head.

"Below the waist, I feel nothing," Nava said, turning her gaze to her mate, reaching up and cupping Saxon's cheek.

"The children?" Elf asked, looking up at Kayden as Doc Lope appeared with someone she didn't know.

"All three of your babies are with your mom, waiting for their mother." Kayden leaned down and kissed her lips softly. "You scared the hell out of me, angel."

"Hell, I scared the hell out of me, too," she said, watching as Doc Lope rolled Nava over.

"Sorry, Nava, this is going to hurt, but it needs to come out. I think what it's doing is slowly drugging you so you can't move." The doctor didn't give her time to think before taking the long needle out of her.

"She was out longer than I was, too," Elf told the doctor.

"Did you have any darts in you?" he asked, looking at her wounds.

"No. I think they thought since they stabbed me a few times that I would be out," Elf said as she glanced over to see Drake lifting a man up by his throat and, boy, was Drake pissed as he shook the man.

"We gave you a place to live, a job, and you betray your own kind and the town that welcomed you?" Drake dropped the man. "Lock them down while we get the women home and healed. We will deal with them in a few hours."

The sheriff and the posse took the three men since the fourth was no more, that is when she noticed the animals were gone.

"Take the ladies back home, boys, I'll bring the children to you," Drake said, and that is when she turned to Kayden.

"Wait, did you say all three of my babies?" she asked, hoping Elf had heard him right.

Kayden smiled, carefully lifting her up into his arms. "Yes, your Willow is a beauty, but I'm afraid the bastard beat her, Elf. She has bruises on her face, and I don't know where else," Kayden growled.

"I'm coming with you, so I can look over the wounds you have. Maybe your daughter will allow me to look at her if she sees me working on her mom," Doc Lope said, as Drake stepped up the doctor, disappearing from the room.

"I must really be out of it if I didn't even see the animals leave," she mumbled, resting her head on Kayden's chest. "You might want to change back. We don't want the children to see your nice package. I'm afraid those pants hide nothing, and damn, the man was impressive."

Kayden placed a kiss on the side of her neck. "And did you like what you saw?" he asked, taking her back to her room, setting her down on the large overstuffed couch.

Elf let out the breath she was holding and looked up at Kayden. "I promised myself long ago I wouldn't even consider giving myself to a man, but you, Kayden, are slowly changing my mind. You are one male I could see spending my life with, but I have to admit, your package scares the crap out of me," she said, feeling her cheeks warm, another first—embarrassment.

He ran his finger down her cheek. "Tonight, we will discuss this fear because I'm afraid, after this, I'm not allowing you out of my sight 'til we join our life forces." Kayden sat down next to her, shifting, new clothes covered him, and damn, he looked sexy as hell.

The door opened, and Willow's cry had her looking up as her daughter ran to her, throwing herself onto her, crying. Yes, it hurt like a bitch as Willow jarred her leg and arm, but having her daughter in her arms was well worth the pain.

* * * *

Kayden reached down and lifted Maranda up in his arms as Elf and Willow hugged and cried. Even he had a knot in his throat.

Darla smiled at him, holding Malcom. "All the girls have been fed; we had a pizza and ice cream. I did get Willow to take a bath and got both girls in PJs." Darla looked over at the door, seeing Doc and Drake come in. "I would like Doc to look at Willow's left side. She has a nasty cut on it, and it does not look to be healing."

Elf pulled back. "Let me see now," Elf said to Willow, who stepped back, her gaze looking around.

"Willow, this is the doctor for this town. He's here to look at you and me. Let him see your side, baby, so we can get you all healed up," Elf informed her daughter as Doc Lope came over and removed the made-up bandage on Elf's leg.

"I was afraid of this," Doc said. "Drake, can you get me towels, please, a few of them. Okay, little lady, can I see your sore?" he asked, turning slightly as he knelt next to Elf.

Willow glanced at him, and his heart swelled.

"He's a good man, Willow, I promise, and so far, I've kept my promises, right?"

The little girl nodded and lifted up her top where a new bandage covered the wound.

"Nice dressing, Darla. I'm going to remove this so I can see what we are dealing with, okay?" Doc said, carefully removing the bandage. "Yep, just like her mother's wound," Doc said as Drake came in with a handful of towels.

"What?" Kayden asked, frowning, seeing the nasty cut on Willow's side, knowing a blade had cut the little girl. He was going to make sure these men suffered.

"So far, on most wounds from knives and such, the instrument in question is coated with a toxin that eats away at the flesh, keeping the wound open and spreading." Doc took a towel and a black-blue jar out of his bag. "Even our kind have trouble healing from it; humans, it would kill them. Willow, I'm going to apply some of this medicine on your wound. It's going to be cold at first then it will warm up, but it might hurt a little. I'm sorry, little one." Doc waited as her gaze jumped to Elf's, who nodded.

"You can do this, and after we are all patched up, we'll watch a movie with popcorn, okay?" Elf said, and Willow nodded.

Doc Lope didn't wait as he started to clean out the wound. Willow didn't move at all, but tears rolled down her cheeks, and once, he heard the whimper.

Kayden looked up at Drake, his dark black gaze met his. "We'll find everyone," he said calmly, but Kayden knew the man was beyond furious.

"Did you find the traitor?" Darla asked, standing next to her husband.

"One of them, yes," Drake said, wrapping his arm around

his wife. "Porter."

Darla shook her head. "No," she whispered. "Why, Drake?"

"I don't know, baby," Drake said, placing a kiss on her cheek. "Elf, did you know any of the men that took you and Nava?"

Elf glanced at him and nodded. "The one that was killed was a guard. The one with the long hair... Let's just say he thought he was a doctor." Elf shivered, and so did Willow.

"Monster had you?" Willow asked. "Is he dead?" The little girl asked, looking at Kayden then at Drake.

Drake knelt down in front of Willow. "Right now, he is locked up. There is no way he can escape. This man will not hurt anyone again." Drake smiled. "You are a very pretty little girl. I have a feeling you look a lot like your mommy when she was small, too."

Willow smiled and looked up at Elf as Doc put a new bandage on the little girl's side. "Okay, you are all set. The medicine will destroy any of the poison left in your system. You'll be sore for about two days but will completely heal. Now, let's clean your mommy up," Doc said, tossing one towel to the ground and turning toward Elf.

Elf frowned. "I really would like a shower before you put the medicine on. I sure don't want to stay in these clothes. They stink. Could I do that first?" she asked, and Doc nodded.

"I want to cover the wounds, so no water gets in them, but you're going to have to be careful in the shower, Elf, so you don't fall. I know this poison makes us weak," Doc said as he began covering her leg.

"Not to worry, I'll be in there holding her up," Kayden said.

"I don't think so," Elf said, glaring at him.

He put Maranda down and stood, stretching before turning to Elf. "Yes, I am. You have three wounds, and you've been beaten up pretty good. I'm taking care of you, so get used to it," he growled, earning giggles from her two little girls.

Chapter Eight

Elf glared at Kayden as he lifted her up and proceeded to move toward her bedroom as Drake and her mother watched the girls. "You can't do this," Elf said. "I can take a shower without help."

"I'm doing it, so stop giving me sass. You are hurt, let me take care of you, Elf. I need to take care of you." He placed her on the counter in the bathroom, closing the door with his foot. Cupping her face, Kayden lowered his head, placing a soft, quick kiss on her lips. "You're mine, Elf. I'm not leaving your side again. I have one of my guys bringing some of my stuff here. I'm sorry if this is fast and too much, but when you were taken, it was as if part of me was missing. I can't and won't go through that again." He nipped her bottom lip as he reached down and started to lift what was left of her shirt.

Elf placed her hands on top of his, scared. "My body, we're not supposed to scar, but... It's not pretty, Kayden."

"Angel, look at me."

Lifting her gaze back up to him, Elf sucked in her breath, seeing the heat in his gaze. "Do you really believe your scars are going to matter to me, Elf? You are my woman, soul, the air I breathe, nothing, and I mean nothing, will ever change that," he said, slipping off her shirt, careful of her wounds on her arms and stomach.

Elf reached up, crossing her arms over her breasts, hating the way she looked. The whip marks, burns from the prod, and other things they created to hurt them.

Kayden took her hands and brought them to his mouth. "Don't cover yourself from me, angel. You know what I see?" he asked but continued. "I see a woman in front of me who was brave and survived. One of courage." He dropped one hand and traced one of many scars on her left breast. "You

138

are beautiful and mine, Elf. Soon, I plan to kiss every single one of your badges of courage, showing you how much you mean to me, but now is not the time," he said, lowering his head and sucking her nipple into his mouth and releasing it just as quick. "Had to have a quick taste," Kayden said, looking down at her pants.

"Elf, I'm going to rip these off of you because I don't want the pants to drag over your leg since it's the worse wound." He started at her waist and carefully pulled her pants apart, ripping them down one leg. "Lift up, Elf," he asked as he pulled the material from underneath her, dropping it to the floor before starting on the other side.

In a matter of five minutes, Elf was naked before him as he started to strip out of his clothes and turning to start the shower. She couldn't help but stare at the man before her. Never had any man caused such chaos inside her but also made her feel so safe when he was with her, and Elf had never felt safe.

Kayden turned, facing her, and all Elf could do was stare at the man who claimed to be hers. "I feel as if you got the short end of the deal," Elf said as he lifted her up and stepped into the shower with her, slowly lowering her legs down.

"I don't want to hear that again, Elf." Kayden growled and bit down on her shoulder. "You are perfect for me, and I'll keep telling you this until you believe it." He reached up and grabbed the bottle of lavender body wash that she loved. "I'm going to really quickly wash you down because Doc is waiting for you."

Kayden did just what he said. But she knew Kayden was checking each and every mark on her. Every time he'd come to a spot where her body was marked, he'd run his finger over the spot for just a second before moving on.

He picked her up and carried her out of the shower. "You counted them, didn't you?" she asked as he wrapped the towel around her body.

"You have thirty-two, and believe me, each man will suffer for each mark that was given to you," he said, his voice almost a whisper, but the anger radiating off of him had her trying to step back, but he held on tight. "Don't." He gripped her hips. "I never want you to be afraid of me. Yes, there will be times I'm angry, but know, I will not lay a hand on either you or the children. We are going to argue, but we'll always go to bed wrapped in each other's arms because nothing is more important than our lives together." He scooped her up after putting on his pants and carried her out into the bedroom, where he found her nightshirt, helping her dress.

Without a word, he carried her out into the living room, placing her back on the couch, allowing Doc to do his work as a knock on the outer door had everyone turning to it. Willow and Maranda both running to her, grabbing onto her.

Kayden growled, looking back at the girls then at the door. "We have a lot to accomplish, but we will," Kayden mumbled as he went to the door.

"Ringo, any word on Storm?" Kayden asked as he stepped aside, allowing her brother in.

"No, Storm is still in surgery, but we went through Porter's home. He's been with this group for a while, Dad. He was here collecting information on different packs, groups, and so on. He had lists." Ringo shook his head. "It's not good, this organization is larger than we believed. Some of the things they did there..." Ringo looked over to Elf as Doc was wrapping her leg. "I don't know how you survived, little sis."

Elf shrugged her shoulders, looking down at the little boy in her arms, her daughters now curled up on the couch with her. "You make do with what you have. When you've been a prisoner all your life, take what you can and make do with it." Elf looked up at Kayden. "That's why it's hard to believe all of this is happening, but we take one day at a time, prepare in case it's all taken away again."

Her mom sucked in her breath, coming to sit next to them on the couch. She reached over and hugged her. "We will do this together, my daughter. You are part of this family, and we're not going to allow anyone to take you away from us again." Darla looked over her shoulder at Drake. "I think it's time for Magic to disappear for a while 'til we find out just what we are dealing with."

Drake stared at Darla then his gaze moved to her and the children. "Ringo, call a meeting. Have the mayor and circle, along with the sheriff. I'm afraid your mother is right. It's been a while since we've had to use this, but too many people are getting hurt. We don't need any more of our children taken from us again." Ringo moved toward the door. "Ringo, two hours. It will give us time to get everything together. Kayden, get the girls in their robes; they'll be staying in the den next to the office so we can make sure they are safe. I'm going to inform Saxon, get him to meet us down there."

"I'm going to help the girls get ready if it's okay with you? I know you shouldn't be moving much," Darla asked.

"I'd like that. There are robes and slippers in the closet for both girls. Storm made sure Willow had a few things here in case she showed up while she was gone. I really wish we could go to the hospital though," Elf said, looking up at Kayden as he moved toward her room.

"Sorry, not going to happen. That hospital is in a town we can't protect. Too many unknowns." Kayden glanced over at her. "We'll have regular updates on her, and I know Matty and Alaster's brother are keeping a close watch on her there." Kayden moved into her room.

"Kayden, I'm going to need diapers and change of..." she smiled as he came out of the room, carrying a small case, her slippers and robe.

"Got it," he said. "But I want you to give Malcom to Darla because I'm going to carry you. You don't need to be walking right now," Kayden said as Saxon and Nava came into the room with Saxon carrying Nava and Ana holding onto Saxon's hip.

"We ready?" he asked as Kayden helped her on with her slippers and robe before lifting her into his arms.

"Let's go." Kayden placed a kiss on the top of her head as the three little girls whispered as they all moved down the hall.

Elf rested her head on Kayden's chest, so tired. It had been one long day, and she would be glad to put this day behind her and start fresh in the morning.

* * * *

Kayden glanced once more at the door next to the one that lead into Drake's offices, which were impressive, to say the least, especially to hold over thirty men in there comfortably. The need to go in there and claim his woman was getting almost impossible to control.

"Relax, we have two men inside and men all around; nothing will get to them," Saxon said, reaching over, squeezing his shoulder.

"It's not that," Kayden barely got out, turning toward his friend, hearing the hiss coming from him.

"Go claim your woman; we can handle this," Saxon said as Kayden glanced toward Drake. So far, they had all agreed it was one more time for the use of the old cloaking device. The original founders of their town found some kind of spaceship that had been hidden in the caves.

Drake turned his head, his gaze meeting his. *"Go, claim your woman. You cannot think while your beast is demanding to claim her. Saxon will update you, but nothing will be done fully until tomorrow morning."*

Kayden knew Drake was right, but he had wanted to give her time, but fates had decreed it was time. Nodding to the man that would be his father-in-law, Kayden went to collect his mate. Tonight, his angel would be in his arms, connected body and soul.

The light was dim as Kayden stepped into the family room; the girls were all curled up eating popcorn, watching a movie, while Elf, Nava, and Darla sat in the back of the room. Elf stood and moved toward him.

As if knowing he was in the room, Elf turned her attention toward him and smiled. But Nava's eyes got big, and she leaned over whispering something into Elf's ear as he made his way to the woman of his heart.

"Darla, Nava, would mind watching the children for a few hours. I'll come by and pick them up..." Kayden started to say, but Darla was already shaking her head.

"You go, we'll bring the children back at ten; that will give the two of you time to be by yourselves." Darla placed her hand on his arm. "Kayden?"

"I know, Darla, I know. I just wish I could have given her

more time. It's my fault; I can't control him right now, but I promise to make it up to her every day of my life," Kayden said, his gaze on Elf's.

"Kayden," Elf whispered as he gently lifted her up into his arms, burying his face into her neck, taking in her scent.

"I need you, angel," he kissed the side of her neck before moving toward the door where Willow met them there.

"We going to our room?" she asked.

"Your grandmother and grandfather will bring you back when the movies are done." Kayden smiled at the bright-eyed little girl.

Just as Willow was going to say something, Darla came over, swooping Willow up in her arms, causing the child to giggle, which Kayden had a feeling that was rare. "Did you forget about our nail painting? Because I have all the bottles at the table," Darla winked at them, moving Willow to the small table where Nava sat, giving Kayden the chance to slip out of the room without any interruptions.

What Kayden wasn't expecting was to see Alaster person-ally following them. Not one to question orders, Kayden moved toward their rooms but stopped and smiled down at her. "I have an idea." He lowered her feet to the ground. "Don't move for a second," he said and turned to speak with Alaster without those sweet ears of his woman hearing.

Giving Alaster the list, knowing others were watching them that could help with his plan, Kayden turned and won-dered how in the hell he had gotten so lucky. Seconds later, Kaden once more had Elf in his arms, heading in the oppo-site direction of her suite of rooms.

With her head resting on his chest, Elf smiled up at him. "You know, I can walk, and I believe you are heading in the wrong direction."

"Nope, you will not do anything tonight but enjoy your-self. I promised you I would wait, but I have to break that promise. I've only broken two promises in my life, one when I couldn't save one of our team members when we were in a hot situation, and now this." Kaden stopped and stared down at Elf. "I'm going to do everything in the world to make this up to you starting tonight." He leaned down and kissed her full ruby-colored lips. "I have a surprise for you," he said as torchlights flared to life as he turned down a tunnel he believed Elf hadn't been in before. Even he had only been down there once, and it had left an impression on him. He only hoped his Elf would be as impressed as he had been.

"This place gets more magical every time I step into a new part of it. It's almost like one of those amusement parks." Elf reached out and brushed her fingers against the rock wall.

"And how did you hear about amusement parks?" Kayden asked as he started to push up the tunnel, knowing they were getting closer to their destination. He just hoped Alaster was able to do as he requested, but hearing the soft music in the distance, Kaden knew the man had come through. He'd have to make sure if Alaster ever needed anything, he'd be there for him.

"Explain to me what is happening. Is it something to do with your other form?" she asked. "Even though there were many different people there, we all learned to stay to ourselves. It hurt too much to see those you care about being hurt."

Kayden took a deep breath, calming his other half when all they wanted to do was go rip someone to pieces. "Among the males of our kind, when we find our fated mates, I've come to find out that seeing you hurt or in danger incites the other half of me. Right now, it's taking everything inside of me to control him so he won't frighten or hurt you. He, no, we need to put our mark on you, start the bonding process so no one can separate us." Kaden stopped before he moved around the corner, staring down at her.

"The first time we make love, my seed, my scent will start the bonding process. Our souls will twine together. No matter where you go, I will know where you are as you will know where I am at. We'll be able to speak to each other in our heads like you do with Nava but more."

"So, when we were taken..." Elf questioned, and he nodded his head.

"My other side has been demanding we bind ourselves together as soon as I found you." He rubbed his cheek on the top of her head. "This night is for you, my angel," he said, placing a kiss on the top of her head before moving around the corner, smiling, hearing her gasp.

"Thank you, Alaster," he said to the man who was now behind him again.

"We will be out of sight but here if you need us," Alaster said, stepping back into the dark tunnel as Kayden moved forward before lowering Elf's legs.

They stood almost on top of the high ridge, a protruding handmade balcony that Drake had put up a railing on. The soft mattress that he had ordered was all set up, with soft-covered throws and pillows. Candles were lit all around them with a bottle of what most likely was one of Drake's best champagnes from his seller.

"You did all of this for me?" Elf asked, looking around as tears rolled down her cheeks. "No one..." she looked up at him.

"No tears, angel. I hope to everyday give you something, show you the world around us. You and our children." He turned her around, so she was facing the view in front of them, her back leaning against him. "There is a huge world out there, and we will explore it together one day at a time," he kissed the side of her neck.

She turned and slid her arms up around his neck, flinching a little. "I'd like that. Show me what it is to love, Kayden." Elf placed a kiss on his chest.

He reached up and unhooked her arms from around his neck. "Keep your arms down, little angel, we don't need to open up your wound. Tonight, I will show you how a woman should be loved, but first, let me see you, angel," he said, reaching, untying her robe and sliding it off her shoulders, throwing it onto the floor by to the mattress.

Elf stood where she was, watching his face. He knew this would be one of the biggest issues for her. "Relax, little angel, you are stunning to me, and that is all that matters." He reached up and cupped her full breast in his hand, seeing the marks of a whip.

He leaned down; Kayden placed kisses on each mark before sucking her nipple into his mouth. She reached up, grabbing hold of his shoulders as he nipped her nipple before releasing it. "Arms down, little angel." He kissed and nibbled on her shoulder as he circled behind her.

"Face forward, little angel," he said, getting control of his other half inside him, seeing the burns, marks on her delicate skin. He knelt down on his knees, licking and placing kisses on every mark of her skin. "I know you don't like your marks; I would ask you to consider maybe a tattoo back here."

Elf glanced over her shoulder, smiling at him. "I was actually thinking about having your beast form tattooed back there. I have to admit, I was kind of impressed by what I saw," she told him, and he growled, reaching around and unbuttoning her nightshirt, sliding it down off her shoulders. She stood there in only a thong she wore.

"You are playing with fire here, my little angel," he growled again, leaning in and nipping her beautiful, round globe before jumping up and sweeping her up in his arms careful of her leg.

Giving her a quick kiss on the lips, Kayden placed his woman on the center of the bed before stripping out of his shirt and kicking off his tennis shoes. "You look so hot laying there waiting for me."

"Why am I burning up? I feel as if my blood and body are under attack; what did you do to me?"

Kayden stripped completely and crawled on the bed with Elf, gathering her into his arms, holding her tight. "Hush, Elf, what you are feeling is normal, little angel. The need to be with your partner, lover, and husband is strong in all of us." He tried to reassure her, seeing she was having trouble understanding the way between mates.

She leaned up on her elbow, looking at him. "Then, love me, my demon, because right now, I feel as if I'm going to burst if something does not happen." She leaned down and scraped her fangs against his chest.

Chapter Nine

Elf didn't recognize herself. She wanted to crawl all over Kayden, and she knew she'd been stupid for not feeding before going down to the family hall. "Kayden, we might have a serious problem here."

Rolling on top of her, he stared down at her and smiled. "All you need to do is ask. Feed, Elf," he said. "But know, I will be taking you into me, also," he said, lowering down, kissing the top of her head.

His cock was thick and long against her skin below. She wanted to feed from him but didn't understand what he meant about him feeding from her; he wasn't a bloodsucker.

Elf ran her tongue across his chest, tasting him. She swore nothing ever tasted as good as he did as she sank her fangs into him. The first blood drops hit her tongue; it was as if lights exploded in her head, as he moved his hips, rubbing his cock on her sensitive skin between her legs. Elf drank, her arms slid around his waist, the strength in his blood replenished her quickly as Elf pulled back, sealing the holes in his chest at the same time Kayden inched his cock inside her, stretching her.

Nothing could compare to the sensory overload she was feeling right then. Her body wasn't hers anymore; it was his, Kayden's. Her mate now lover. She sunk her nails into his back as he pushed further into her.

"Kayden," she whispered against his chest, rubbing her cheek against him, wondering if she were also part cat because Elf swore she was purring. Pleasure rushed through her as he rocked slowly back and forth working himself into her.

"Wrap your legs around me, angel," he growled, and that's when she noticed that his skin was thicker and a pink color. Her man, the both of them, were loving her, showing Elf

147

what it was to be loved by a man. Giving her everything he had but gentle like that of a baby until fangs sank into her neck shocking her and driving her body even higher if that was even possible as he fed from her.

"Yes," she whispered as he sank fully into her and moved in and out of her, slowly as if he were trying to find... "What..." was all she got out when Kayden angled his cock inside her, hitting that same spot again, sending her over a mountain.

Pleasure, lights, and stars filled her head as her body shook, having no control over anything right at the minute. The pressure on her neck was released as Kayden threw his head back, growling, thrusting into her three more times before warmness filled her, starting inside her pussy and spreading through her whole body.

Leaning down, Kayden rolled them once more to where she laid on top of him. Her body sweaty and coming down from a high Elf would never be able to explain. Tears filled her eyes, a knot formed in her throat as she buried her face in the crook of his neck, not able to hide the tears anymore.

Kayden sat up, pulling her into his arm. "Did I hurt you?" he asked, setting her back, searching her face and body.

"No, if anything, you were so gentle," she said, wiping the tears away.

"Then, why are you crying, angel?"

"Because I just realized how much they have stolen from me," Elf said, hating that her lip was trembling, the tears threating to come back. "From you." She looked up into his eyes. "They took what should have been yours."

"Aww, angel, don't cry. Don't you know you have given that to me already?" He pulled up the cover, it was soft as he tucked it around her. "I got to give you what any woman should have, love. To me, it was your first time. We will have many firsts, little angel, but we must remember to not allow those who stole from you to win. Every new experience is a win in my book. Look out there at this view, the world is waiting for us, and I plan on sharing with you every single day."

She placed a kiss on his chest and looked out at the city

below. The stars were bright as the moon shined bright in the sky. "You know they most likely took my eggs," she said. "What if I have children out there?"

"You, Nava, Darla, and the other females will start your search soon, and we will be standing beside you. I don't care if there are twenty little ones of you out there. We will find them and bring them back to the family, our family." He picked her up and placed her on the bed, getting up.

"Now, I think it's time for us to celebrate," Kayden said as he poured two glasses of some bubbly drink and turned to hand her one of the glasses. "A new first, your first taste of champagne."

Joining her on the bed, he tapped her glass. "To hundreds of new firsts to share together. It will be like I'm experiencing it again," Kayden told her, watching as she lifted the glass to her lips and sipping the liquid.

It was sweet but not too sweet, the bubbles tickled her nose. It was different that was for sure. "Strange, sweet, but good," she smiled up at him.

"It should be good. I have a feeling your father paid a pretty penny for that bottle," he told her, wrapping his arm around her.

"We should head back; Mom will be bringing the children back to our rooms soon," Elf said, resting her head against his chest. "Are we really mated now?" she asked, taking another little sip.

"Yes, I have marked you, taking you into me, and my DNA is running in your body now. You are mine, and I'm yours. We'll leave in a minute. I just want to hold you and enjoy the view around us with my woman in my arms." He kissed the top of her head.

"Tell me, are you one of those jealous types my father told me about?" Elf asked, remembering her father, wishing he were there with her.

"You're talking about your blood father? The one that was also in that place?" he asked.

"Yes, just like me, he was a prisoner. I don't know how they kept him when his people are like Storm and can move from place to place. Eventually, I'd like to see if we can find his family, would you mind?" Elf asked, peeking up at him.

"Elf, you can do what you'd like. You are free, but of course, we can search for them." Kayden frowned. "If he was an elf, that means you are, also. Why can't you do the things they are able to do?" he asked, looking down at her.

"My father didn't talk much about his kind. They had listening devices and cameras everywhere." She looked up at him. "He'd been there longer than I had been."

"We'll find every single asshole out there, and we won't rest 'til we do. Come, let's get dressed and go back to the room. It's getting chilly out here." He reached down and grabbed his shirt. Why don't you put this on and wrap that blanket around you 'til we get back?"

"I do have clothes," she looked around, frowning. "What happened to my clothes?"

Kayden smiled. "Um, I'm afraid I kind of threw them off the balcony."

Elf laughed and shook her head at the expression on his face. "You know that was..." She frowned. "Do you think Storm is okay?" she asked as he helped her dress in his shirt before he slid on his jeans.

"From what Ringo has told me, Storm is out of surgery. She's made it that far and is holding her own. We just have to wait. The next twenty-four hours are the important ones." Kayden lifted her up in his arms.

"Don't forget the champagne; we don't want to waste it," Elf said, bending down and grabbing the bottle as he smiled at her, shaking his head.

"Do you think we can go visit Storm? She's done so much for all of us. Did you know she also helped the other women with their clothes? I don't know how she stays in business when she gives away all her works."

"Tell me something. What did you do to pass the time? Were you allowed to read, do school work?" Kayden asked as they moved around the corner and down the hall toward her suites.

"No, they didn't want us to learn anything, but we were lucky there. Books and magazines were snuck in. The older people there taught the younger how to do math and to read.

I made sure to start both of my girls early. I also taught them to write. I'm not that great, but I can print at least."

"You know they have a great program in town to help adults if you'd like to get your high school diploma. They also have many different programs you might be interested in, computers, writing, design, all sorts of thing. Then, there is the apprenticeship program. Most store owners love to have people come and apprentice under them. Hell, I'm sure your mom would love to show you all about her business," Kayden said, stepping up into their wing.

"I sure would. We could see a mother-daughter store together if you'd like," Darla said, meeting them in the hallway with her children and Drake holding Willow in his arms.

"Did you know this lady can draw? She made me a picture; I'm going to frame and put it in my office, right beside our two little girls' pictures," Drake said, smiling down at her two sisters.

"I know, and it sure does not come from me. I can barely manage smiley faces. How did the meeting go? Is everything okay?" she asked as Kayden lowered her down on the sofa in her family room.

"The men that had you are in the hold and Tormac..." he growled lowering Willow to the floor. "He's been taken care of and will never again bother or hurt another."

Elf closed her eyes, resting her head back against the sofa, releasing the breath she had in her lungs. "Did he tell you anything about the others?" she asked, looking up at Drake.

* * * *

"Why don't we speak of this tomorrow. I think tonight, we should spend it with the girls after you feed this little guy." Kayden smiled, lifting Malcom out of Darla's arms. "This little guy is so alert, and he knows his momma's voice," he said as the boy started to whimper as he went to place him in her arms but looked at the t-shirt and then him.

Elf laughed, getting up slowly and moving to the bedroom. "I'll be out in a minute, but you can change him since I really smell him right now. The diapers and wipes are by the couch," Elf said, laughing and closing the door.

"That is our cue to leave you all to bond," Drake said,

slapping him on the back. "Congrats; welcome to fatherhood, son." He laughed, escorting out Darla and shutting the door behind him.

Both Willow and Maranda giggled as he sat down on the ground, looking for a blanket to put the little guy on. "Willow, would you spread out the throw on the floor here for me," he asked, wrinkling his nose as she did what he asked.

"So, are you our Daddy now?" Willow asked.

"Yes, is that going to be okay with you two?" He placed Malcom down and started to unsnap the cute one piece on him when his fingers slid into something warm and very stinky. He moaned, and the two girls giggled at him. "Maranda, hand me those wipes, will you." He pulled out his hand as Maranda pinched her nose, handing him the wipes.

"My brother stinks," Maranda said.

"That he does. I think it's taking you an awfully long time in there," Kayden yelled over his shoulder.

Sliding Malcom's legs out while cleaning each leg, putting each wipe in the messed-up outfit. As far as he was concerned, the thing could go in the trash along with the diaper as he took it off, rolling it all in the outfit after cleaning the little guy up. It took everything in him not to gag at the stink, but he was going to do this. Prove to his little angel, well right now, he could swear she had a little horn on the top of her head.

"Oh, you might want to watch out, seems my son has..." her words were cut off as she came out of the room, her warning too late as Malcom decided to pee. His aim was right on, hitting him in the face, mouth, not to mention himself.

Kayden grabbed he diaper and placed it over his little member and turned to glare at his mate who had just grown two little horns. But seeing her bent over laughing with tears rolling down her face, all he could do was shake his head and start once more cleaning himself and his son up.

"You, little guy, are going to be a wild one; I can just feel it," he said, placing a kiss on the little one's cheek and handing a clean little boy to his mother to eat. "Now, if you will excuse me, I'm going to wash my mouth out and scrub my face." Moving toward the bedroom, he stopped and looked over his shoulder. "Girls, why don't you climb onto the bed, and we can all watch some TV together tonight, curled up together."

Elf looked over her shoulder at him smiling. "You wouldn't mind?" she asked.

"You are my family now, Elf, all of you. But you should have warned me about that little guy's bombs. That outfit is going in the trash, too."

She smiled, standing, following the girls into the room.

"You aren't going home?" Willow asked.

"You guys are my home now. Where you go, I go. For now, we'll live here 'til we decided where we want to live. Plus, it's safer here now that security has been upped, until we can make sure every one of those bad guys is caught," he said, moving into the bathroom, grabbing a towel and started to wash his face.

After washing off the soap, he opened his eyes to see Willow there next to him, handing him the towel. "You really are going to stay, protect us?" she asked again, almost afraid, her eyes showing that this child had seen too much.

He lifted Willow up and placed her on the counter. "You are now my daughter. I protect what is mine." He reached up and tucked a piece of her hair behind her ear. "Why don't you go get the brush. When I'm done here, I'll braid your hair for you. If I'm not mistaken, I saw some cool beads on the dresser out there, too, we can use," he told her.

Her eyes got big. "You'd do my hair?"

"Of course. I might not be too good at it. I used to braid my sister's hair for her, but I'll try to do my best," he told her, picking her up and placing a kiss on the top of her head before placing her on the ground and watching her run into the room past Elf, who stood in the doorway.

She moved into the room and wrapped her arms around his waist, resting her cheek on his chest. "Thank you, Kayden. I don't know how, but I love you, and I can't wait to share my life with you."

He turned, wrapping his arms around her and tried to kiss her, but she shook her head and backed up, laughing. "Nope, you haven't brushed your mouth yet, not going to happen." She giggled and tried to get out of his arms.

"Woman, give me a kiss," he growled, and she giggled again as Maranda came in and wrapped her arms around his leg.

"I want to play, too," she said, smiling.

"Oh, you want kisses, too?" He went to reach for her, and she squirmed out of his reach, laughing as both women took off into the room, leaving him standing there.

His mom had been right. His mate not only connected with him on an emotional level, but she was also his world now, and so were the children. Kayden's life was complete. Now, all he had to do was find those that threatened to take it away from him and keep his family safe at the same time.

But he wasn't alone. No, this group had made some deadly enemies attacking their city, and none of them would rest until each one was dead. Hearing the giggling, Kayden hurried up brushing his teeth, not wanting to miss one smile, laugh from his family.

Storm's Magic Halloween
Little Angel Rescue, Book 3

Chapter One

The beeping of machines, the smell of disinfectant, and sickness threatened to drown her in the horrors of her past, but Matty's voice anchored her, which she kind of hated to admit. He slowly brought Storm back to reality and pain. That is when she remembered the concert and the explosion.

Storm had covered a child's little body then pain. If she were full pixy, like most believed, Storm would have been able to heal herself, but that was obvious it didn't happen. Did Matty and Nolen know her secret? She listened, not moving to listen to them speak to each other as she tried to figure out where she was and how bad it was.

"I know you're awake, Storm. Open those beautiful green eyes, baby," Matty whispered, leaning down, he placed a kiss on her cheek.

The back of her head throbbed, but as she opened her eyes, Storm wasn't expecting the light to blind her and a sharp pain to shoot through her skull.

"Light," her voice cracked as she tried to cover her eyes with her arm but was stopped by the pull of the tubes and stuff connected to her arms.

"Easy, little lady, don't pull your IVs out," Nolan said, taking her arm and lowering it to the bed. "The lights are down low. How much pain are you in?"

"Well, if I was human... Wait, I am part human... Crap," she moaned, hating her big mouth. Whenever in pain, Storm always did shout out what she had been thinking without thinking about it.

"Pain, yes, pain... Headache from hell and those little beeps on the machines don't help," she whimpered, her mouth was dry. "Water?"

"You're allowed some ice chips, but that is about it, my little pixy," Matty said, and she sighed.

"I'm not your anything yet, Matty," she mumbled around a piece of ice he gave her. "How many were hurt?" Storm asked, her headache starting to fade, which was weird. "Okay, which one of you is healing the headache?"

"We won't allow you to be in pain if we can help," Nolan said. "And you are ours."

Storm ignored his statement as Doc Lope came in followed by what she thought was another doctor. "Storm, finally you are awake. You gave us a big scare there, young lady." He pushed Nolan out of the way, reaching in, squeezing her hand and placing a kiss on the top of her head.

Nolan growled, glaring at her adopted father.

Doc Lope glanced over his shoulder at Nolan, and Storm laughed-moaned at the same time knowing the look he was giving Nolan. "Don't do that," she said.

"What?" Doc Lope asked, turning back to her with an innocent face.

"You know what, giving Nolan that look you give to anyone who questions you. I've seen it enough times over the years," she said, and he just winked at her while taking her pulse.

The other man moved over to where Matty was and tried to get by him, but he, too, growled, refusing to leave her side.

"Back up, Matty, now. This is Doctor Keyys. He's the one who did the operation on Storm's head. If it weren't for him, she wouldn't be here right now. Even I couldn't save my little girl this time."

Matty grumbled but stepped back as the doctor stepped in and smiled down at her. "How do you feel? I have to say, when Doc Lope called me in, I was amazed you were still alive. I couldn't believe you were actually talking. Can you lean your head down?" he asked.

She frowned at the doctor, not liking him instantly. His scent was off, and the way he acted was strange. Just what he said about her being dead wasn't right. She leaned her head down but glanced over at Doc Lope, and he, too, was frowning at Doctor Keyys. He started to unwind bandages from her head.

"Sorry, we had to cut all that purple hair away, but you had splinters of wood in your head we needed to remove," he told her, his cold fingers running over her scalp, pushing on a certain spot on her head had her yanking away from him.

"That hurt, damn it, and you cut all of it?" Storm felt the tears start to form, and she closed her eyes as she reached up and found that she was totally bald.

"Sorry, but I need to see if there is any infection. As I said earlier, you are lucky to be alive; your hair will grow back." The doctor stepped back, frowning down at her. "I'm going to leave the bandages off for now. You are healing nicely."

Storm didn't know what was going on, but she was getting a really bad vibe from this guy, and as soon as he left, leaving Doc Lope, Storm glanced at him. "Where did you find him? I have to say, Doc, he just isn't... there is something off about him. Were you in the operating room with him?"

Doc Lope nodded, frowning at the door. "Yes, he might be good at what he does, but he still does not understand the other half of you. His bedside manner needs some improvement also, but he is right on the hair. It will grow back, Storm; plus, you know there are tons of different wigs you could wear 'til then." He patted her arm.

"It's not the same, and you know it," Storm said, leaning back. "Do you think I could get something to drink now?"

"I'll have the nurse order up some coffee and a liquid diet for now." Doc Lope moved to the door and stopped, looking over his shoulder.

"Matty, a word with you and Nolan, please," he said, stepping outside.

"Hey, you can talk in front of me," Storm said.

"Rest, Storm, and that is an order," Doc Lope growled at her, and she stuck her tongue out at him.

"You're lucky I love you, old man," she mumbled and curled up but not before her favorite blanket covered her.

"Don't do that again, young lady. You've been through a major trauma to your body. You need to build up your strength. No more magic for the next day at least," he ordered, going out into the hallway followed by Nolan and

Matty.

"No magic? Please," Storm mumbled but had to admit she was now very tired. She closed her eyes, curling up in her blanket and flinching when she tried to move. Yep, this was a fine mess. She really did hate hospitals, too many bad memories that wouldn't go away. Not to mention pain mentally and physically sometimes.

* * * *

Nolan Moree followed his mate Matty and their Doc Lope out of Storm's room. He had found his mates in one day to almost lose one in an explosion from some frantic group that was now on his family's list to be destroyed.

He glanced over his shoulder at Storm as she cuddled with the old blanket as the door slowly closed from her room. "What is this about you knowing more? Do we need to hunt someone?" Nolan asked, turning to face Doc Lope.

"Follow me; we will not speak of this out where everyone can hear us," Doc Lope said and lead them to a nearby room, shutting the door when they entered it. He turned to stare at both men. "You are her mates?"

Matty frowned. "You know we are. What is this all about, Doc?"

"Matty, you know I adopted Storm. What you don't know is I'm the one that brought Storm here from New York. I found Storm in an alley scrounging for food. She had a black eye, burn marks on her back, along with whip marks. I knew instantly what she was, but she didn't."

"Did you find the one who marked her?" Nolan snarled.

Doc Lope shook his head. "She didn't remember, or that is what Storm informed me at the time. Now, do I think she knows who did it? I've asked her repeatedly if she knew where her mother or father were, but she just smiles at me and says it's not important now that she has me." Doc Lope growled. "She should have her mother, but that isn't what worries me. This will bring on the night terrors as she calls them, but I know for a fact they are dreams about what happened to her in the past."

The doctor looked at Matty then at Nolan. "The both of you have to get to the source of her fear. I have a feeling she's hiding here, that someone is searching for her because Storm was supposed to go off to school in New York. She won a designer contest, all was paid for. It was a once-in-a-lifetime chance, but I found out a week later she had turned it down. No, there is something in New York that is scarring our Storm. I thought with Drake and Darla hosting their annual Halloween Ball this year, maybe you could go pick up costumes to bring back here or something. Whatever it is, it needs to be dealt with."

"Your best guess on how old Storm is?" Nolan asked.

"No guess, Storm told me she was twenty-eight. She does not remember when her birthday is, but Storm knows she is that old."

"Another question, what is wrong with the doctor that came in Storm's room? Because, I tell you right now, he's lucky to be still alive. I swear, he hurt her on purpose, and the way he behaved toward her, I won't have it again," Matty stated.

"I agree. I say we keep the creep away from her. Any idea when we can take her to your place? Where exactly does Storm live?" Nolan frowned and glanced at Matty, who was also frowning.

"She never told me. Storm would just disappear. Doc?" Matty asked.

"She has a room at my home, but I believe Storm has her own space, but even I haven't seen it." He smiled. "My daughter does think I don't know where her apartment is. Anyway, she has a little place up above her store, and she's got half of her belongings at home. I asked her, but she just shrugged. Saying it was better this way."

"Well, it seems to me we have a lot of walls to break down and to earn a certain pixy's trust. What do you say we ask Storm to say at your father's home, with Elf and Nava? Maybe say with this group of fanatics around, we don't want to take a chance they capture her, which is true in many aspects. Even my brothers agree the town needs to be on alert more. With so many different species living here, this group would have a field day capturing children and such." Nolan glanced to the door. "My brother is here, Alastar, along with your father, Matty."

Doc Lope moved away from the door, allowing Drake and Alastar in. "What's going on? Any more attacks?"

"We need to move Storm out of this place now." Nolan's brother stared at him then at Matty. "It's not safe. My first sweep when Storm was brought in was fine but not anymore. Others are here, and I don't know what they are. My pets are uneasy also, and they are never uneasy."

For his older brother to say that much, Nolan knew that Storm was in danger. He glanced at Matty, who nodded his head.

"Matty, your wing has been prepared. Your mother has opened up the master suite there, and all the rooms are ready for Storm and you two. Welcome to the family, Nolan, sorry it's under these circumstances, but we will deal with this new threat to our family. Doc, get Storm ready to move. I have the car waiting below; Dagr and Ivarr are guarding the car as we speak."

In a matter of twenty minutes, Nolan and Matty had Storm wrapped up and in Matty's arms as he moved behind them covering their tails. His brother in front with Drake and Doc Lope on either side of them.

It was an impressive sight, but it would seem this didn't even phase Doctor Keyys as he stepped in front of his brother, Alaster. Nolan smiled as Alaster lifted the doctor up and moved him to the side. "Do not move," his brother snarled, Alastar's eyes going red as Matty walked out the door of the hospital with his father and Doc Lope.

Doc Lope turned and frowned as Doctor Keyys ran out following Alastar. "You can't take her. Are you out of your mind?"

"Doc, if that man is a friend of yours, I'd really get him out of my brother's sight, or he isn't going to be around much longer," Nolan said and got into the car behind Drake. "We'll meet you at the estate," he stated to his brother and the doctor, closing the door and nodding to the driver, Ivarr.

"I really don't like that man," Storm mumbled, pulling her

old blanket around her tighter, the end of it brushing his hand. At once, his gift kicked in.

Chapter Two

Storm hadn't given Matty or Nolan any fuss when they had informed her that they had to move. She had felt the shift in the hospital as she was sleeping, waking her instantly. She would have used her magic leaving the hospital, but even Storm knew she was too weak to do that much right now.

Her being hurt, knocked out, they had been able to find her, and the good old Doc Keyys was with them, whoever they were. Storm didn't know what these men wanted but never did she take a chance, she had learned her lesson the hard way as did her mother with her life. Why they saved her, Storm didn't know. But for some strange reason, the ones that had killed her mother wanted her, at least that is what she thought.

Trish Larrs, Storm shivered and pulled her blanket, the only thing she had left from her real father, closer. With only a few memories, Storm cherished the old blanket, always repairing and keeping it close, remembering happier times with him.

She had learned early on that it had been her father that had kept her safe, away from her mother's psychotic behavior. After his death, she had taken Storm and ran away from everything she had known.

Drugs, humans had been her world. Storm knew how bad it could be being kept prisoner by humans. For years, she had been beaten, tortured, and touched, her mother only laughing while pushing the needle into her veins.

No, they weren't the monsters; Storm had seen what true monsters were. The ones that had starved a little girl, kicking and hitting her when she cried out for daddy.

"Easy there, little pixy, you're safe," Nolan whispered, leaning over and placing a kiss on her cheek. "We're right here and won't allow anyone to hurt you."

"Too late for that, not even you two can keep monsters away," Storm whispered and curled up closer to Matty, closing her eyes.

"Night or day, Storm, monsters can be defeated. Believe me, over the last hundred years I've destroyed my share of them, and I'm not going to stop until yours are all gone, a memory, sweetheart." He tucked the blanket around her. "But, Storm, we are going to talk about this. If your father is the kind of man I see, and I do see him, Storm, he'd want you to tell us so we can help."

Storm glanced up at Nolan, meeting his gaze, and she knew right there that he had seen the pictures of her father. "Maybe," she said when Drake leaned over, pulling the blanket away from her face.

"The hardest battle you will face is your past. What would you say to Ana, Nava's little girl? Should she hide, bury the pain, forget those that had hurt her?" Drake asked.

She glared at Drake, earning a smile as he sat back. "That isn't fair. There is nothing you can do for me. These monsters that I fight are humans, druggies, my mother took me into their homes. If you can call it that. The other, I honestly don't know what it is, in the hospital. Every time I'm hurt or my defenses are down, they come, searching for me." She turned and buried her face against Matty's chest but not before saying, "I honestly don't know what is coming after me. Who my mother has hooked up with, and I don't want to know. My mother is dead."

Both Nolan and Drake said nothing, but Nolan tucked her blanket once more around her, rubbing her leg. Storm really didn't know who or what was coming after her, but after all that had been done to her, Storm wouldn't put it past her mother to find the lowest, scariest thing out there to come after her.

Her mother's mind had been far gone from this world. She closed her eyes, and at once, there he was, her father. His long black hair pulled back into the braid she had always held onto when they went anywhere.

His magic had been strong and always created a bubble

around her when they went somewhere. Her mother would be furious, yelling that she didn't need such protection, but her father ignored her mother always when it came to Storm.

Storm sat up quickly, flinching. "He had brothers, my father had brothers. Do you think we could find them?" She frowned and slunk down again against Matty's chest. "Maybe not. What if they blame her for his death?"

"There are ways to find out without them knowing where you are," Nolan offered. "Do not do that again, Storm. You are not healed yet, even though I have a feeling you are healing much faster than normal, we don't need you opening your wounds."

"How could you find out without them knowing you are searching for information? My father was one of most powerful of our kind. Well, that is what I remember, but it could be a little girl's love for her father, too," she sighed. "I don't know what to think anymore." Storm closed her eyes but opened them up and slowly turned to face Drake.

"Before the explosion, while Nolan and Matty were arguing..." She peeked at Matty who snorted.

"We were talking, working things out." Matty grumbled.

"And have you worked things out?" she asked.

"No, but don't worry; the most important thing is you, Storm. The other stuff will come. But what were you going to say? What did you see?" Nolan asked.

One thing was for sure; when Nolan spoke, her hormones had a habit of doing jumping jacks or something. Even here and now, hurt, she was affected. "Knock off the voice, please," Storm told him before turning toward Drake again when she felt Nolan's breath on her ear.

"Sorry, Storm, but this is my normal voice; you'll have to get used to it and so will Matty," he said, earning moans from Matty and her.

"Okay, enough, the three of you. I want to hear what she has to say." Matty's father laughed, shaking his head.

* * * *

Nolan grinned even though Matty had kicked him in the leg

and Storm had glared at him, it would seem his mates were just as attracted to him as he was to them. All they had to do now was find out who was after Storm and wait for her to heal before they could seal their bond.

One thing was for sure, Nolan didn't have that much patience, but for Storm's health, he'd wait even if it meant jerking off in the shower. He turned his attention once more on Storm, who was glancing at Drake.

Storm was nervous, staring at Drake. "This could be nothing, but I found it strange that Ringo was speaking with Porter before the explosion. I saw in Matty's thoughts that Porter had been the traitor, and well, they were arguing about something. Again, maybe it's nothing," Storm said.

Both Matty and Drake said nothing, staring at Storm. "Does Ringo know Porter well?" he asked, not afraid but needing to know.

"Everyone at the house knew Porter and his wife. They were regular visitors. No, he can't be in on this," Drake sat back, growling.

Nolan swore Drake was going over Ringo's movements over the past weeks while sitting in the car.

"To steal children, even hurt Mom?" Matty asked.

"Ringo could have been recruited. Remember, your mother was taken before you two were even born. Did Ringo know about his mother being taken before all of this went down?" Nolan asked, sending the information to his brothers, knowing they would move carefully to see what they could about Ringo without hurting his new father and mate.

"Yes, this is why I can't understand why... I mean, sure, he wasn't too happy when Matty was born, but... This just does not make sense," Drake growled. "But then, Porter's visits... I remember seeing Porter and Ringo speaking sometimes but stopping when they spotted me."

Drake sat forward and glanced at each of them. "This does not go anywhere until we find out for sure. Darla has been hurt enough with Elf." Drake turned and looked at Nolan.

"You've spoken with your brothers. I'm leaving this up to them. They will report to me when they find out anything. Nolan, I'm counting on your family keeping this from Darla because this is going to destroy her."

"No shit," Matty grumbled and hugged their woman tight.

Nolan reached over and squeezed Matty's arm. "Whatever the outcome, we will work this out as a family. Even if he has some connection to this group, we'll work it out together, that I promise. All of you are family now, and my brothers protect their family. But Drake, if this is the case, it will have to be explored to see how much damage was done to the city itself since Ringo knows all our security information."

"Nolan, I would like you and your brothers to move in the wing where you are staying. Also, ask your cousins to stay. They can take Elf's and Nava's wing for now. Matty, do not, and I repeat, do not leave Storm with anyone but Nolan's brothers, understood?" Drake ordered.

"Dad?" Matty questioned.

Drake sighed. "We can't take the chance, Matty."

Storm glanced back and forth between Matty and Drake. "I'm sorry. I didn't mean to cause trouble."

Drake reached over and touched her nose. "No, I should have seen this before, that something was going on between the two. You just brought it to the forefront, which is good. We need to make sure and cross the dots because we know this group is once more reforming and will be back again. My goal is to wipe this group from this planet, and I will do it."

Nolan sat back, pulling Storm's legs onto his lap, rubbing down her feet. "That is a big task, especially since their numbers have risen from the last time your wife had to deal with them. May I ask, did you know Darla when this happened? Or was this before you found her?"

"Before. We didn't think she could have children after what happened. Didn't know if they had destroyed her chance at having children or not. But with Doc Lope's help, Ringo was born and then Matty. She wanted more children, but the pressure of just trying was too much. We both agreed we would not try anymore. If it happened, it happened. When Nava showed up, it was the first time in a long time I'd seen that light in Darla's eyes. Don't get me wrong, she loves our boys, but Darla's always wanted to give me a daughter." Drake laughed. "Now, I have four and soon to be five." He glanced over at Storm.

"This is why I don't understand why Ringo would do this after what happened with his mother." Drake glanced out the window.

"We will find out before anyone knows and allow you to handle this." Nolan reached over and squeezed Matty's arm. "My brothers and family are here to help. We'll figure this out and take care of it together. All our problems," Nolan said, his gaze moving to Storm, seeing her rub her bare head.

"It will grow back, little pixy," Matty said, placing a kiss on the top of her head.

She sees the humans as monsters, but this threat that was at the hospital was bigger than a human. I hadn't felt that much power except when your father got mad the other day, Nolan told Matty through their blood bond they had formed the night before.

I know. One day we'll find those humans if they are still alive and drain them, but for now, do you have a clue who we are dealing with, those back at the hospital? Matty asked, looking up at him.

The signature, patterns were the same as our woman's, but much, much stronger. If I had to guess, it would seem her family has come searching for her, but that is for us to find out before they even approach Storm.

Agreed, she does not need to be hurt again, Matty said.

"This woman would like to be in on this investigation you are planning. I'm not a wilting flower. If this is my family, I will be there with you," she said, turning her head to stare at him, surprising both him and Matty.

"We will see," Nolan said as the pulled up to the Drako estate. Every time he got out and took in the great place, Nolan felt small.

Chapter Three

Storm opened her eyes, looking around. The last thing she remembered was giving a piece of her mind to both Nolan and Matty when she had just gotten so tired. Yes, this stupid explosion had taken a lot out of her and brought up the old nightmares she had thought she'd put to bed, but it was obvious she hadn't.

One thing for sure, the room she was in now was one of the most beautiful she had ever seen. Whoever heard of having a small waterfall in your bedroom, but what was amazing were the stone walls.

"Stunning, isn't it?" Nolan said, coming into the room and sitting on the edge of the bed. "This is our master suite. Darla has gone out of her way to try and make us all comfortable." He nodded to the other side of the bed, and Storm turned to see a huge rock in the corner.

"Do I dare ask what that is?" Storm asked, smiling.

"Supposedly, it's a boulder from my hometown in Ireland. Darla called it a Galway kissing stone. Don't know how she figured out all of us were mates and to have it here so quickly, but I know one thing, I'm not kissing the thing."

Storm couldn't help it and laughed. "I have to agree. I won't be kissing the stone either. You never know where it was, but you are right, Matty's mom is a smart one and sweet. When I first got here with Doc Lope, she was there bringing me clothes and telling me all about the city, at least the good parts. Maybe she knew then that I was going to be part of her family." She shrugged. "I don't know, but Darla will always be the mom I never had."

"Well, that is good to hear because your mother has brought you some food and you are going to eat it, young lady. Doc said you could have soup and a little bread, slowly build up. So, let's not tell him about the cake, shall we?" she said. "Help her sit up, Nolan."

Nolan's lip twitched, and Storm saw the laughter in his eyes. He leaned over, placing a kiss on her cheek before helping her sit up. "If you're up to it, you can even soak in a hot tub. Your wounds have finally closed, so it won't hurt anything." Darla placed the tray over her, and Storm stared at all the food.

"Of course, I had to give you soup since the doc ordered it, but really, who heard of having soup for breakfast. I know you love your oatmeal and bacon. I also brought some cinnamon rolls that you love and, of course, your coffee cake, coffee, orange juice, and water." Darla leaned over and kissed the top of her head.

"I also had a few wigs sent over for you to try on." Darla looked over at the door, where Matty came in carrying about eight different boxes followed by Drake with the same number of boxes.

"A few boxes? Darla," Storm shook her head, popping a piece of bacon in her mouth, moaning. "So good. Now, how are Nava and Elf?"

"We're fine; you're the one that went and got hurt so bad she ended up in the damn hospital. What the hell?" Nava grumbled, following Elf into the room.

"I have to agree with Nava; what is up with getting hurt? But I owe you big time for protecting my baby, thank you," Elf said as they both came over, giving her a hug and kiss.

Storm couldn't smile, eating her food. "God, I missed you two. Did Martha show you the back rooms? I know you three wanted to check out the space," Storm asked, smiling, thinking of the older widowed wolf lady.

Darla laughed. "Martha was a hoot. I have to say, it has been a while since I've been in your store, young lady. I am so impressed at the amazing work you have done. But you need to send your clothes out further to the other cities."

"I send them out, just not to stores. I usually take a bunch of things to the shelters for the children and women, but I make enough here. I don't need much, and my bank account is fine," Storm mumbled around a bite of coffee cake. She didn't know what was better—the coffee cake or the cinnamon buns.

The room got quiet, and she looked up to see everyone staring at her. "What?"

Darla once more leaned over and kissed the top of her head. "You amaze me, and I'm proud to have you as a daughter. Eat, I'll be back later to collect the tray, and you two, make sure to take good care of her." Darla started to move out of the door and stopped.

"I forgot to tell you. We are doing a fundraiser at the Halloween party. We are asking for donations for the house at the end of town. Nava's and Elf's mates thought it would be a wise purchase. A place we can place families that might show up, looking for help."

Storm nodded. "Count me in for clothes. We can set up a room in the house for clothes—children's, women's, and men's. Wait, when is Halloween?" Storm frowned, her days totally messed up.

"We have a few days to go, and not to worry, I'm sure you'll come up with the best costume," Darla said, going out the door, and she smiled, looking down at her food.

"Oh no, you don't. You have an idea for costumes? Because we need help big time," Nava said.

"Well," she glanced at Matty and Nolan.

"Okay, you two, out. We need to plan, and it looks like you guys are getting a surprise," Elf said, waving her hands and pointing at the door. "Go, join our men watching the little ones. We'll call you when we are done."

"Really? We're getting kicked out of my own room?" Matty grumbled.

"I wouldn't be worried about that if I were you. Storm wants to surprise us for their costumes; you know this could be bad," Nolan said and glanced back at Storm, who was smiling from ear to ear.

"Storm, what are you up to?" Matty said, frowning.

"Me?" she asked, and Matty groaned. "Storm, no magic and really? I thought I was past this?" Matty said, and Nolan had to smile as he pulled his hair back into a braid.

"You still owe me," she said as Elf shut the door on their

faces.

"You really are going to have to make up with her. Wait," Nolan pushed the door back open and peaked in. "Do not get out of that bed without us, Storm. I mean it. You know how to call me if you need me." Nolan's gaze met hers, and she sighed, nodding.

"Good, have fun." He closed the door, moving down the hall with Matty.

"How is it she'll listen to you?" Matty grumbled.

"I didn't hurt her," Nolan said, reaching over and squeezing his cheek. "But Matty, she clung to you when we were carrying her from the hospital. She needs you, but I believe she's still scared." Nolan stopped him before they exited his wing. "Are you going to accept our mating?" he asked.

Matty ran his hand through his hair and met Nolan's gaze. "Yes, I accept our bond, but like I said before, I won't do anything 'til Storm is with us. I hurt her too much and refuse to even take that chance again."

"Agreed, but..." Nolan reached around, grabbing the back of Matty's neck and pulled him closer before covering his mouth with his. Both of them fought for dominance as their tongues battled, tangled until Matty sighed and relaxed, giving Nolan what he needed—acceptance.

Nolan ran his fang over Matty's bottom lip, nipping it, sucking the little bit of blood into his mouth. "You taste like the finest wines. Soon," he said and released Matty. "Let's go see if our brothers need any help with our nieces. Plus, my brother is going to meet us there and tell us what he found out."

* * * *

Storm waited until she knew her men were far enough away that they wouldn't hear a thing she said. She shook her head and took a sip of her coffee, sitting back. Two freaking men. Of course, the fates had to mess with her heart and head again.

It wasn't bad enough she had one alpha man biting at her back end, she now had two, and if first impressions were right, Nolan was not as easy going as Matty had been. Yea, her gentleman had changed; Storm saw it in his expression as he held her earlier as they had come from the hospital. So much like his father when he was furious.

The bed dipped on both sides as Elf and Nava surrounded her. It was the first time Storm had allowed herself to have friends. Even as a child she had played, but no one was every brought close to her home, even when Doc Lope had brought her back to Magic.

She smiled, staring at each woman, each of them still fighting their own demons inside. "So, my idea. I don't know if you will like it, but I thought we could dress as the *Elvira* sisters. Since it's only fitting our parents are throwing the party, or if you don't like that we could go as..."

Both women were shaking their heads, smiling. "I've seen this woman a few times, and it's perfect. I say we even get wigs, too." Elf grinned, putting her hands together.

"There is no need for you two to wear heavy wigs when I can, well I hope I'm allowed to use my magic by then. I really need to speak with Doc," Storm said.

"You called?" her friend-father figure came strolling through the door. One thing was for sure, the man was impressive, and Storm was lucky she had him.

"Are you behaving and listening to what I said?" He frowned at her plate. "I'm really going to have to speak with Drake about his wife. I said a liquid diet," he grumbled and went to take her tray.

"Don't you touch my food," Storm grumbled. "It's all my comfort food, I'm allowed." She pouted, and he laughed.

"Fine, but if you get sick, I'll tan your hide, stubborn woman. Now, what did you want to ask me? Lower your head, little pixy, so I can see the wounds."

Storm did as he asked as Elf scooted back, giving him access to her. "When can I start using my magic?" she asked, flinching when he touched a sensitive spot.

"Sorry, your skin has healed over the wounds, but you are going to be sensitive back here." He placed his fingers under her chin and lifted her head, so she was staring at him.

"This means that you will take it easy for the next couple

of weeks while your head heals. As for your magic, a little a day will not hurt, but this does not mean you can go floating around like you have been, Storm. Two weeks for everything. That means if you need anything from your place, you will have your men help you bring it here, understood?" the alpha wolf ordered, and Storm knew not to push him.

"Fine, and how did you know about the apartment?" she grumbled.

Doc Lope knelt down, taking her hand and squeezing it. "The first night you didn't come home. I was frantic, so I hate to admit it, but I went hunting. When I found you, all curled up in your little apartment, I didn't have the heart to bring you home. But Storm, you will always have a room at our home." He stood and winked at her. "So, if those two men of yours give you any trouble, you can come home."

"Okay, Matty, Nolan, I thought you two were going to go help Elf's and Nava's mates?" Storm said as they moved into the room.

"Not a chance if the doc is checking on you," Nolan said. "Well, how is she, and for the record, Storm, will not be going anywhere. We work this out together always." His gaze landed on hers, and Storm swore his eyes were swirling with bits of fire in them.

"Two weeks, she is not to use her total magic. Walking is fine but not to overtire her. Since it's obvious she can eat, and it is staying down, just make sure she does not eat too heavy today. No more cake today, young lady."

Storm stuck her tongue out at him, and he laughed. "Be good; I'll check on you tomorrow, and if you're going to the Halloween party, no heals."

"Well damn... but I don't need heals for what I have planned." Elf and Nava laughed. "Okay, Nava, Elf, you two are going to help me into the bathroom for a nice bath." Her gaze jumped to Nolan's then to Matty's. "No, my sisters will help me for now, but when I'm done, I'd like to go to my apartment. If I agree to stay here, I want to bring a few things here."

Elf leaned over and grabbed the tray. "You're done, right?"

"Yep, you don't mind helping, do you?" Storm asked Elf.

"Not at all; you helped us both when we needed it. That is what sisters do for each other, help each other. Plus, I owe you, little sister. Now, do you need help to bring over your belongings here?" Elf asked when she got up, putting the tray down away from the bed.

Before she or Nava could come over to help her, Nolan was there lifting her up into his arms. "I will carry her," he said, giving her one of his looks.

"Why do I get the feeling you are going to be a pain in my ass," Storm grumbled, wrapping her arms around his neck.

"Because you know I will tan that gorgeous butt." Nolan leaned down and nipped her nose, but before she could reply, everything went black.

Chapter Four

*N*olan threw his head back and howled. Their mate was gone, and she had been taken out of their bedroom, but worse, out of his arms.

The door burst open as Alastar and Drake came running in. "They were here," he stated.

"Who was here? What the hell are you talking about? Where is our mate?" Nolan glared at his brother, stepping up to him. "You knew something would happen?"

"Back up, Nolan, and take a deep breath. Her family took her. Storm was lied to, her father is very much alive, and from I was told, they have been looking for her for a while," Alastar informed them.

"They took her from my arms, Alastar. We have no idea where they are or even how to get to where they are," Nolan yelled and spun away from him so furious at his brother. "Matty and I should have been told immediately there was a threat that they could come into our room and take her.

"Dune!" Drake yelled, making even him jump and spin around just as a man appeared in the room.

He had long blond hair, almost to the ground. "You bellowed."

"Don't push it, Dune. I'm calling in that favor. My daughter was taken from our home, pixy; I want her back," Drake snarled. "Contact Briar Neverstream; he'll be able to find out what is going on."

Dune whistled. "Wow, you know royalty." The man disappeared when Drake started to snarl. "Alastar, I suggest you find that man you were speaking with since it's obvious they set you up."

"It's done." Alastar spun to leave.

"Alastar..." Nolan called out and moved to his brother.

"I'm sorry," he said, looking up at his brother, who grinned.

"Do not worry about it. I have a feeling I will be calling you and Matty for help soon enough." Alastar reached out and squeezed his shoulder. "But I promise we'll get her back today."

Doc Lope moved up to them. "Why don't we go down to the kitchen and wait. I know Darla had coffee and cinnamon buns sitting on the table. If this man is her father, he won't hurt her; well, he better not," he growled and moved out the door as Elf and Nava stepped out being met by their men and kids.

"I've been to their world. If this does not work, I can take us there and get her back ourselves," Saxon offered. "Or we can go now. I mean, I couldn't sit and wait."

Drake growled. "If we go to their world, it could be declared a sign of aggression."

"And them coming into our home isn't an act of aggression?" Matty growled. "I say we go now." Matty glanced at him.

"Agreed. Sorry, Drake, they stepped over the line. Saxon, if you would," Nolan asked.

"Shit, not without me you're not going. Kayden, let's go. Ladies, inform my mate what is going on." Drake growled, "Alastar, you're with us, too."

Within minutes, they were on a hill overlooking a small town. At once, Dune was next to them with another man.

"Reason for this?" the man said.

"Your people come in our bedroom and stole our woman," Nolan growled, getting fed up, needing to find Storm.

Drake placed his hand on his shoulder. "Gentlemen, this is Briar, my contact in this world. As you heard, my daughter was taken from my home. She had just been taken out of the hospital because of a threat and is still not healed," Drake informed the man.

The man glanced down at the small town. "My cousin Flix. Come, but I warn you now, I will protect him and his family. They have been through much searching for this child."

Nolan stepped forward. "And I will kill any man that has harmed my mate. I don't care if he is family."

"Are you threating me?" the man asked, stepping into his personal space.

"No threat, a promise, and the one that entered our room will be hurt," Nolan said as his brother growled, drawing the man's attention.

The man actually stepped back, glancing from Alastar to him. "Follow me," was all he said, leading them toward a home off to the side of the city.

"We find her, you and Matty take her home, we'll deal with these people," Alastar said, nodding to Saxon, who nodded.

"We will wait to see what they have to say," Drake said, looking at Alastar. But if she's hurt, believe me, nothing will step in our way or anyone."

Briar mis-stepped but caught himself glancing back at Drake then to Alastar. Nolan would have laughed, but right now, he was barely keeping it together. Next to him, he could hear Matty's little growls.

Nolan reached over and rubbed his back. "Easy. You don't want to make Storm upset again," he said.

"After this, she is not leaving our sight for a very, very long time," Matty said.

"Agreed on that," Nolan said as a very tall man stepped out of the house, followed by the doctor that had been at the hospital.

Nolan didn't know he had been growling when Drake grabbed onto him, holding him. "I suggest you have that so-called doctor out of here or he's dead."

Briar turned and glanced at Drake. "Shit." Briar dropped and knelt to the ground, which would not be good at any normal time, but right now, the smirk on the doctor's face was too much. Shifting, never had Nolan lost control of himself, but this was one time there was no control. The animal inside of him broke loose as he jerked out of Drake's grasp, rushing toward the doctor.

But the damn man vanished. His growl even had his ears ringing as he turned to see the doctor standing behind a woman and man.

"Someone better control him because if he tries to attack

the royal physician again, I will have no choice but to destroy him," the man said next to the lady.

"You touch my little brother..." Alastar snarled and released his little zoo around him.

"Enough, Alastar, pull them back. Matty get Nolan under control now, and King Neverstream, never threaten my sons. Your family entered my home and stole my daughter from her mates. That so-called man you call a physical hurt their mate and was rude. He will not go near my daughter."

The king turned and glanced at the doctor as Matty wrapped his arms around Nolan from behind. "I need a levelheaded man here, Nolan. Dad is ready to go to war here, and we don't need that," Matty said.

"No, we don't," Storm stood in the door, holding onto the doorway. "Okay, beast man, I could really use your strong arms about now," she whispered, leaning against the door.

"Storm," the man that had come out the door yelled and moved to grab her, but Nolan was there before him, growling as he carefully lifted her up in his arms.

He shook, holding her tight, moving her away from everyone except for Matty, who followed close, growling at everyone, watching their backs. "Storm, are you hurt?" he finally got out. "Did he hurt you?"

"Easy there, wild one. Looks like we have some major talking later, don't we?" She nuzzled his neck as he sat down on the grass, where Matty reached around and hugged them both.

"Two scares in a week. You will not be going anywhere alone for a long time, our little pixy," Matty growled.

"Tired, father, Lope was right, too much magic... Kept the fool away from me. I really don't like him," she said, and Nolan lifted his head, snarling as his gaze found the doctor's, who had the good sense to step back. "No war, sleep," she said before falling asleep in his arms.

"Saxon," Nolan said, and in the next minute, he and Matty were back in their room, but they weren't alone. Said man with the long blond hair had followed them.

Saxon growled and stepped in front of him. "You dare to enter our home again?"

"I didn't enter it in the first place, and I'm not leaving my daughter again. I allowed you to bring her here because it was what she wanted, but I'm not leaving her. My name is Flix. Storm was stolen from me when she was but four. I've been searching ever since then for her."

Storm moaned as Nolan put her down in their bed. "He can stay; we have much to work out, but be warned that if that doctor even tries to come here..." he snarled, and at once, Storm reached out rubbing his arm.

"Shhh, wild one, here," she whispered.

Doc Lope came rushing in. "You fools left without me. How is she," Doc Lope came over to the side of the bed, leaning down, placing a kiss on the top of her head. "Little pixy..."

"Okay Doc, okay, tired. You were right," she rumbled to Nolan, who knew their woman had gone into a deep sleep.

Storm swore she had just been in this same boat yesterday or was it the day before. It would seem the days were starting to blur together, and it was pissing her off. She had work to do and to help her sisters find the little ones taken from them.

But there was one difference from before, there was a warm body on each side of her, wrapped around her. She cracked her eye open, and sure enough, Nolan was smiling from ear to ear at her. As she turned her head, Matty smiled down at her.

"Do you know how long we have been waiting for you to wake up? You scared us, little pixy. Even Doc Lope is furious, to say the least." Matty leaned down and kissed her lips softly. "Morning, love," Matty said, moving out of the bed naked as the day he was born.

It would be wrong if she didn't stare, the man had a body she could drool over easily and had done so many nights lying in her bed alone.

"I do believe our little pixy is fascinated with your body, Matty," Nolan said. "Which I do have to agree. I so love the dimples right up above his butt cheeks, not to mention the tattoo he has on his ass," Nolan said, leaning over and kissing her cheek. "But alas, people are waiting to see you, my dear, and since you didn't get a bath yesterday..." Nolan growled, moving out of the bed, naked too.

Her gaze jumped to his, to see he was still very pissed off. "Wild man, it wasn't my father that took me from our room; it was that creep doctor. He really is off, Nolan, Matty. There is something not right about him." Storm went to scoot out of the bed when she noticed she was also nude. "Okay, why am I naked?" she growled.

Nolan glanced over his shoulder, heading toward the bathroom. "When you're in our bed, you will always be naked. Stay there; I'm going to start the bath. Matty, tell your dad to give us an hour so Storm can enjoy her bath. Her father owes her that, at least." Nolan growled the last part.

"Why are you mad at him? He did allow me to come back here," Storm asked and regretted it as Nolan spun around, glaring at her, his eyes black as the night.

"Allowed? Do not even go there. We are bonding, you know this, and after you almost died on us, to be taken out of my arms..." he snarled. "No, I'll shove *he allowed* up his damn ass first. If he knew where you were, your father should have come here and asked to see you. But no, he sends some half-quack doctor to retrieve you, not caring that you had people that would be scared shitless about where you had gone. Not to mention, did he even try to inform us that you were where you were, no. Instead, he comes out ready to confront us." Nolan turned around and marched into the bathroom.

Matty sighed. "Nolan is right, Storm. Your father is lucky he was allowed to stay here, and he better tread lightly today when it comes to you because..." Matty glanced back at the bathroom door.

Storm closed her eyes and took a deep breath. Both of her men were right, but he was her father, but so was Doc Lope. Just the mechanics of it all. She felt sorry for her real dad, and Storm wanted to ball like a baby that she had missed out having him as a father. But then, she wouldn't have met the doc or her mates.

"Quit worrying. I promise not to attack the man, but I can't promise the doctor if he shows up here again," Nolan grumbled and lifted her up into his arms as he came back into the room.

She went to grab at the covers, but he was quickly pushing them out of the way. "I've seen your body, little pixy. Even though I haven't explored you thoroughly, which I will soon, now is not the time or place." He stepped into the tub, still holding her and sat in the bubbled water without a slip.

"Impressive, wild man, now you going to tell me about

your other half?" Storm asked, a little embarrassed as he picked up a sponge and started to wash her. Matty stepped in a few seconds later, and Storm now realized why the tub was so large.

"Father has been told. Breakfast will be ready in an hour. Nolan is right, Storm, now is not the time. We have a party to get ready for and a family to get to know. But we do need to find out what is up with that doctor because I have to agree with Storm, something was off about him. I've been around pixies, and he's just not the same. Not to mention the fact he's hiding something."

"And he enjoys handing out pain. Do you know when I first got there, the asshole once more grabbed onto my head, trying to see what was going on was his excuse? Needless to say, he never touched me again. I didn't know where I was, but the moment I saw my father come into the room, well I kind of flipped out."

"I can understand that, little pixy, but I want to know why he had the court's physician looking for you?" Matty said, reaching over and lifting her foot up and starting to wash her leg.

"Actually, it was her cousin that found them, I believe, and I have to say, I feel sorry for that SOB because when my brother finds his butt, well, there isn't going to be much left. You do not lie to my brother, not to mention take one of our family."

Storm looked over her shoulder at Nolan. "He won't kill him, will he?"

Nolan kissed her nose. "No, but he'll be feeling some pain that is for sure. Enough of this, Matty and I have something for you. Matty..." Nolan said, nodding to him.

Matty lowered her leg and held out his palm. "May I have your left hand, please?" Matty asked.

She looked from Matty to Nolan. "What are you two up to?" Storm asked but placed her hand into Matty's, but what she wasn't expecting was the ring he slid onto her finger.

"Marry us, Storm, be our wife, lover, mate, and the keeper of our hearts," Matty asked, his gaze holding hers.

* * * *

In between smiling and growling, Nolan was ready to bite the ass sitting across from them. Storm was grinning from ear to ear, staring at her hand and listening to her father.

"Okay, it's obvious you are distracted here. Care to share, Storm?" Drake asked, grinning and winking at Nolan.

"I'm getting married," she waved her hand at everyone. Elf, Nava, and Darla all screamed and came over, giving Storm hugs, careful not to bump her head.

Doc Lope laughed, leaning against the wall, watching as her father frowned. "From what I've heard, you have just met Nolan, and Matty you were having problems with, do you think this wise?"

The room grew quiet except for Nolan's growl. Storm reached over and rubbed her hand over Nolan's shoulder. "You promised, wild man," she said and leaned over the table, starting at her father.

"I know you are my father, by blood, but these people have kept me safe, and I love them. Is it fast? Yes, it is, but from what I heard, the mating bond is always like that. Weren't you mated to my mother?" Storm asked.

"I'm sorry and no. I'm afraid it's my fault your mother was like she was. I met your mother at a party my human friend was having. She was beautiful and the sweetest thing I had been around in a long time. I took her out a few times when we found out she was carrying you, Storm." He leaned over and squeezed her hand.

"You were my world. I invited your mother to live with me, told her I'd take care of her, but I didn't realize until it was too late what our world would do to a human not bonded to someone. I promised myself right then and there I would take care of your mother and you, but somehow, she got away from me and took you, too. I found out later it was a friend that had brought her back to this world, not realizing what he had done. You were only four when she took you away from me. I don't know how your mother hid you from me, but I've been searching for years for you. Do you know where your mother is now?" he asked, and Storm shivered, pulling back, curling up close to Nolan and Matty.

Doc Lope came over and sat down. "I found your, daughter."

"Our..." Storm interrupted. "You are my father, too," Storm said, glaring at Doc Lope, who laughed.

Doc Lope laughed. "Sorry, little pixy, just didn't want to step on toes. *Our* daughter in an alleyway in New York. She had been beaten, starved. Storm didn't even realize what she was for a while when she started to heal. It took a good year before Storm would sleep in her bed instead of a corner of her room with a blanket wrapped around her. But in school, our daughter was number one in her classes. Darla here noticed Storm's love for clothes and sewing and those things. Needless to say, after about twenty different classes online, Storm started to design and create her own clothes. Our daughter is amazing and has a heart of gold, clothing all new ones that come here, including her sisters."

"Not to mention that our Storm has also been asked by many New York fashion houses to design for them, but she has turned them down again and again. When she has extra clothing, she goes to nearby shelters and gives them away," Darla added, winking at Storm, who moaned.

"You're making me sound like a saint here," Storm grumbled.

Doc laughed. "Do you really want me to get into the other side of you, dear? Like the fact you made your mate wear tight pants for the last two months."

Drake grumbled. "Or the spell you put on him every time someone touched him."

Nolan smiled, seeing Storm's cheeks pinken. "I do believe you are blushing, little pixy." Nolan leaned over and nibbled her neck.

"Storm, don't you think it's time to tell us what happened to your mom?" Nolan asked, hating to when he knew it brought her pain, but his woman needed to get this off her chest if she was going heal inside.

Her sad green eyes filled with tears, and Nolan couldn't help but lift her up, placing her on his lap. "Tell us, little pixy, get it out into the open. It will help," he encouraged.

"They killed her. In the end, she tried to protect me, but they killed her," Storm cried and buried her face into his chest. "She said she was sorry, that it was time for her to go that someone was coming to take care of me." Storm looked over at Doc. "She knew you were coming. I don't know how, but she saw the life I was going to have with you. The only thing she didn't admit was about you." Storm glanced over at her father. "I think in her mind you were dead in the end. You see, Mom started with the drugs right off the bat as soon as we left you. Things went from bearable to a nightmare in a matter of weeks. By the time I was eight, I was trying to find food for both of us, but the men... It wasn't pretty."

"Who killed her," her father snarled.

"Is that why you won't go to New York? Are you afraid of someone there?" Doc Lope snarled. "Are they the ones that marked your back?"

"Yes, but I don't want to talk about it, and I won't go back," Storm said, her gaze snapping to Doc's. "You will stay away from there, too, please."

Doc's chair flew back, and he snarled. "They threatened me, didn't they? Whoever this is found you and threatened me!" he snarled. "I want to know who, Storm Marie Lope!"

Storm flinched. "But..."

Doc Lope reached over and grabbed her chin. "Little pixy, they're not going to hurt me, I promise, but these people hurt you and should be taken care of. The thought they came here, in our city, and threatened you just pisses me off. Not to mention what Sheriff Theo is going to say about this."

Nolan glanced over his shoulder as Theo pushed into the room. "You called?"

"Well crap," Storm mumbled, glancing at him. "A little help here?" Storm asked.

"Sorry, little pixy, I agree with Doc Lope. When we have children, do you want to risk these people coming here with our children?" he asked.

"That's not fair," she sighed and rested her head on his shoulders. "It's not a person but a gang. Mom, for some strange reason, thought tying herself to the gang, they would protect us. Boy, was she wrong." Storm rubbed her cheek on his shoulder. "They call themselves," Storm smiled and glanced up at Doc. "The Wolves."

"The Wolves! This is rich. Theo, have you heard of this group?" Doc Lope asked.

"No, but that means nothing if they are not from around here," Theo said, leaning against the door. "Have they been here in the city?"

Storm ducked her head. "Yes, a few times."

"You are damn lucky you are an adult because right now..." Doc Lope stomped out of the room furious.

Storm went to jump up, but Nolan held onto her. "No, Storm, he needs to cool down. He'll be back."

Tears rolled down her cheeks. "I couldn't lose him, too," she whispered, but Nolan knew the doc had heard her as he snarled and howled in the next room.

Chapter Six

Storm knew everyone would be furious with her, but she needed the air and to be alone. She held up her hand and smiled. The ring on her finger was the most beautiful thing Storm had seen. One single diamond with rubies surrounding it. She didn't know how they had known that the ruby was her favorite, but Storm didn't care.

She curled up in her window seat, staring down at the square that had been destroyed. Storm could have been killed down there, but she'd do it again if it meant Malcom survived. She glanced up at the clock and smiled. Thirty minutes until she could go visit the little boy that had captured her heart when they had rescued everyone at the one facility.

From what Storm had heard so far, not one of his family members had been found. Alex was seven years old and a bear shifter. Even though there weren't any bear shifters around here, Alex hoped that she and her men could still adopt him.

Today, she would ask Alex if he would like to be part of her life. Her father was alive and wasn't going anywhere, it would seem, that was after he got back from New York. Both he and Doc had taken off together, promising to be back later that night.

Slowly getting up, Storm grabbed the bag she had for Alex and was about to leave when Matty and Nolan stepped into her apartment followed by Sheriff Theo. Oh yea, she was in serious trouble here by the look on Matty's and Nolan's faces.

"Explain," Nolan growled, stepping up to her, taking the bag in her hand.

"I have business, and you can't come. It wouldn't wait. He wouldn't wait," she said, picturing Alex when he got the game system she had purchased for him.

Her wild man growled. "I'll kill him. What man?"

Storm rolled her eyes. "Look in the bag," she said, waiting.

Nolan looked in the bag, frowning. "You purchased a game system for a man?"

"There is no man, for Pete sakes. It's for one of the little boys we rescued. We have a standing date on Tuesdays, and I missed the last one. I want him to be part of our family, but he has to want it first. He's different, so I want to make sure he understands I'll do anything for him."

At once, both of them relaxed. "Storm, you are hurt. You shouldn't even be out walking around," Nolan grumbled.

"I've been taking it slow, plus I promised him I'd be there, and I wasn't. He's had so much happen to him. They beat him, Nolan. I saw the whip marks. He won't tell me what happened yet, but I see so much pain in his little face."

Matty reached up and cupped her cheek. "You've bonded with him, haven't you? Why is he different, Storm?"

"He's a bear shifter," she said and sighed. "Yea. The first two nights I stayed with him. He reminded me of you, Matty. He wears his hair the same way, and now that I think of it, he has your eyes, Nolan."

Nolan swept her up in his arms. "We'll come back and get your belongings, but for now, let's go meet this boy who has captured your heart."

"I really do love him already. I didn't want to say anything to him until they made sure he had no family." She looked at Theo as they moved down into her warehouse. "Theo ran checks on all the children, and he didn't find anyone. Now, I know there is a chance later on that the mother or father might show up, but we can't leave him there wondering. He doesn't even know any family. All he's know is the prison they were in."

Theo nodded and opened the door for Nolan. "I'm afraid Alex was one of the bad cases of mistreatment we found. There were about fifteen children that seem to bear the brunt of the abuse when it came to children," Theo snarled.

"I can't wait 'til we wipe these assholes out," Matty said, and Storm could see the worry on his face about his brother.

She looked up at Nolan, who shook his head. "Nothing yet," he whispered.

Matty reached over and squeezed her leg. "Father is still looking. We have to take this slow."

"What's going on?" Theo asked, glancing at Matty and Nolan.

"Nothing right now, but as soon as we figure this out, believe me, we'll contact you," Matty said as the four of them moved down the street toward the old Norton Estate. "The children still at the old Norton Estate?" Matty asked, coming up to his car. The lights blinked as he opened the door for Nolan.

"Yes, Topper and her sisters updated everything, and there are enough rooms, so the children don't feel cramped. Everyone has been taking turns staying with the children, including Storm. You take care, little lady, and next time someone threatens you, I better hear about it." Theo growled, and she nodded.

"I'm sorry; I was just so afraid for Doc. Seeing what they did to so many people, including Mom." She shivered. "Do you think Doc and my dad are okay?" She looked up at Nolan then at Theo.

"Doc is a powerful man, and he didn't go alone," Theo said. "He took six of his best men, not to mention a few of Saxon's. Let's not forget that Flix does not seem like a pushover either. Believe me, these humans don't have a chance." Theo smiled at her before turning and moving down the main street.

"Look at him. Ever since he found Gwen and her sister, he seems to be at peace. I haven't had time to get over there, but I did send a box of baby things and a box of maternity clothes for her," Storm said as Nolan helped her into the back seat, handing her the bag.

Nolan jumped into the passenger side as Matty got into the driver's side. "You really do too much Storm, and when did you volunteer to stay at the estate? Why didn't I know about it?" Matty grumbled.

Storm smiled, looking out the window. "If you will remember, we weren't speaking much, Matty. I had to find something to do with my time. Plus, it gave me more time with Alex," she told them.

* * * *

Nolan stood back and watched as Storm and Alex hugged each other. Yes, their woman had bonded with the child already. Tears rolled down both of their faces as Storm took off the scarf she had been wearing, showing Alex the wounds on her head.

He had given her another hug almost squeezing her too hard when Nolan cleared his throat, and he stepped back.

"Alex, these two men here with me are my mates. Do you know what that is?" she asked.

Alex frowned and shook his head. "They're big," he leaned over and whispered to her.

"Yes, they are, but they would never hurt you. You see, they are going to be my husbands. Matty has the black hair like you and Nolan has your eyes. See, they are both like you in some way."

Nolan and Matty knelt down and held out their hands to Alex. "We've heard a lot about you, little man. It would seem our woman would like for you to come home with us to live. How would you feel about that?" Nolan asked the child, not waiting for Storm to say anything since she had been hem-hawing all around the subject for the last thirty minutes, and Nolan could see she was getting tired.

"Really? I'd come to live with you in a real home? It would be my home?" he asked, his eyes getting big and round.

His gut twisted at Alex's words, and it took him a few minutes to get himself together, but Matty had that covered.

"Yes, you would. Right now, we are living with my parents, but we have our own section of the house. You will have your own room and lots and lots of family if you agree."

Storm placed her hand on Alex's shoulder and just sat on the ground. "If your real parents show up, we know you would have to go with them, but for now, we want you forever if you want to come."

Alex frowned, staring at Storm. "You're still sick, aren't

you? That's why Nolan was carrying you." Alex crawled into her lap, resting his head on her chest. "I want to come home with you. You need someone to take care of you," Alex said, and Nolan stood, smiling.

"I'll be back; let me tell who is in charge that Alex is coming home with us. Matty, why don't you go with Storm and Alex to gather his belongings. But, Storm, you do nothing, and when we get back, it is a nap for you after we settle Alex in."

Alex got up, helping Storm up. "You really don't have to. I've spoken with Theo, and Lacey is staying tonight with Frost. They both know what's going on, matter of fact." She laughed as a small suitcase appeared on the floor along with a black teddy bear. "I got the bear for Alex after I saw him shift. It looks just like his bear, the black fur and all."

"We'll have to take Alex to the pond. I know he'll love that area and plenty of space for him to shift and run," Matty said.

"You know we can all go running with Alex," Storm said, smiling as they made their way toward the front of the estate where Lacey stood with Frost, smiling.

"We have something for you. Now, I wouldn't give this little guy away, but Storm has been sneaking visits with him, and I know he is yours to love," Lacey said, reaching around the counter to lift a big fluff ball out of a box.

"Taz," Storm squealed, and the little puppy barked and whined, wiggling his tail.

"Frost has a twenty-five-pound bag of puppy chow outside on the step for you, plus dog dishes and such. He is now potty trained, so it's going to be your job, young Alex, to look after Taz."

Matty moaned, and Nolan laughed as the little puppy squirmed almost falling out of Alex's arms. "Matty, grab Storm. Little Alex, why don't you let me hold the little furball 'til we get into the car? Then, you can take care of him 'til we get back to our quarters. He's going to have to be introduced to my brothers' animals, so they leave him alone. I've asked my brothers to meet us at our rooms," Nolan said, taking the little puppy, getting his face all wet with puppy germs.

Storm giggled, and Alex laughed, even inside his head, Alastar and Cahir were teasing him. "You owe me, little pixy," Nolan mumbled as they all climbed into the car. Frost, putting the dog food and items in the trunk, turned to him.

"Alex still has nightmares. We found out he had a little sister, and she was taken to another place about a year ago. There is much inside that little one that hasn't come out yet, but he's a good kid," Frost said and shook his hand. "You, Matty, will be good for him. He'll see that strong men don't have to hurt children and women."

Chapter Seven

"*No! You can't take her; she needs me. Leave her alone,*" *Alex cried and attacked the man who held him, trying to get to the little girl in the other man's arms.*

The little girl had a scar on her cheek, and she was whimpering, calling for Alex.

Alex was lifted and thrown across the room, his head hitting the concrete wall, but it didn't stop him as he shifted, charging across the room toward those that held his sister. But the bite of the whip on his shoulders had him screaming out in pain as it next wrapped around his neck, holding him in place.

Storm woke, sweating and hurting. She was alone in bed, but that was because she had fallen asleep needing a nap, but something wasn't right. Throwing the covers back, Storm dressed herself before getting out of the bed, allowing the rush to her head to recede before standing.

Something was wrong with Alex. The last she knew, he had fallen asleep as she had read him a story. Moving slowly, Storm opened their door, leaning against the doorframe. She blocked everything out, hearing the little whimpers coming from Alex's new room.

She rushed across the hall only to be swept up into Matty's arms. "Easy, little pixy. Take a deep breath. You don't want to go into there being upset. He needs us to be strong and steady," he said.

Nolan stepped in front of them, running his finger down her cheek. "Matty is right. We do this as a family, so Alex can see we are all there for him." Nolan pushed into the room, seeing Alex now in the form of a bear all tangled in the bed sheets, snarling and ripping apart his pillow.

Stay there, Storm, Nolan told her as Matty lowered her

194

feet to the ground, his arm wrapped around her waist. Matty held her in place and placed a kiss on her neck.

Be careful; they say it can be dangerous waking someone from their sleep. Plus, I'd hate to see his claws sink into you. I mean, after all, you two are the bloodsuckers around here, Storm tried to tease him all the while she wanted to pick up Alex and hold him.

Nolan peeked over his shoulder and lifted his eyebrow at her. *Really?*

Hey, I'm worried here. It was the best I could come up with at short notice and not clothe you in steel."

"We are all worried, little pixy," Matty said into her ear as Nolan stepped in closer to Alex, calling to the boy softly, trying to wake him out of his nightmare.

"I'm warning you right now I'm going to replace his pillow when he wakes enough. I don't want him to feel guilty about tearing that up, and he will," Storm whispered to Matty.

"Of course, but nothing else since it's obvious you have already clothed yourself." Matty's fangs scrapped her neck.

"I had to hurry. Matty, have you ever heard of being in someone else's dreams or nightmares?" Storm asked, looking up at Matty.

"I've heard of it, but we'll talk about it later." He nodded toward the bed where Nolan was now running his hand through Alex's fur. The bear seeming to settle down, Storm replaced all his bedding that had been torn up.

Slowly, not to spook Alex, the bear, Matty and Storm moved up to the bed. As soon as Storm sat on the bed next to the little black bear, well not so little creature, as it carefully crawled into her lap.

"I know, Alex. We're all here, and we promise to find your little sister. I saw her, Alex. I can let everyone I know what she looks like, so they will find us when they rescue her." She leaned down, rubbing her head on the bear's, tears rolled down her cheeks onto his fur.

Both Matty and Nolan ran their hands through the little bear's fur, comforting him, allowing him to gather himself until he was ready to shift back to that of the little boy they knew. It didn't take long until the eight-year-old was shivering, wrapping his arms around her neck and holding on.

"She couldn't see well. They beat her one time when I wasn't there, hurt her bad. I have to find her." Alex's little growl was fierce.

Nolan leaned over, covering the boy up with a blanket. "We'll find her. You are very lucky this whole town has vowed to help find those that had been taken and hurt. We'll be here for her, all of us," Nolan said, lifting Alex up and standing him onto his feet. "Go hop in the shower, Alex. Dinner will be ready here in a little while, and you have a whole bunch of family to meet. I'll take this little guy outside since it's obvious he has to use the restroom, too."

Alex smiled at the puppy, reaching out and petting him. "He was afraid of my bear, wasn't he?"

"Your bear is twice his size, and you were not in a good mood. Any puppy would have stayed away, but that does not mean he doesn't love you. Now, off with you, we have much to do tonight."

Nolan got up and turned to her. "I'll take this little guy out, but Storm, no more magic. You've done enough today. Tonight, we are taking Alex to get fitted. I need you to tell me colors," Nolan said, and she frowned.

"I don't understand? For the Halloween party? What is he going to go as?" Storm asked, smiling.

Nolan shook his head, moving toward the door. "No, little pixy, for your wedding. We're having it at the Halloween party."

"We're what?" Storm yelled, jumping up. "Are you out of your mind?" Storm reached up and rubbed her bald head, shaking her head. "No. I want my own hair when I marry, Nolan." She plopped down on the bed and stared down at her hands.

She knew it was Nolan in front of her now, hearing the puppy in his arms. A finger to her chin a little pressure and Storm was looking into his dark eyes. "No matter if you are bald or have hair down to your ass, you are the most beautiful woman in the world to the both of us, Storm. We will marry Halloween night," he cupped her cheek, holding her still as he lowered his head, covering her mouth with his.

He was warm, tasted divine, and in a simple, gentle kiss, Nolan had claimed her right where she sat. The man didn't have to do anything fancy as he lifted his head, placing a kiss on the top of her head. "Seeing you this way reminds Matty and me how close we came to losing the one thing that means everything to us. Our world... shit" Nolan growled and looked down.

Storm fell back on the bed laughing so hard she had tears rolling down her cheeks, holding onto her stomach.

Next to her, Matty smiled and leaned over her, placing a kiss on Storm's cheek. "Good to hear you laughing, Storm. I missed the smile in your eyes. But Nolan is right even though he is covered in dog pee."

"Keep it up, you two, and I'll get even. Come on, little guy, let's make sure you are finished," Nolan grumbled and spun around.

"Nolan, if we are really going to do this on Halloween, my dress is going to be black and red," she grinned when he stopped and looked over his shoulder.

"What are you up to?" he asked before reaching for the door where Darla, Nava, and Elf stood with Charm. All four of them glanced down at the puppy then the spot on his clothes, smiling.

"Don't say a word. Darla, we are going to count on you to keep Storm from using her magic while she's with you ladies," Nolan grumbled and moved out of the room. That is when she heard the little girls laughing before they came running into the room.

* * * *

Nolan took a deep breath; rain was going to move in soon. He had always loved when it rained; it always washed away the scents of so-called civilized people. Nolan had stripped his ruined shirt off before coming out to the gardens.

For living in the desert, Darla and Drake had created a world onto itself in the caverns. He had seen at least three different areas with different landscapes, each one more beautiful and different from the first.

"I figured you'd be out here," Alastar said, coming to stand next to him, his other brother Cahir on the other side of Nolan. "Heard puppy had an accident on you?"

Nolan heard the teasing in Cahir's voice, but he chose to ignore it. "Any word on Doc Lope and her father?"

"They found a few of the members but not the ones that did any of the damage. Also, I've heard the royal physician has gone missing." Alastar grinned.

"What did you do? I don't need trouble now with us getting married on Halloween night. I want Storm's night to be perfect." Nolan glanced at his brother, who was shaking his head.

"It wasn't me, even though they thought so, paying a visit to me just a few minutes ago. I told his royal highness that something was not right with that man. Even the beasts wanted to tear him apart. It took everything in me to control them. Plus, I don't know why, but they have a thing for your woman. It would seem she made an impression on them when they were hunting a few weeks ago and came across Storm."

"Do you think we have to worry about the doc. I hate to say it, but even calling him Doc just does not sit right with me," Nolan growled. "Did his scent remind you of something? I know I've smelled it before, but I can't place it."

Alastar reached down and picked up Taz. "Maybe that is why the beasts have been acting up. Cahir, what do you think?"

"The one room with all the blood and medical equipment in it. Where we found the dead man when we rescued Elf and the others," he said.

Nolan froze and turned to Cahir, who was never wrong when it came to scenting anything or anyone.

He nodded. "I walked by..." his brother glanced around them, stiffing up. "We have company."

"Hello, gentlemen, was looking for my brother, have you seen him?" Ringo asked, coming toward them. He'd been in the gardens, and Nolan could kick himself for not realizing he was out there.

"I'm right here," Matty said, moving into the massive garden, joining him.

"Mom told me you were getting married Halloween night; congrats. Was wondering if you needed any help planning. I'd love to help my little brother," Ringo asked, and Nolan frowned, sensing a lie in those words.

"Of course, we would love to have you stand up with us as my brother's will," Nolan said, reaching over and wrapping his arms around Matty, knowing right now was difficult for him. Nolan scrapped his fangs against Matty's neck. "Also, we have a few of our family flying in tonight for the event. Is there anywhere they can stay in town?"

"I'm honored to stand for you. Mother will not allow family to stay in town. I'll inform the staff to get a few rooms ready. How many of your family are coming?" Ringo asked, moving past them, heading toward the tunnels.

"All of them. I'm afraid they threatened each of us. If we ever found our other halves, they would all be here," Alastar smiled. "We kind of gave our family hell growing up."

Ringo threw his head back and laughed. "We haven't opened up the lower caverns in a long time, but it looks like we will need to. On it. See you guys at dinner."

A few minutes later, when everyone knew he was gone and there were no others in the garden, Matty growled and pulled away from him. "He lied to us! My own brother lied to us. I had hoped, but..." Matty shook his head and looked up at Nolan. "He won't be at our wedding. Something is going to happen on Storm's night; I can feel it."

Nolan nodded. "I feel it, too, that is another reason we called in our family. Well, Alastar did. Cahir?"

"He was meeting the good doctor. I could smell him on Ringo as soon as he walked up," Cahir said as Drake and the king of the pixy walked into the gardens.

"My physician was here?" he asked, glancing at his brother, and Nolan snarled.

"Don't even go there. If my brother had done something to this man, he would have told you. He hides nothing," Nolan hissed. "Drake, we need a private word with you, please."

Drake glanced at the king. "He is right. My men would inform you if he destroyed him. He hides nothing, not even his pets, I'm afraid." Drake gave Alastar a look, and his brother snorted.

"They have minds of their own. Sometimes I can control them..." his brother left it at that, lowering Taz to the ground. "If you excuse me, I have work to do. We are meeting Mom and Dad at eleven tonight to inform them what is going on."

"We'll be there. Don't lose him," Nolan said.

"Lose who?" Drake asked as the king looked around then vanished.

"My brother. He lied to us, Dad. Told us he would be at our wedding and lied about it. Not to mention he was meeting with the good doctor you two were looking for," Matty said with disgust. "They're both part of this hurting and kidnapping."

Drake snarled. "We're not sure of that."

Alastar walked by Drake but stopped. "You will be on Halloween night when everyone in town but your son is coming for this Halloween party. I already have my cousins in the room, but I need help. With the pixy around here zipping in and out, this man can place anything, including bombs, around. I'm going to ask Doc Lope if he has any men that can sniff out the explosives." His brother glanced at him. "I'd move the wedding to Ireland, away from all of this. It would be safer."

"Not if the good doctor knew where we were. Plus, this town is Storm's home." Nolan shook his head. "Hell, in the short time we've been here, even you have fallen for this city of Magic," Nolan said, and his brother nodded.

"The three of us were meant to be here, but it still does not mean it is safe. Excuse me." Alastar left.

Drake glanced up at Nolan. "You know he's right. Ever since this, we can't even say that. This GSP was here before we knew about Nava. If I had Porter's skinny neck in my hands again..." Drake snarled. "Since it seems the good doctor is part of this, it's only fair that the king supply some of his warriors to help guard our home." Drake spun around and followed after Alastar.

"Well, that is not going to go very well. Let's hope with Dad's temper he doesn't start a war with the pixy this night,"

Matty said as he scooped up Taz and started to head toward the dining room where everyone would be meeting for dinner.

"Was the so-called doc the only scent you picked up that was pixy?" he asked his brother Cahir. "And can you tell the difference by scent for their species like we can for shifters?"

"They are different, but did we rescue any pixy from the compound? I would need to know this before I could tell if there were more," his brother said.

Chapter Eight

$\mathcal{N}$ails and toes done thanks to Charm, owner of Enchant-ed Charm's Parlor, she smiled looking at her hand. "Well at least my hands and toes will be ready for Hallow-een," Storm said, glancing over at Elf and Nava.

Traveling down the tunnel toward the kitchen, the chil-dren in front of them so they could keep an eye on all of them. "Elf, you every remember a so-called doctor at the compound with blondish hair with a few streaks of black in it. His hair was to his shoulders, eyes green, I believe, and a nasty bedside manner, loved to dish out pain."

"No, but then again, I was kept separate from a lot of chil-dren and others. Why?"

"Maybe it's nothing, but I have this weird feeling about this doctor that works for the royal family. He's off some-how." Storm rubbed the back of her head where he had hurt her twice.

"No wonder Nolan wanted to destroy the man," Nava said, and Storm smiled, seeing little flames dance around her eyes.

"What's wrong, Momma?" Ana came running back, look-ing around.

Storm couldn't help it and laugh. "You are too much, my dear friend. Believe me, the man got a nice zap, the second time I was so pissed, which I didn't tell Nolan or Matty about. They were all ready to start World War III. Plus, I have a feeling not even my father knows what is going on with the creep."

"Twice," Nolan growled as he wrapped his arms around her from behind.

"We really need to find that piece of..." Matty stopped his words, seeing the children around.

The children started to giggle, even Alex was smiling as he

bent down and scooped up his puppy, Taz. "Is it true he peed on you?" Alex asked, causing everyone to break out in laughter again.

"It was my fault; I didn't get him outside quick enough. So, when the little guy tells you he needs to go, you call one of us, and we'll take him out," Nolan informed Alex.

"Do I really need one of you to come with me?" Alex asked as they started to walk again toward the dining room.

"Afraid so, Alex. I don't want those idiots to get their hands on you again," Storm said and ruffled his hair.

"They come for you, too," Alex said.

"That you are right, which is why Storm will not be going anywhere by herself for a while 'til at least those around here are caught," Matty said, glancing at Storm.

"You know I can disappear, right?" Storm said.

"And if what we think is right, so can a few of them. Maybe tracking you, too. No, Matty is right. All of you do not go anywhere alone," Nolan said.

"Elf, are you listening to him?" Kayden asked as he and Saxon joined them.

"Let anyone try and take my grandbaby," Nava's long-lost grandmother said from behind them.

Storm laughed when Flask appeared next to Calamity Jane. "Who are you going to kill now, little lady?" he asked, yanking her into his arms, once more taking the weapon from her hands. "You don't need to carry your gun all the time, Calamity Jane," Flask said as the gun disappeared.

The woman turned and glared at him. "Just because you're my mate does not give you the right to take my guns, damn it."

"Ohh, Grandma is mad," Ana said.

Storm smiled when she peeked over her shoulder and winked at Ana. Every time Storm had seen the woman, she was a big softy when it came to the children. It was weird though; Nava's parents had only visited a few times.

They all pushed into the dining room to stop in their tracks. The dining room was covered in blood, and Storm knew it was her father's blood. Storm rushed and lifted Alex up in her arms, moving into the hall. Matty, right next to her, took Alex and wrapped his arm around her.

Following her out the door, Nava and Elf carried their children, both of their mates beside them. "I will kill whoever did this to my home," Darla screamed inside the room and stormed out of it as Drake and Alastar came running toward them.

"Is everyone okay?" Drake asked, wrapping his arms around his wife.

"How do they keep getting into our home? I want this stopped, Drake, now. How can we keep our children safe if we can't stop these attacks in our own home," Darla growled, both of the twins hugging her legs, tears running down their cheeks.

"I can clean it up." She looked up at Matty, who shook his head.

"Not right now, but thank you. We're going to have to find out whose blood that is," Matty said and looked up as Nolan stepped out with Theo and Doc Lope.

"We already know," Nolan said as Doc Lope stepped up to her. "I'm sorry, Storm. One minute we were on our way back, then your father said he was being summoned home. I should have known something wasn't right when he thought it was weird."

Storm shook her head. "I just found him. Are you sure it's him? Maybe he's still alive, they just used some of his blood?" she asked, glancing at Nolan, who came over and swept her up into his arms.

"No, Storm, there is just too much of it. The king is in there now. They are trying to locate the body," Nolan informed her, moving out of the hallway and back into the tunnels.

She said nothing, just numb, resting her head on his shoulder, tears rolling down her cheeks. Was it the gang? Had they found out that her fathers were looking for them? "Doc!" Storm screamed, and he came running down the hall.

"What's wrong?" he growled, scanning around, half beast.

"Don't go anywhere alone. It could have been the gang. Please. I can't lose you, too." Storm pleaded.

"Oh, baby girl, nothing is going to happen to me, but to

make you happy, I'll have my betas follow me around like the puppies they are." He groaned, and she smiled.

"I'd like for you to say that to Tarek's face." She squirmed until Nolan put her down, and she went into Doc Lope's arms.

"Please, I'll clobber him," he grumbled, hugging her tight. "Don't you worry about me, and Storm, we'll find who did this, I promise," Doc Lope said.

"I didn't even get a chance to know him. I knew you two should have never gone there." Storm stepped back into Nolan's arms. "If it was them, they're not going to stop. That was just a warning."

"Well, we'll just have to finish it because no one kills my family." The king appeared next to Doc Lope. "Alastar has asked for help, and I'm granting it. Anyway, Nolan, Matty, meet Travis and Zack. They are now Storm's personal bodyguards. I also have ten other men searching the grounds for your father's remains. We'll find him. In the meantime, you will go through with this wedding. He'd want that. If you don't have anyone yet, I'd like to offer my services. I've married a number of people, and I'd consider it an honor to marry you three."

Nolan bowed his head. "Thank you, we would be honored to have you."

"But," Storm glanced over her shoulder at Nolan then at Matty, nodding. "We'll do it and screw the assholes."

"That's my girl," Doc Lope said.

* * * *

Nolan glared at his brother. "How the hell did this asshole get into this place let alone kill her father, a warrior for the damn king?" He snarled, pacing in his brother's room.

"You know that was a personal threat to Storm, that whoever did this is not going to stop," Alastar said, drumming his fingers on the small table. Around him, the Beasts of Tuamgraney snarled and paced back and forth, smelling the blood even from this distance. "If this gang is human, which I don't think they are, there is no way they could have done this to her father. So, it's going to have to be someone else."

"I know. I've spoken with Theo and Matty about this after we got Storm and Alex settled in our suite. His mom and Doc Lope are staying with her right now along with the other women." Nolan glanced at Matty, who leaned against the wall, listening. "I agree on the gang theory, too. I have to ask this. Is there any way that Keyys and Ringo were in on this? We knew he lied about being at the wedding and that he is now speaking with the disappearing doc."

Matty growled as Drake glared at him. "Are you sure Ringo was with that doctor?" Drake asked.

Matty sighed. "I'm sure. I could even smell Keyys on him earlier. When Nolan asked him to stand up for us, he lied, saying he'd be there and he was not happy their family is coming here, too. I hate this," Matty snarled, swinging around and slamming his fist into the wall. The wall gave way but not without some damage to his mate's hand.

Nolan moved to him and took his hand. "I know this hurts, and I'm sorry. I wish there were some way to make this right for your family. Do you think maybe they have something on Ringo? Maybe trying to blackmail him or something like that?" Nolan asked, cleaning off Matty's hand with a towel Cahir handed him.

"I have no idea. Ringo has become so secretive in the last four years. We used to do everything together; now, he's not even here most of the time," Matty said as Nolan wrapped his hand as Storm flashed into the room next to them.

"What happened?" she asked, taking Matty's hand, lifting the towel, and looking at the wall. "I see it was a tie, both are damaged."

"And what are you doing here? Didn't we ask you not to use your magic anymore today?" Matty asked, frowning down at her.

Storm waved her hand, dismissing his question. "Like I wouldn't come. You are hurt, dummy." Storm rewrapped his hand. "You're going to need some ice until the swelling goes down."

"Don't," Nolan said, wrapping his arm around her and yanking her back. "Matty is right to ask you that question.

His hand is nothing compared to what you have been through, little pixy."

"Agreed," Doc Lope growled from the door where it was obvious he had run all the way there.

Storm ducked her head. "Sorry, Doc. But I had to make sure he was okay."

"This is as much my fault as it is hers. Sorry, Nolan, Storm, Doc." Matty leaned down and placed a kiss on her cheek. "I'll be fine. Go back with the doc, and we'll join you in a few as soon as we're done here."

"Storm, did you know the wolves are a mixed gang? From what Doc was told us, he scented wolves, blood drinkers, witches, and a few like your father. Your father, before he left, informed Doc that there were at least two from his world that were associated with this gang," Alastar said, getting up as the beasts gathered around Storm.

"Okay, brother, your pets are getting a little docile here," Nolan grumbled as Storm slid down to the ground and started to pet the wild ghostly creatures.

"I didn't even know what I was, Alastar. How could I recognize others? My mom and I stayed in a run-down hole in the wall in downtown New York. It was off an alley that hadn't been touched in years." She smiled. "It used to be a dress shop. When mom was clear-headed, which didn't happen often, we would have fashion shows. Dress up in the leftover clothes there. It's one of the things we had in common. Mom loved to dress in nice things, well did until the last year or so."

Doc Lope came over and went to pick her up when the ghostly animals growled at him. Doc Lope growled right back, lifting Storm up off the ground. "Come on, my little pixy, you need to rest and eat. Plus, I believe Alex is waiting for the food with Darla. Don't be long; Saxon and Kayden went to pick up food from the Krazy Kettle," Doc Lope said, walking out the door with their mate.

Nolan turned and stared at his brother. "We'll find them," Nolan snarled.

"It's already in the works. We have men searching for every last one of them. Two of Doc's men stayed and met up with a few of my men. We'll find out at least what is going on with this gang. But for now, we keep Storm surrounded. As for the wedding and the party, with the king's help and others, the town will be sealed off tomorrow. Nothing will get in or out," Drake said, moving toward the door. "Let's go, gentlemen. I, for one, am not passing up food from the Kettle. Plus, Darla will have my head if we are not there," Drake grumbled, which had Matty snorting and Nolan smiling.

There was one thing for sure, he and Matty would do anything to put a smile on Storm's face. But the next few days were going to be hard on their woman, knowing Storm would have to go back to her father's place to take care of his belongings. Their honeymoon would have to wait until they knew for sure there wasn't someone out there targeting their woman.

Storm stared out at the garden. Taz was out there running around doing his business. It was late, and both her men were snoring so loud Storm couldn't hear a thing, let alone sleep. So, she had gotten up and grabbed the little thing while checking on Alex.

For a change, Alex was finally sleeping, and she had a feeling Doc Lope had done something about that. She sat down on the bench, pulling her legs up and wrapping her arms around them, her toes peeking out of the nightgown she had put on. Storm took a deep breath, breathing the night air in.

It had been a long day, and tomorrow would be even longer. In the morning, the king was going to take her to her father's home. She had asked him. For some reason, Storm didn't believe her father was dead. Something was missing.

Her father was a warrior through and through. No, something was up, and she refused to mourn someone who Storm believed was alive. She rubbed her cheek on her knee and glanced down, wincing when she noticed Nolan's brother's pets staring up at her.

"Please, tell me your master isn't around, too," she said and looked around. Sure enough, Alastar came strolling toward her carrying Taz, and she knew Nolan would be there any minute. "You big squealers," Storm hissed at them. "See if I give you treats next time."

"Storm," Nolan said behind her, placing his hands on her shoulders and squeezing. "And you are out here by yourself because…" he asked as Alastar placed Taz in her lap.

She looked around. "Is there anyone around us? I'd like to ask you two a question without others around, well Matty could be here, but we'll tell him when we get back since I know he's awake." Storm covered her mouth with her hand.

"Sorry, kind of wound up for some reason."

Nolan lifted her up and took her seat, placing her onto his lap. "No, no one is around. What do you want to know, little pixy? But we will be speaking about you coming here alone later." He placed a kiss on her cheek before reaching over and rubbing Taz's head.

"I don't think my father is dead. I believe someone did that to make it look like he is," Storm said.

Alastar frowned and glanced at Nolan. "It was a lot of blood, little sister, and from what the king... Shit. We took his word that it was his blood."

"Not to mention the fact there was just too much, even if one of us drained someone, there wouldn't be that much blood," Nolan said, rubbing his chin on the top of her head. "But why would he do this, or why would someone do this?"

This was where she knew Nolan was going to blow his top. "I've asked the king to take me to my father's house. I told him I wanted to visit where I grew up."

Nolan stiffened under her and snarled. "And when were you going to inform us of this? Were you going to inform us?" he snarled and turned, so she was staring at him.

"I'm not that damn stupid," she snapped back and moved to get up, but Nolan pulled her back up against him.

Nolan took a deep breath. "I'm sorry. I shouldn't have snapped. Is there a reason why you are going there?"

"I don't know if it means much, but when I was small, I had a secret place in the house. My father showed it to me. Told me if anything ever happened, Mom mostly, to go there. I know I was little, but every night he told me this before I went to bed, without mom knowing about it. He told me it was our secret, and with my mom acting so crazy, I didn't tell her about it. Hell, half the time she scared the crap out of me. But then, there were the times she was normal in the head, but I still wouldn't tell her."

"You want to go to this secret place?" Alastar said.

She nodded. "I don't know why. It's like I have to go there. I didn't explain it to the king. No one but you two, and I'll inform Matty too when we get back to the room. Do you think we should mention this to Drake, too? If my father left a note or something, he might know what to do. Maybe he put a spell on the place, and it's drawing me? I have no idea."

"I'm here," Drake said, coming out of the tunnel. "Matty called, worried. Not to worry, no one is with me. I'm afraid I can't go with you to your father's home. If I did, they would wonder why I was there, too. Take Nolan, Matty, and Alastar. Since Alastar always watches after his brother, it will be normal."

Alastar snorted. "Just like you have this creepy way of sneaking up on all of us, including my pets." Alastar glanced down at the little creatures. "First, you take treats from Storm, and now this, some beasts you are," Alastar grumbled and started to walk toward the tunnel. "I'll be there, Nolan, just let me know when. Oh, and little sister, no more walks alone. You can't sleep, wake one of the bumbling idiots up; it's their job to protect you. I still can't believe she got out of the bed without you knowing about it." Alastar shook his head, grumbling about women as he left the tunnels.

"Come, I'll walk you back to your quarters. I would speak with the three of you," Drake said.

Nolan swept her up in his arms. "Is everything okay?" Nolan asked.

"I don't know if my son has mentioned to you yet about Darla's abilities to sometimes see things? It's one of the reasons I wanted to speak with the three of you. Darla would be here also, but usually, after she has one of these flashes or whatever you call them, she sleeps for a good six hours."

"Why do I get this feeling that this flash thing is going to connect some dots to what is going on around here?" Storm said, and Drake nodded.

"You are very perceptive, daughter."

* * * *

Nolan held onto Storm, refusing to release her, afraid she would once more disappear. They were going to have a long talk as soon as Matty's father left. She couldn't keep disappearing and leaving them wondering if she was okay.

Matty and he had come to an agreement. That night, they

would bond with their mate. Sealing their bond with his mates like that in the old days. Loving her thoroughly, joining their souls and hearts, so they beat as one always. No matter where their little pixy disappeared, the two of them would be able to find their heart.

They stepped into their main room, where Matty came over and took Storm out of his arms, hugging her tight. "Not again, little pixy, not again," Matty whispered, placing kisses on the top of her head, sitting on the sofa as Drake shut the door, looking around before taking a seat across from them.

Nolan glanced over at Matty, and he, too, looked worried as he placed Storm between them. "Dad, what's wrong?"

"I had to force your mother to sleep tonight. She is beyond angry and hurt." Drake looked up. "Ringo has disappeared. His room cleaned out except for a note to your mother, blaming her for her own capture with this horrific group." Drake looked up at Matty. "Your mother is going to need all of you. She has the twins, but she's going to need all of her children, Elf, Nava, are going to be the key to keeping her focused. I've informed Theo and the others what we believe since your mother now knows what is going on." Drake got up and started to pace. "Her dream, she saw him in a room with that animal Keyys. What I saw in your mother's head... What they were doing with some of the children and women..."

"Do you think Ringo knew about Elf? That she was family?" Storm asked, and Drake turned to her, nodding.

"I have a feeling it's the only reason why she wasn't hurt more than she was. Keyys, Ringo, and three others, from what I could see, were in charge of the compound we destroyed, but there are others, we all know this."

"Maybe he was trying to get her out of that place? Undercover type of work?" Storm said, trying to give them some hope.

Matty reached over and squeezed Storm's hand. "No, if Ringo knew Elf was our sister, he should have gotten her out long ago with her children."

Drake nodded and moved toward the door. "I know the three of you were planning your wedding on Halloween, but I'm hoping by then Darla will slowly come back to us all. It gives us not much time to find out what is going on. I've spoken with Theo and a few of the men of our town; there will be no trick or treating in town. We're going to have a party for the children here after your wedding."

Nolan sat back and nodded his head. "Our family will be here, and we'll have plenty to help in case we are attacked. But Drake, do we trust this king? Do you personally know him?"

"What I tell you stays here," Drake said. "We found dead bodies at the compound. Children and adults. Most of them were from his world. These idiots couldn't keep them locked up, just like they did with Elf's father, he was killed. No, what they couldn't control, they destroyed."

Storm stiffened. "My father?"

"I don't know, Storm. Go to his home with your mates. I'm sure Alastar will keep the king busy while you search, but watch yourselves. If you feel anyone watching you, do nothing. The king should be fine. But right now, I wouldn't trust anyone around him. Especially with Keyys disappearing like he has." Drake stepped out into the hall. "Storm, no more taking off by yourself. I want all my children to stay safe, and that means staying together. I have called in a few pixies to help. Our rooms have now been protected. No one will get past them or in who mean us harm." Drake turned to them, his eyes were black with shots of red shooting through them.

Matty stood and moved to his father, pulling him into a hug. "You and Mom mean the world to me. Please, be safe," Matty said.

Drake sagged against him and hugged him back, closing his eyes. "If what the evidence is pointing to, I'll have no choice, Matty. You will lose your brother. Your mother and I will lose a son," Drake said, looking defeated as he placed a kiss on his son's cheek and moved down the hall.

Matty turned, tears rolling down his cheeks as he stepped into the room. Both Nolan and Storm moved to him, hugging him tightly. "We are both here for you," Storm said.

"Thank you, having the both of you is what is giving me the strength. Now, explain why you thought it would be smart to take a walk in the middle of the night by yourself?"

Matty asked as Nolan stepped back.

Nodding to Matty to continue, Matty scooped Storm up and moved toward their bedroom. It was time to make both of them his. Tonight, their family would become one, and let someone harm one of his family, they will see the damage the Moree family would bring down on them.

"Come, wild man, you are growling again," Storm said as Matty lowered her to the ground.

"Strip, both of you," he snarled, closing their door, knowing they would hear Alex if the nightmares started again.

Storm glanced from Nolan's gaze to Matty's and knew to-night that there would be no turning around. The both of them wouldn't wait any longer by the look on their faces. She reached down and lifted her nightgown up and over her head.

She was naked underneath, and Storm knew they had seen her body before, but this was different. Under their heated gazes, her nipples hardened, and her body woke from the dormant state it had been in the last few years.

Nolan moved like a panther after he stripped out of his clothes, coming to their sides. "You, my little pixy, take my breath away." He cupped her breast at the same time Matty leaned down, sucking the other nipple into his mouth.

Her legs shook as Storm grabbed onto Matty's shoulder and Nolan's arm. Nolan's eyes never left hers. "Are you ready to belong to us fully?" Nolan asked, leaning down, scrapping his fangs along her neck.

She smiled, her legs shook. "I've been yours, but are you two sure?"

Matty growled, lifting his head, and there was no denying he was his father's son, the red dancing in his eyes. "Storm," he snarled.

"On the bed, now." Nolan scooped her up and waited for Matty to crawl on the bed before placing her into Matty's arms. Nolan crawled in the bed, sandwiching her between the both of them.

What was the sexist thing Storm had seen was when No-lan reached over, grabbing the back of Matty's neck, pulling him forward and covering his mouth. Storm worked her way down Matty's body, kissing and licking. She had dreamed of touching and exploring him, and tonight, she would do so.

Matty had the six-pack many women worshiped, along with a tattoo of a dragon that covered his skin. Storm placed a kiss on the top of the dragon's head. She had always thought of getting a tattoo, but she had thought of having one on her lower back or one that wrapped around her breasts that would cover the scars she had.

Both men reached down and pulled her back up. "Hey, I was having fun," Storm moaned as Matty kissed and licked the scar on her left breast.

"We love you just the way you are. If you would like a tattoo, I have no problem with it, but it will be done by someone we trust if we're going to allow them to see what belongs to us," Nolan said, tracing the one scare on her side. "We'll find the others of this gang one day."

Storm glanced over her shoulder. "Don't bring them into this, please. I want our night to be special, to forget."

"I'm sorry, little pixy, shouldn't have said that. Let me make it up to you," Nolan said, kissing a path down her back, squeezing her ass cheeks as Matty covered the front of her.

"Well, damn," she muttered, grabbing onto anything she could. The nip on her butt cheek had her jumping, but they held her down, not stopping. Her body warm, started to tingle with all the kisses and nips to her skin.

Nolan sat up and took one of her legs, lifting it up, as Matty moved down, opening her pussy lips, kissing and licking her. "I knew I would be addicted to your taste. Apples, I swear you taste of caramel apples," Matty mumbled, burying his face into her, his tongue sliding in and out of her, driving her nuts.

"Move over," Nolan growled and lay down next to Matty, her leg falling onto Nolan's shoulder.

She didn't know whose tongue was whose as they both touched and explored her. Two fingers slid into her pussy before moving and sliding them back to her ass. "Hold still, little pixy," Matty said, placing his arm up on her stomach, holding her.

Storm didn't know she had been moving, but now that they held her still, loving her with their hands and mouths, Storm whimpered. "Guys..." She reached down to grab onto them to drag them up but grabbed onto the bed as someone hit the spot inside her that had her trying to either yank away or grind her pussy against them more.

One thing she hadn't even thought of was her magic, but now, inside her, Storm could feel something different. "Stop, oh, my god, stop," she pleaded, but both men only increased the pressure and the pleasure.

Her ears rang, magic floated all around her as her body sang a song Storm had never heard played. It was magical, and the intense pleasure had tears rolling down her cheeks as both Matty and Nolan kissed their way up her body.

The orgasm shook Storm to her core. She was still slowly coming down; it was the most intense yet different orgasm than any other she had ever had. When she could catch her breath, Nolan pulled her up over him. "Put me in you, my heart," he said, lifting her up by the hips, waiting as if she weighed nothing.

With her arms shaking, Storm did as he requested. His cock was thick and stretched her as Storm slowly sat down on top of him, moaning, a small orgasm rushed through her body. "What is going on?" she mumbled and looked down at Nolan as he reached up to bring her down for a kiss.

"Your body is preparing yourself and us for our union. It's normal, little pixy," Nolan whispered, reaching back and separating her ass cheeks, lifting up, nipping her bottom lip. "Never be afraid."

Behind her, the bed shifted as Matty slid on a condom. Storm watched as he grabbed a tube of what had to be lube and spread it over his long cock. "Relax, Storm, you're ready for us both," Nolan said into her ear, nipping it. "Do you allow us to feed from you tonight, my little pixy?" Nolan asked, scraping his fangs across her neck before covering her mouth in a kiss that she swore stopped her heart.

The feelings, the love her man put into the kiss melted her. Their tongues seemed to melt together, swaying back and forth, dancing to the music that wasn't there but only in their minds.

"I love to watch you two kissing," Matty whispered in her ear as he slid his cock up and down the crack of her other hole before he started to inch it inside her. "Relax, we're here for you, little pixy. We're never going to let go of you, Storm. You're ours." Matty grunted as he slid in another inch. "So damn tight; will... not last long..." he said.

"You..." she moaned, breaking the kiss and resting her forehead onto Nolan's chest. Matty was now fully inside her, they ran their hands up and down her, placing kisses, whispering words of love to her while waiting for her to adjust to them both inside her.

* * * *

Nolan nodded to Matty, and they both started to move inside their woman, syncing their movements. Not only was she tight as Matty had said, but Nolan could also feel Matty's cock rubbing up against his.

Matty was right, they wouldn't last long, but he and Matty had made a promise to make sure Storm's first night with them would be something to remember. One of the cherished memories all three of them would look back on.

Nolan released the gift he had, waving his hand. Orange, brown, black candles lit up around the room. Storm's favorite flowers, lilies and roses, had spread around before he and Matty sank their fangs into the sides of her neck, drinking from her, connecting them to her for life.

Her body tightened up, she let a small cry loose as her body shook. Her magic and theirs coming together, surrounding them, joining them. There would be no Nolan without Storm or Matty. They were now a family as both he and Matty released their seed into her, sealing their bond.

That was when he felt it. "Storm," Nolan growled, releasing her and healing the holes in her neck. What he wasn't expecting was her to bury her own set of fangs into his chest drinking from him. It would seem her father hadn't explained everything to them after all.

He thrust into her four more times, his cock still hard and releasing his seed. Yes, this night was special for them all.

She lifted her head, licking the blood from his chest, sealing the holes, as Matty slid out of her, falling to the side of the bed and pulling her to him.

Storm cuddled up on top of Matty before burying her new fangs into Matty's chest, drinking from him as she had from Nolan. Was she a drinker now like them? Nolan had no idea. He got up and grabbed a condom, his cock still hard, needing to finish his claiming.

Matty moaned as Storm lifted her head, her fangs disappearing, placing a kiss on the little mark he knew Matty now carried. Their woman claiming them as they had claimed her.

"It's time, Matty," Nolan snarled as Matty set Storm on the bed and rose. His cock hard, leaking still.

"Yes, it is, but what makes you think you are going to do the claiming this time, my mate," Matty challenged, making him smile.

"I so do love a challenge," Nolan stated, as both Matty and he circled each other. Matty was a handsome man. Storm had been right. Matty took after his father with the dark hair and eyes, but he had his mother's mouth. One he loved to kiss, and soon, his cock would be between those thick lips...

Matty struck, grabbing Nolan around the waist and his hand on his cock, stroking it. Nolan allowed Matty to touch him, but all too soon, Nolan couldn't wait, stepping around Matty in one move, he had Matty up against the bed his ass rubbing against his cock.

"It's time, my mate. I need you," he said, nipping at Matty's shoulder. "I want your cock in her pussy while I claim you. Storm, get your cute butt down here and spread them for our mate," Nolan ordered and watched as a big-eyed Storm slid to the end of the bed.

Matty grabbed onto her legs, separating them and pulling her to the edge of the bed. "That's it, Matty, claim our woman," Nolan whispered.

"This isn't over," Matty challenged. "I'll have that fine ass soon." He looked over his shoulder at him.

"We'll see, now love our woman." Nolan guided his cock into Matty's ass, not giving Matty the time to think.

Matty snarled but slid his cock into Storm's pussy. "Beautiful," Nolan said, surging forward, pushing Matty into

Storm.

She grabbed onto the bed, sweat covered her chest, face. Her skin flushed from their previous round of loving. By the time they were done, Storm would sleep well in their arms.

Nolan picked up speed, thrusting in and out of Matty's ass. He reached under Matty, cupping his balls. Matty leaned further over Storm, sucking her nipple into his mouth. "Such beautiful breasts, aren't they, Matty, so full," he growled, leaning down and sinking his fangs into Matty's neck."

The scent of their loving and the blood that filled his mouth, Nolan couldn't hold back, but a little pixy had a surprise for them both, too. A pulse of magic ran over his skin, like a caress from her hand, sending little electrical pulses through his body.

Matty snarled, reaching down, and Nolan knew he was paying homage to that nicely swollen clit, sending another pulsing orgasm through her at the same time theirs hit them. Nolan sealed the holes in Matty's neck and glanced over his shoulder at their little pixy.

Her gaze met his, and she smiled. "I thought I would help a little bit," she grinned.

Storm ached in spots she didn't believe possible. Not only had Nolan retaliated, but they had also made sure Storm couldn't even move to clean herself, which was embarrassing in itself. When she had finally come out of her sexual stoup, she had noticed the candles and flowers. Of course, Storm had cried, acting like a total fool.

Both of her men had held onto her as she let go of everything that had happened to her over the last two weeks. But Storm had a feeling both of her men were going to be impossible when it came to sneaking off to do the things she wanted.

Doc Lope had come by that morning and had demanded to check her out, giving both Matty and Nolan a look that had her laughing her ass off. Not only that, he made sure to give them a lecture that he'd be watching them to make sure they did right by her. Yes, Doc Lope was an amazing man, the father she never had. But to finally meet the man who was her father, alive then have him ripped away from her was too much.

She watched Alex play with his puppy, waiting for Nava and Elf. They were going to watch the children while Storm and Nolan went to her father's house with Nolan's brothers and the king. You would think she'd be impressed to be around a king, but right now, Storm didn't know what to think of the royal family, especially after meeting their so-called physician, who also had a bedside manner of gremlin.

Early this morning, all three of them had met Elf and Nava in the family quarters to visit with Darla, who hadn't wanted to leave her room. Matty had decided to stay with his mother. All of them had tried to spend some time with her. Even Elf had sat on her bed, holding Darla's hand. The things Elf had shared with her mother had Darla crying, holding onto her, promising her they would build new memories that she just needed time to come to the fact that her son had betrayed them all.

By the time Storm had left, she wanted to find Ringo herself and turn the asshole into a pile of dog shit. Matty and his whole family were suffering, and there was nothing she could do about it.

Dog shit? I'd like to see that, but not to worry, my heart, Mom is doing a little better. Doc Lope was here and demanded she eat. I have to admit that man can be scary when he has to, Matty grumbled, and Storm knew he was thinking of earlier that morning, too.

This talking in her head had Storm frowning. It would take some time to get used to.

All the more reason not to piss him off. Believe me, Doc can be as stubborn as anyone I've seen. I think that's why they call him the alpha, Storm said.

Okay, smartass. You will listen to Nolan and his brothers, right?

Hey, now, that's not nice calling your heart a smartass, Storm laughed as the puppy attacked Alex and tripped him, sending him to the ground where Taz attacked again with puppy kisses. Such an innocent when so much had happened to him.

Nolan stepped up behind her, laughing at the two in front of them, his arms coming around her, holding her tight. *We will give him the time he needs to be a child again, and we won't stop searching for his sister.* Nolan kissed the side of her neck at the same time Alastar and Cahir stepped into their suite followed by Nava and Elf. Their children and Matty's twin sisters with them.

"So, what do you guys have planned today?" Storm asked, hugging Elf and Nava.

Elf glanced back at the door, laughing when Saxon and Kayden came in their arms filled with beach stuff. "We've decided to take everyone to the pond. We're going to have a picnic. If you guys get back early, you should join us. Matty is trying to get Darla to join us this afternoon. It will do her some good to be around her grandchildren and her other children."

Storm nodded and motioned Alex to her. "I've put a swimsuit on your bed. Why don't you go change? There are some flip flops for you on the floor, too." Storm said, ruffling his hair. "Remember, Matty is here if you need him. We shouldn't be long."

Alex threw his arms around her and hugged her tight. "Thank you so much." Alex held onto her.

"For what, sweetie, for loving you? It's easy, and we'll all be here for you whenever you need us," Storm told him, knowing he needed the reinforcement.

Alex stepped back and stared up at her. "You love me?"

"Of course, now off with you. You're going to love the swimming hole, but until you have lessons, you will stay in the shallow end and wear a safety vest."

He moved toward the door and glanced back over his shoulder at her but didn't say anything, going to his room.

"I do believe you just shocked our cub," Nolan teased, kissing the side of her neck before turning and stepping in front of her.

"Sir," Nolan said and lowered his head a little to the king while Alastar and Cahir moved up beside her. "We will be going with my mate to her father's house. With everything happening around us, I cannot allow Storm to leave without us."

"I would expect no less. Come, there will be no one there since her father lived alone. If I may speak with Storm?" the king asked.

"Of course, you can speak with me. Nolan, get out of the way, jeez." Nolan wrapped his arm around her and pulled her to his side, refusing to let go.

"What would you like to speak to me about?" Storm said, giving a quick glare to Nolan before turning her attention back to the king.

"I wanted to let you know you do have family. You have two uncles and an aunt. Plus, your grandparents are still alive, also. They are all asking to see you. They were wondering after seeing your father's home and belongings if you would meet with them?"

"Right now is not a good time, but our wedding is in two days. Maybe they would like to come for that since my father won't be there. It would be nice that family would attend, even though I do have my adopted father, Doc Lope."

"I hadn't realized that you had been adopted," King Neverstream said, frowning.

"Why? Didn't you think anyone would want me?" Storm glared at the king. "My father Doc Lope is an amazing man, and he will be giving me away. I missed getting to know my real father, but no one will replace Doc Lope."

Storm was actually growling, she was so pissed, almost not wanting to go to this other world.

"Easy there, little pixy." Nolan placed a kiss on the side of her head.

"Is there a reason for this?" Nolan asked.

"Please forgive me; we should go," the king said as Alex came running in and hugged her.

"You're going to come back for the picnic, right?" he asked.

"We'll try; I see no reason why we wouldn't be back. King Neverstream, met my son, well he's going to be my son, Alex, as soon as the papers are drawn up." Once more, the king frowned but bowed to Alex.

"It's a pleasure to meet you, young lad. Are we ready?" he asked, and once more, Storm glanced at the man.

"You know, I think I need to do this another time with Matty's mom not feeling good. I'm sorry to be a pain, King Neverstream, but I'm going to stay here for now. Maybe after my wedding I'll feel up to venturing there. If you will excuse me, I'm going to go change into my bathing suit so I can spend the time with Alex." Storm spun, needing to get away from the man. Something was way off with him, and her skin was itching, and her ears were ringing, which was weird, to begin with.

"Wait; are you sure?" the king asked, everyone in the room looking stunned, but she didn't care; something in her gut was telling her not to go with him, and she always listened to her gut.

* * * *

Storm, what's wrong? Nolan asked as the king glanced at him then at her.

Something is wrong with him. I don't know why, but my gut is saying we stay here, and I always listen to it, she told him, and Nolan could mentally see her shrug as if he didn't believe her.

Later we will discuss this fear you have of us not believing in you, but for now, stay in the bedroom while I get rid of this man. Nolan turned his full attention on the man in front of him.

Is it possible for someone to be impersonating the king? Storm whispered to him again doubting herself.

Alastar, Storm believes this man to be an imposter, not the real king. Can you tell? Nolan asked his brother, sliding a little closer to the man in question.

At first, I assumed that all royalty scent was like this Keyys, but I have to agree with your woman, Alastar stated and turned to Saxon, nodding his head but slowly made his way around the man as Drake stepped into the room and behind him the real king.

"Keyys," the king growled and waved his hand as he stepped into the room. "Why?"

Saxon and Kayden pushed the children and women out the door, including Storm, who had come out joining Alex. What she was wearing, he would deal with later, too, but right now, Nolan didn't take his gaze off of Keyys as Matty and Doc Lope joined him in their suite.

"Why do you want Storm?" Nolan growled as Keyys shifted and laughed.

"That is for me to know. As for yo sir. You have been lax, ignoring what needed to be done," Keyys said and was gone before anyone can do anything.

"What the hell? I thought you had him. Why did you release him?" Nolan snarled.

"I didn't. It would seem my former physician has learned more than I believed, but it also shows me he isn't the only one from my world who is working with these people, but why?"

"Well, now that you are the real king, would you mind if I go to my father's home just for a few minutes? There is something I want to check out. It might give us the answers we need," Storm said, coming back into the room with Kayden next to her.

"The others are on their way to the pond. Storm said she needed to come back," Kayden looked down at her. "We weren't going to allow her to come by herself."

Nolan held out his hand, and Storm placed hers in his. "This is important, Nolan. I have to go to my father's home."

You sure as hell are not going anywhere dressed like that, Matty growled in both of their heads, but Nolan didn't say a word, glancing down at Storm.

I don't know what all the fuss is about. I thought you would like my suit? She looked up at both of them, grinning right before she changed her clothes. "Is this better?" she asked out loud.

"Storm, on this, I have to agree with your men," her father said, coming over next to them. "I don't know if it's a great idea for you to go, young lady."

"I have to go, Doc. Just like I had the feeling about Keyys earlier, I have this same feeling and need to go, almost stronger. Like my other father is asking for me to go."

"Doc Lope is right, but if we make this trip quick, no one can penetrate your father's home but me. We're going to go right inside. You will do what you have to then we will leave," the king said, and in the next minute, Nolan was with Storm, Matty, and Alastar.

I don't like this one bit, Nolan snarled, scanning their surroundings, holding onto Storm as Matty also did. *There are men outside waiting. Storm don't say a word.* Nolan connected Alastar to his mates.

"They can't hear us for now. Go do what you have to do, young lady, and make it quick before they can sense you." The king stepped in front of the big window. "They can't see us either. At least, I have an idea who to deal with and not to trust."

Storm pulled Nolan and Matty down the hall. "Do not leave me," Storm said and knew she was scared.

"We're not going anywhere, little pixy, but hurry," Matty said as they raced into a room that was pink and frilly.

"My room," she said, running to her dresser and opening it up. As she moved something, a small opening in the wall, opened.

"I've got it all. King Neverstream, now," Alastar said, grabbing everything in the small compartment as they all once more disappeared, reappearing in their suite.

"They knew you were there. I don't know how, but they knew," the king said, frowning, studying Storm as they were once more standing in their rooms. "Storm, could you come here, please? Doc Lope, what exactly did my physician do to your daughter. I know you were in the room; I can see that, but Keyys could do anything and you wouldn't have seen it."

Both Matty and Nolan held onto Storm as she stepped forward close to the king. Too close to him, but so far, the man had proven himself.

"Would you turn for me so I can see the wound?" the king asked.

Storm turned around; at the same time, Doc Lope stepped up to him. "What do you think? Do you think he put something inside her?"

"I know he did. That is the reason why the last time he hurt you. He activated that little metal thing in your head," the man said.

"What? Get it out?" Storm spun around grabbing onto him and Matty. "Make him get it out of me, Nolan, Matty."

"Easy, little pixy," Nolan said, placing a kiss on the side of her cheek. Matty rubbed her back but not taking his gaze off of the king.

"Can you take it out without hurting her?" Matty asked, and Doc glanced up at the king.

"I can, but I don't know what or if he placed some kind of trap if it was found. If I move it, who's to say the thing doesn't explode as soon as it is detached from her tissue?"

"What?" Storm squeaked, her grip on his arms grew tighter as her legs gave way.

"I've got you, Storm." Matty swung her up in his arms and moved to one of the couches, sitting down with her in his lap.

"May I ask how you called on Keyys to help you with Storm?" the king asked Doc Lope.

"One of the other doctors I work with recommended him. I've worked with this doctor before, and he's one of the best," Doc Lope said.

"We'll have to check him out, too. As for getting that out of her head, I can remove it as fast as he put it in my way. But as I said, Keyys could have left something else in there to hurt Storm. What we need is... my brother. I'll be right back." The king disappeared.

"Drake, how well should we trust this king? Because right now, I don't want to trust any of them," Doc Lope said. "I let that monster touch my daughter." Doc Lope snarled.

"You didn't know, Doc. Alastar, anything in the box?" Storm asked.

Chapter Twelve

Storm slid down on the floor, leaning on the back of the couch. Both Matty and Nolan behind her watching as she slowly went through the box her father had left her. Jewels like she had never seen before filled one container.

But when Storm dug deeper, she found the letter, and it was new. It hadn't been sitting in the container. Hell, all but the jewels were recently put in their secret place, not having any dust or anything on them.

She took a deep breath and opened the letter, knowing her men waited as did the others.

My Little Storm,
I don't have much time. As it is, I wasted what time I had to travel with your doc. We didn't find the ones we were after, but I did find out this gang is also connected to whatever this GSP is that you and the others are searching for.

As soon as I knew that Keyys was up to something, I was ordered to go undercover. Whatever they say, I am not dead, just can't allow my presence known to anyone, including you, my little girl. I am on my way to another location in or around Texas. Somehow, I will get word to you. Know I am with you on your special day, and I want lots of pictures. Please, give this other envelope to your mates, my little Storm.

Love you, my little Storm, always will.

Tears rolled down her cheeks as she looked down in the box seeing the other envelope. "Perfect timing," she said, lifting the letter up, standing up, wiping her face. "This is for you two. If you'll excuse me, I'm going to go throw some cold water on my face."

She leaned down and kissed Nolan's cheek then Matty's, making her way into the bathroom. Her mind partially blocked, Storm shut the bathroom door behind her and disappeared from the room. Going out into the desert, her favorite place, she would sit and watch the sunset.

No, if she were going to live, this thing inside of her would be gone for good. Storm sat down on her rock and stared out at vast canyons of the desert around her. It was time to remove this thing and take her life back.

But before Storm could do anything, she was once more back in their suite of rooms, staring at two very pissed-off mates, the king, and another man she didn't know.

"This is our mate, Storm. Eldon. If you can help her before we spank her cute ass, please do," Nolan growled, flames danced in Matty's eyes as he leaned against the wall, watching.

"Hello, and I was going to remove the thing away from everyone, so no one would get hurt," she glared back.

Nolan grabbed hold of her chin, his nose touching hers. "And what would happen if you removed it and it blew up? You think to sacrifice yourself? Did you think of Alex? Us?"

She pulled away from Nolan, glaring at him. "Why do you think I left?" Storm looked down at her hands. "I'm not about to let anything happen to you three or my father." Storm glanced over at the door where Doc Lope stood. "I'd rather die than let that happen."

Doc Lope growled as did her mates.

"I think we can prevent this," Eldon said. "If you would stand up, please."

That's when Storm turned her full attention on the man. Eldon looked nothing like his brother. Where the king had almost white hair, his brother had black-as-night hair, down to the back of his legs and the deepest blue eyes Storm had ever seen.

"Storm," Nolan growled as she got up and turned around, smiling.

You keep adding it up, little pixy. Your butt is going to be red by the time I get hold of it. You don't need to be looking at him. Nolan growled.

Cool hands touched the back of her head, pushing her head down. "I knew it. Keyys is an armature, which is good news," Eldon said right before the onset of pain in her lower head.

"Storm will have a headache and a little pain, but nothing was damaged, and the thing is out. Keyys had the right equipment, but the idiot didn't know how to work it," Eldon said, stepping back as Storm plopped down on the bed, curling up on it, closing her eyes.

"Little pain," Storm grumbled. "I really do hate headaches."

"How bad, Storm? Like your migraines?" Doc Lope asked as she felt the bed dip and knew he was beside her.

"A little more intense, I'm afraid," Storm mumbled.

"It's not really a headache but a small bruise where the offending thing was. It should ease up in the next hour or two as you heal," Eldon informed her and Doc.

"In other words, for me about four hours," Storm moaned.

"I don't understand? Why would it take you longer to heal?" Eldon asked.

"Storm is half human. Everything runs slower in her," Doc Lope explained before he leaned down, placing a kiss on the top of her bald head.

"Interesting. Anyway, did Briar, you, or her father inform her mates about what happens after being mated for twenty-four hours?" Eldon asked, stepping back away from the bed.

Storm opened up her eyes. "What happens to my mates? They don't get hurt, do they?" Storm asked.

"No, they gain a little of our abilities, also. Ones that will control little pixies who take off by themselves," Eldon said, giving her a look as he moved out of their bedroom but tripped over a rug that appeared out of nowhere.

"Stormmmm," Doc Lope growled, glaring down at her.

"What? I didn't do anything. Plus, I meant to put a rug there anyway," she grumbled.

Eldon threw his head back and laughed. "Yep, she sure does take after her father. I'll never forget the time he got Briar with a bucket of oil and feathers. His mom was furious, but I never laughed so hard."

The king coughed, but Storm had seen the smile.

"Yes, let's take this into the outer rooms, so Storm can rest," Drake said from the doorway.

Storm said nothing but curled up with the pillow. Both Nolan and Matty came over and placed a kiss on the top of her head.

"Rest, little pixy, we'll be back in a few minutes," Nolan told her, closing the door behind him, leaving her alone.

"Finally, I thought they would never leave," the screechy voice of Keyys said behind her. "Time to go bye-bye," Keyys said, but Storm vanished before he could touch her, appearing at the pond where the others were.

"Nava," Storm whispered before falling to her knees.

"Momma Storm," Alex screamed as everything started to go black.

"Keyys bedroom," she managed to get out she hoped.

* * * *

Nolan spun around and ran for the room, but Eldon was already there leaning against the wall. "The weasel didn't think I'd know he was in the room. See, brother, this is what I mean, half of these cowards are lazy," Eldon glared at Keyys as Nolan stepped toward him. "We would like to question him before you destroy him. I believe right now Storm needs you. Someone named Saxon is bringing her here."

Nolan spun around, heading for the door, Matty ahead of him. "I get his ass when you are finished," Nolan growled.

"We'll see if anything is left when I'm done," King Briar said, disappearing with Keyys and his brother.

Running down the hall, both of them met up with Saxon, a crying Alex, and Darla, who came around the corner from the other direction.

"What the hell is going on? Why are these people getting into our home?" She turned and glared at Drake. "How can we keep our children safe if they keep getting in? I thought you had a pixy put safeguards up?"

"I'm working on it, Darla. I'm afraid I'm going to have to change everything," Drake said, wrapping his arm around her, holding on to her tight.

A single tear rolled down her cheek. "Ringo," she whispered, watching as Doc Lope took Storm from Saxon's arms.

"She's used to much energy, magic. See how her skin is clammy, Nolan, Matty?" Doc Lope said as they made their way back to their rooms. "She used to do this in the beginning when Storm learned she could do things. But it would wipe her out for a whole day. With the pain from them removing that thing from her head and this, she's going to be out at least a day."

Doc lowered Storm down on the bed and covered her with a sheet. "Is it going to be safe to have this wedding?" Doc Lope asked, turning to Drake.

"We're going to have a small one with just family and a few friends. The party has been canceled with everything going on, but we have offered to host the little ones' Halloween party. We can't disappoint them," Nolan said, pulling Alex over to him and hugging him. "She's going to be fine. Just needs lots of sleep. I tell you what, why don't we have that picnic here. We can start planning the wedding and your Halloween party."

Darla nodded. "I'd like that. Something to take all of our minds off what has happened. Drake, you get with whomever you have to and get security done. I want our children safe. We've already lost one," she whispered.

"Done, and I'll have the cook bring up more of this fried chicken he cooked up for Elf and Nava. I'm sure they would love to come help plan the party, too," Drake said as they all moved into the family room where Saxon and Kayden and their mates stood waiting.

"Do you mind having your picnic here?" Nolan asked. "I really don't want to leave Storm." Nolan sat down on the floor, pulling Alex down into his lap as Matty sat down next to him.

"Not at all. We need pads of paper and pens so we can write all this stuff down. Saxon, in our room..." Nava said, and he nodded.

"Got it; anything else while I'm there?" he asked. "You want dry clothes?" he asked, and his woman laughed.

"Yea, just grab what I was wearing earlier and Ana's clothes, too," Nava said, looking over at Doc Lope, who leaned against the door, watching as everyone sat down on the ground.

Nolan knew it had to be hard for Doc Lope to watch his mate as a child, especially since this child had been hurt. Yes, Doc Lope was a special man, and he was proud to have him as a father.

"Crap," Nolan said as he heard the voices coming down the hall.

Matty laughed. "Family, I take it?"

"You won't be laughing long when they all pile in here. I have a feeling we're going to have to move to someplace bigger." He frowned and glanced at the door where Storm slept.

"You two go and plan. I'll stay here with my daughter 'til you are done," Doc Lope said as Ana came over to him, smiling up at him, holding up a picture to him.

"For you," she said, holding up a colored picture. "It's a picture of you as a wolf. I dreamed of you running in the woods last night. You were so sad," the little girl said.

Doc Lope knelt down, taking the picture. "I was worried about my little girl. Storm is in there sleeping. Thank you for the picture, Ana, I'll keep it always. What are you going to dress up as for the Halloween party?" he asked.

"I'm going to be a bride," she leaned over and whispered. "I know it's not real, but one day, we'll have our wedding." The little girl touched Doc Lope's cheek. "I know," she said and turned, skipping back to Nava, her mother.

"How?" he asked, looking up at Saxon, who shook his head.

"She has visions, our little Ana. We believe with Ana being more relaxed and safe that her gifts are coming into her slowly." Saxon glanced over at Elf as he moved in behind Ana. "Even Elf has noticed a few things she can do now that she had no idea she could."

Kayden snorted. "And sometimes at the worse times," he snorted, and Elf smacked him on the head, glaring at him. "What?" He reached over and yanked her into his arms, careful of the little one she carried in her arms, kissing her.

Ana giggled. "They do that a lot, and so does Momma and Daddy." Ana leaned over. "Kind of disgusting. I mean, think of all the germs."

Nolan laughed at the doc's expression. "You sure you don't mind?" Nolan asked.

"Go, I have no problem spending time with my daughter since I don't get to see her much anymore. Plus, I have a beautiful picture to stare at," Doc said, winking at Ana as Nolan's family started to come in the room.

The first ones being his mother and father with Alastar and Cahir leading them. His mom came right to him, wrapping her arms around him. "I've heard all that has happened. Rest assured, we are here to help. But, sweetie, this room is a little small for our family," his mother whispered, and Drake snorted.

"Let's go to the room where the Halloween party for the little ones will be. We can get a feel of it and plan." Drake moved his two daughters in his arms toward the door as Darla came over and introduced herself.

"Mom, Dad, this is Matty, one of my mates," Nolan yanked Matty over to get kisses from his mom and a firm hug from his father.

"Please, follow us, Mom, Dad," Nolan said, urging them toward the door when everyone stopped and was staring behind him. "So help me, if you are out of bed, I'm spanking your butt," Nolan growled and turned to see Storm leaning against the doorframe.

She smiled. "I had to say hi since your family came all the way from Ireland."

Nolan ran for Storm as her legs gave out. "Storm, you just don't listen," he grumbled, kissing the top of her head.

"I know how important your family is to you."

He sighed as his mom and father came over and placed a kiss on Storm's cheeks. "You get some sleep, young lady. We'll have plenty of time to get to know each other since we just learned Alastar might have met his mate, too, it would seem?" His mother trained his brother with a look Nolan knew too well.

"Mom," Alastar growled.

"Alastar, you do not growl at your mother." His father smacked him upside the head, and Nolan couldn't help but laugh.

"Just wait, little brother, just wait," Alastar grumbled as Doc Lope came over and took Storm out of his hands.

"Go spend time with your family while my daughter and I talk, and she rests," Doc Lope growled.

"Mom, Dad, this is Doc Lope, Storm's father," Nolan said.

"Adopted," Doc Lope said.

"Father," Storm said back, glaring at him, and he laughed.

"Even when she is sick she's sassy. It's a pleasure to meet you both. We'll speak soon, I'm sure." With that, Doc Lope took Storm back into the bedroom and slammed the door.

Matty laughed and wrapped his arm around Nolan. "I do believe Storm is getting talked to." Matty escorted him and Darla out of their rooms, leading his parents toward the small ballroom, Darla called it, which it wasn't unless you call a football field small.

Chapter Thirteen

Storm stared up at the ceiling in Elf's room. She, Nava, Elf, Darla, and a few women from Nolan's family had all stayed there the night before, giving Storm a bridal party. But it was a surprise to them all that Nava and Elf were also celebrating, too.

The three of them were going to get married at the same time. Saxon and Kayden had spoken with Matty and Nolan, all four of the men planned the party and her day. First, they each had a spa day at Enchanted Charm's Parlor. Who would have thought little Charm, owner of the parlor, had a damn sadist streak in her?

She rolled over and groaned. "Wait 'til I get hold of Matty and Nolan," she mumbled. "Brazilian wax," Storm growled. "They're toads."

"I don't know what you are complaining about," Nava growled. "I still can't believe he told them to wax my mustache! I didn't have one, did I?" she asked, sitting up next to her.

"What time is it?" Storm asked and looked at the clock, smiling. "It's still early. Do you think they are still sleeping?" Storm smiled. "Let's wake them up, shall we?" Storm asked as Elf and Darla sat up smiling.

"Now, I don't normally agree with this..."

Nolan's mother snorted. "I say we fry their asses. Really, who the hell has a damn wax on their private parts? Not to mention our men had to go there and ask for this stuff. Two hundred years I've been with that man, and he asks for this. Oh, he is so going to pay."

Storm laughed. "I was actually thinking of a nice ice-cold shower, plus Nava does the fire stuff."

"Ice is good, really good. Get their blood pumping like

ours was when we were screaming," Fancy, Nolan's mom growled.

"I have a feeling I'm really going to like you," Storm laughed and said a few words, waiting.

Storm! Both Matty and Nolan yelled in her head.

"Good morning; was it painful," she growled in their heads and out loud she was so pissed off, showing them the pain she had been in. Both men calmed down, telling her how much she would appreciate it in the end. "Then, you go and have yourself waxed down there. Wait, I'll make the appointment," Storm snapped. "No, cancel that; they can't see you down there. I know. We'll have our own wax party tonight, and I get to wax the both of you."

Darla fell off the bed, laughing as tears rolled down Elf's face she was laughing so hard. Nava shook her head. "They couldn't handle it. After the first yank, they'd be coming after us."

They all turned to the door and smiled, hearing the pounding on it. "Well, I spoke with my men, and they know better not to come here, so who do you think?" Storm asked.

"Mine," Elf said.

"Mine," Nava repeated.

"Nope, mine," Fancy said. "Stay right there and watch, ladies." Fancy marched into the outer room and threw open the door so hard it banged the side of the wall. "You have a damn problem? Well, let me tell you about what my problem was about," she growled when Storm heard the yelp.

"Woman, what the hell did you do?" Jared, her husband, asked.

"I pulled out only a few hairs; now, you had a little taste of what I went through, you air biscuit," Fancy squealed.

Storm leaned over to Darla. "What is an air biscuit?"

"Fart," Darla said as she winced, hearing Drake yell from the other room.

"My turn," she said. "You three are not to come out of this room," Darla pointed to the three of them. "If your men come here, believe me, I'll send them on their way."

Sure enough, Darla was a tie when it came to handling her man, too. But all too soon, Storm, Elf, and Nava were sitting on chairs getting their hair done by Charm and two of her best people. She actually apologized, saying they had to do it fast or it would have hurt them worse.

However, Storm still didn't believe so and told Charm she wouldn't be going through that again any time soon and so had Elf and Nava.

Charm stood behind her and smiled. "I have something for you. I saw it last month and had to buy it. Now, I know why. I've worked with it some, but I really think this will look stunning on you to match your dress." Charm turned and opened a large box, pulling a wig out, but when the hair touched her leg, she knew it was real hair.

Black hair with red strips, but what was really stunning was the small orange lilies weaved through it. "Are they real?" Storm asked, and Charm nodded her head.

"I worked on it this morning. I want the three of you to have that special day. This town has been through so much, but you three... Well, it's time for you to have a good day, and today is that." Charm put the wig on Storm's head, and Storm smiled, seeing how long the hair was.

"I've always wanted to have hair this long but never really tried to grow it. I just might have to after seeing this," Storm said as Charm danced around her, fixing this and that.

"Okay, ladies, you're going to eat now before the ceremony. Also, we have some things you have to have on your wedding day," Nolan's mother said. "This gift is from Darla for all three of you. It's your something blue."

Storm laughed, knowing it was the garter, but she wasn't laughing when she saw the jewels on it. "Darla, are these real?" Storm asked.

"Mom, and of course, they are real. This one you will wear, while..." Darla nodded to the box. "That one will be thrown. Each of you will give this to your children's mate. Yes, you will all have at least one girl, that much I have seen," Darla said, looking at her, and she smiled.

"I hope she has Fancy's and your temper," she said, all of them busted out laughing.

"Next is mine. It's something borrowed," Fancy handed each of them a small box. "I had a hell of a time trying to think of something, but Darla gave me the idea. Each of those broches is part of the Ireland jewels from our family. Storm, you have my great grandmother's broch, she had a thing for black diamonds." Fancy turned to Elf, whose dress would be green, honoring her father who had been killed. "Elf, you have the emerald; it was my husband's great grandmother's, and Nava, since your dress is red for fire, a ruby belonging to Darla's great grandmother."

"Now, something new..." Darla and Fancy handed each of them another small box. "These are from your men."

Storm slowly opened it up and sucked in her breath. "An ankle bracelet?" she asked, and Darla nodded. She lifted it up and stared at the black diamonds. "My god, it's stunning."

"That is one thing, both of our boys have wonderful taste," Fancy said as Nava held up a ruby one and Elf had the emerald one.

"So, for the old part, there will be no tears, is that understood? I already see them in your eyes, all of you, but you will ruin your makeup. First, Elf, we know your father can't be here to walk you down the aisle, so Drake would like this honor, but Elf, your natural father's family is here. Your grandmother is here, his mother and she has something for you." Both women stepped aside as a woman with bright green eyes moved into the room wearing a formal green dress.

"My name is Sorenta. You are the last person to see my son, but I see him in your eyes. I give you this, Elf. He would have given it to you on this day, but since he can't, I do." She reached out and took Elf's hand and placed an emerald four-leaf clover in it. "It is ready to be worn in your hair. Your father had that made up for his bride, his mate if he ever found her, but now, it is yours."

Both Darla and Fancy sighed as Storm wiped the tears away, and so did Nava and Elf. Elf stood and hugged her grandmother. "You will stay after the wedding so I can share with you what he told me? Plus, you have three grandchildren that would love to meet you." Elf asked.

"Yes, she is already set up in a room in your wing, her and your aunt," Darla said.

"Thank you, Momma," Elf said as she sat back down when the ghost parents of Nava showed up.

Nava stood. "I was so hoping you would be here," she whispered.

"This is all new to us. We have to save our energy to be here with you, but your father will walk you down that aisle, and here is old, even though you have..."

"Don't you say it, Granddaughter," Calamity Jane growled, following behind Nava's parents.

Storm laughed as did everyone else. "Well, this is your grandmother's, and now yours," Nava's mom said, shaking her head at Jane.

"It's not much, but my momma gave it to me when I was small before she died. I want you to have it now," Jane said, holding her hand out. A small bright gold band was there. "It should fit on your pinky."

Nava cried. "I want to hug you, but I can't."

"Bullshit," Jane stepped up to Nava and pulled her into a fierce hug. "Soon, your momma and papa will be able to do this when they get older," she informed her and looked over at Elf. "Your father's spirit is around, but right now, he can't do anything, Elf, until his body is found, I'm afraid."

"Really?" Elf said, getting up and moving to Jane. "You just gave me one of the best gifts. He and Nava are the ones that kept me going, well until my little ones came. I've missed him so much. Thank you." Elf hugged Jane as everyone stepped away from her.

Storm wiped the tears and glanced to see Doc Lope coming into the room, holding two boxes. He leaned down and kissed her cheek. "You make me so proud. I found this at home on my bed. It's for you."

She took the box and opened it to see a small note inside.

My little girl,
Even though you will not see me, I can promise I will be watching as you walk toward your destiny. Matty and No-lan are two fine men, and I couldn't have picked better for my daughter. And if I couldn't walk you toward your men, I'm happy that Doc is doing it for you. He is an honorable

man and loves you as much as I love you...

Storm stopped reading, the tears now rolling down her face non-stop.

Darla sighed and handed her a small towel. "I knew we should have given you three these presents beforehand. We are lucky we have Charm here to help us again."

She wiped her face as Doc moved behind her, rubbing her shoulders. Storm took a deep breath and looked back down at the letter and continued to read.

I heard you needed something old. So, I give you your great grandmother's earrings. By the way, my parents will be coming, so be prepared; they can be overpowering, but they loved you when you were tiny. Love you, Storm, and know I'm there watching.

Storm closed her eyes and turned to bury her face into Doc Lope's chest, crying.

"I know, little pixy, we're both here for you. Now stop the tears and open my box." Doc Lope said.

She frowned, wiping her face. "You've given me too much," Storm said but took his box and opened it. "What? I can't accept this. You should give it to Ana when you marry her?" Storm said, looking down at the little wolf necklace that had been his mother's.

Doc Lope shook his head. "I have something for her. No, this is for you. Even my mother knew when you first saw it that it was going to be yours. She'd be right there in the front row if she could, little pixy. Grandma Susan loved you so much." Doc Lope leaned down and kissed her cheek. "Now, turn around and let me put it on ya."

You okay, Nolan asked, but she knew Matty was listening, too. *You shouldn't be crying on your special day.*

I'm fine, my fathers are just once more showing me how much they love me. I'm very lucky to have two papas like our children will have, Storm said, turning around and allowing Doc to place the necklace on her. The piece was so dainty she was afraid she'd break it.

"I remember Grandma telling me the story of this. Of how Grandpa had given it to her," Storm smiled. "For being so big, your daddy was a teddy bear," Storm said, which earned a snort from Drake as he came into the room.

"Chap Lope was far from a teddy bear. That man could rip you apart with one paw. Where is the old buzzard?" he asked Doc Lope, who laughed.

"Afraid after mom passed, he was restless. He's traveling to the different packs. I think, he was even thinking of going overseas, too. Last I heard, he was in Maine, heading up into Canada." Doc Lope kissed the side of her neck and stepped around her. "He is late checking in though." He tilted his head to the side and laughed. "Well, it would seem your grandmother has given my father a lecture on shirking his duties as a grandfather."

"What? You can talk to Grandma?" Storm asked.

"Yes, I've been speaking with her for the last two weeks. She's not ready to make an appearance yet, but she'll be around, Storm. But she is highly pissed at my father right now." Doc shook his head. "I would expect a visit very soon, little pixy," Doc smirked.

"Okay, everyone out. We have to feed these girls and get them finished up. Come back in two hours, gentlemen. Drake, how are Nolan and Matty doing with the ring bearer?" Darla asked, walking her husband out.

"Little Bear is doing great, more so than his fathers, who keep pacing back and forth. Not to mention our two demons who keep biting everyone's heads off if they get close to them. I swear, you'd think they'd never get to see you three again." Drake leaned over, giving Darla a kiss that would heat up Niagara Falls in the wintertime.

"It would seem someone else has missed his woman," Storm teased, earning a look from Drake before he left.

"All right, ladies, it's time to get serious. Let's eat!" Darla said, moving into the other room where Storm was impressed. The spread of food here was amazing.

"Let me guess, Susanna did this?" Storm asked, popping a twice-baked finger, as her friend like to call them. "She sure does know how to do some great food for Halloween. I can't wait to see our cakes."

Chapter Fourteen

$\mathcal{N}$olan rubbed his arm, glaring at beef man, Doc Lope's father, Chap. Even his mate Matty next to him was growling and glaring at the man.

"I can't believe he threatened to neuter me if I hurt her again," Matty grumbled.

"That's nothing; he told me if I allowed you to hurt Storm, I'd be speaking with my cock up my ass. Man, that man has a vocabulary even bad for our family," Nolan grumbled as Saxon came up to him, glaring at the same man.

"The old coot even got Kayden and me. Kayden is still outside trying to put himself back together. Told us since Storm considered Nava and Elf family, they were his granddaughters, too. I would have called him out, but Ana came in, and I swear, I never saw a man that big go down so hard when Ana handed him a picture." Saxon ran his hand over his face and scanned the room.

Orange, black, red flowers were everywhere. The room itself wasn't as big as the hall they were having the party in for the children, but it would seem half the town was there for their weddings then there was Nolan's family.

Matty nudged him. "I do believe your family has taken up one-third of the seats."

Alastar joined them as Kayden stalked down the flowered path toward them, but he kept looking over at Chap Lope, growling and showing his teeth at the man. "Boy, is he pissed. What the hell did the wolf say?"

"He told Kayden to quit thinking with his cock and get ready for the wedding. It was Kayden's first night alone without Elf, and needless to say, he hasn't taken it well," Saxon said.

"Well, if I'm not mistaken, neither did you," Alastar said,

looking at Saxon. "Didn't I catch you peeking around at the women's door in the middle of the night? But then again, my little brother was right behind you."

"Keep it up, Alastar, and I'll make sure your woman knows all about your little trips home," Nolan snapped.

"I have nothing to hide." His brother frowned and turned to scan the room.

"What?" Nolan asked.

"Others are here," Alastar said.

Chap stood and moved toward them. "I was to inform you that Storm's grandparents from the pixy world are here, plus it would seem the king and queen are joining them." Chap tilted his head to the side. "The king has brought guards, and they are waiting for your orders, Alastar. They are here to help with protection. Oh, and the king is going to do the ceremony?"

His brother nodded and moved toward the king and the other couple. The room darkened, and the roof of the room turned to sky above as candles lit up the room.

"Impressive," Chap muttered and turned to look at each man. "I would give my life for each of you. You are my grandsons. When it is your turn to be papas or grandpas, you'll know where I was coming from this night. Welcome to the family, all of you." Chap grinned. "My mate has informed me I was a jackass and told me to get my ass over here and apologize. Done that, but don't think I won't be watching." He turned to leave and reached up and rubbed his arms. "Woman, when I get a hold of you," he growled.

Saxon grunted, but Nolan could see the big smile on his face as did Kayden. "He's still a pain in the ass," Kayden grumbled before glanced at them. "Are we ready?"

Nolan glanced around the room, the night sky, candles, flowers, and turned to the orchestra and nodded. "Gentlemen, I do believe it's time." Nolan watched as the king of pixies came up, nodding to each of them and taking his place at the front of the altar.

Matty leaned over. "I swear, I've never been this nervous, even in damn school."

Nolan wrapped his arm around him and squeezed. "We

are giving our woman that magical night she so deserves. All three women have been through hell. This Halloween night is their night to shine and to be loved," he told Matty, but both Saxon and Kayden nodded as they stood to wait.

They didn't have to wait long when Elf's oldest daughter appeared dressed in her Halloween dress. She was stunning with her hair all done up with little pumpkins twined in her hair. Glancing over at Kayden, Nolan could see the proud look on his face as Willow glanced toward him and smiled.

The tension from her body disappeared instantly. Nolan leaned over and whispered. "You have gained their trust quickly. I'm impressed; that little girl sees you as her father," he told Kayden.

Kayden nodded. "It took a few weeks, but Willow is one of the smartest little girls. She does us proud."

The music changed as Willow moved forward, and Ana appeared next dressed in her orange wedding dress with candy corn barrettes laced through her curly hair. Her big eyes meeting Saxon's gaze and smiling.

Matty leaned over. "Saxon and Doc are going to have their hands full with that one. She's going to attract the boys."

Saxon glanced at them, smiling, and it was a mean one with his demon side showing. "Human fathers might need a baseball bat, but I don't."

Nolan laughed but stopped as Alex and Elf's little girl Maranda stepped out into the hall. Alex being the ring carrier, or whatever they called it, while Maranda, the flower girl, too scared to do it herself, Alex had volunteered to walk down the aisle with her at the same time.

When Nolan had heard what Alex had offered, he knew his son, and Alex was his son, would be an honorable man. Nolan nudged Matty. "Our son has a very protective streak in him, look at the way he hovers over Maranda."

"We need to find his sister." Matty glanced at him, and Nolan took his hand and squeezed it. "We will, and we'll destroy any of the assholes who have hurt her." Nolan let out a small snarl, and Alex's gaze met his, worry in his eyes.

I'm fine, Alex, just thinking of something. You make Matty and I very proud to have you for a son, Nolan threw in, and instantly, the boy smiled and helped Maranda down the aisle as she spread her flower petals as they came toward them.

Both Matty and Nolan had exchanged blood with Alex. The night after his nightmare, Alex had come to Nolan and Matty, asking for the exchange so he would know where he was. All four of them had discussed it before actually doing it. But now, Nolan was glad the child had brought it up.

Saxon sucked in his breath as Nava appeared on the arm of her father. She was beautiful with her wavy hair streaked down her body. The way the beautician had done her hair, it appeared as flames were dancing down her body.

"I do believe my friend is going to have a hard time waiting 'til after the party," Matty teased, earning a glare from Saxon.

"I wouldn't be teasing because I have a feeling he's not going to be the only one," Nolan said, nodding toward the entrance where Elf stood, Drake standing on one side and Darla on the other.

Nolan glanced at Elf's dress then at Nava's, yep they were in so much trouble. "Matty, look at the dresses," he whispered, knowing that Storm had created the brides' dresses, and sure enough, when he glanced at the entrance, there she was. Their Storm.

Her dress was black as the night, a slit on both sides, showing her long legs and the black garter she wore. The front of the dress outlined her full breasts, and the cutaway allowed everyone to see the swell of them, black diamonds around her ankle and ears, a small wolf around her neck, as she glanced at the man at her side, Doc Lope.

Matty moaned. "I'm in so much trouble." The whole audience laughed, and Storm smiled. Even Doc Lope had a smile on his face as he placed a kiss on the top of Storm's head then glanced down the aisle at Ana.

Storm leaned over and whispered something to Doc Lope, and he smiled, nodding as they made their way down to them. His heart beat fast, and for the first time, Nolan was nervous something would take away this beautiful woman from him.

Nolan scanned around, seeing his brothers in the back. Alastar nodded to him.

We are fine. Doc even has some of his pack sniffing for any bombs and such. We have you, little brother. No one will ruin this day for you.

* * * *

Storm held onto Doc and stared at her men standing at the altar waiting for her. She was really going to get married, and her men never looked so good in their black suits, orange shirts for the Halloween theme. Even the ceiling was a canvas of the night sky.

The scent of flowers, hers and her sisters' favorites, were scattered around the room, but what had her more surprised was to see so many people from town there. What was supposed to be a small wedding sure wasn't that small after all.

Susanna from her favorite place to eat, Lanny from Sweet Tooth, Charm, even Theo, and his new wife were there. Then, she snorted, hearing Matty's moaned words.

"I do believe Matty is having a difficult time," Doc said to her. "I do have to admit you have outdone yourself, Storm. All three of you look breathtaking. You and your men have made this evening magical. Look at the way those two men stare at you."

"I'm very lucky. I have to admit, with Matty, I didn't know if I would get here." Storm glanced over at Matty just in time to see him growl and rub his arm. "I have a feeling my other father just saw what Matty had done to me," she giggled.

I just informed my soon-to-be son that if he hurt you again like he did, I'd be paying him a visit. But, my baby, you look stunning. I love you, Stormy, her father said into her head. As she started to walk down the aisle, lightning flashed across the ceiling, and she smiled, remembering when she had been afraid of storms.

You were born during a storm and had a temperament that could outlast any storm, her father told her as Storm joined Nava and Elf up at the altar with their fathers.

The king smiled. "Who gives these lovely ladies to their

men?"

Nava's father growled, Drake growled, and even Doc growled. All four men straightened but didn't move an inch. Behind them, Storm knew the audience was smiling.

"Her mother and I do," Drake said first followed by Nava's father, and then, Doc looked down at her with such love tears filled her eyes.

"Don't you dare," Darla whispered to her, and Storm laughed, closing her eyes for a second to gather herself.

"I do, her father, and I know her other father would also give her to these two upstanding men if he were here," Doc said and leaned down, placing a kiss on her cheek. "Love you, Storm, be happy." Doc Lope moved her to Nolan and Matty, where they stepped up on each side. "We are trusting you with our hearts, don't disappoint us," Doc said, but Storm heard another growl behind them, and she glanced around her father to see her grandfather growling, too.

"Love you, Gramps," she whispered, and he nodded but kept glaring at Nolan and Matty. She looked at her men, who glared back, and Storm sighed. "Knock it off, Gramps," she said, and at once, he sighed and flinched as if someone had smacked him.

Doc Lope laughed. "It would seem your grandmother is not happy with him either," he said, stepping back as the other parents moved to their seats.

The words were a blur, but when the king and his queen joined them at the altar drawing all their attention, Nolan didn't know what to expect.

"With all the sadness and hurt these three ladies have gone through, I give them each a gift to help them, guide them toward the children they are seeking to help. The three of you are now and always will be children to the court of the pixy. Live a happy and full life, all three of you."

Storm stood there as what felt like being shocked but through her whole body. She swore her blood was hoping all over the place. But the king was not done. He looked at each male and smiled, nodding.

Without warning, each of them jumped and snarled, rubbing the back of their heads. "You now have the gift of going any place you wish, including our world." The king stepped back and wrapped his arm around his wife before vanishing.

Did you know he was going to do that, Storm asked her father.

I had no idea, but my grandparents might have since they are best friends with the king and queen. But it is a great honor. I must leave, Storm. I will speak with you again soon, and with those words, her father was gone.

Nolan turned her to him and cupped her cheeks. "He'll be around. I have a feeling he's going to give Matty and me hell, but it will be worth it because we have the biggest prize of all—you," Nolan told her as he covered her mouth with his.

His tongue sliding into her mouth, dancing the first dance with hers, claiming her for all to see. All too soon, he broke the kiss. "Ours," she said and turned to face Matty.

Matty had tears in his eyes as he took her hands into his, kissing each one before dropping one, wrapping it around her and pulling her up against his body. "I have been a fool. I could have lost you twice, and I promise you here and now, never again, Storm. You are finally mine, ours, and I will cherish you every single day." Matty lowered his head, sealing his words with a kiss that had her toes curling and her heart singing.

Her life went from living on the streets to having a city of Magic turn her fear into love. Her Halloween wasn't just normal, but nothing about the town of Magic was, and she and her sisters wouldn't change it for the world as the three of them turned to face the crowd as they all stood and cheered for them.

"You do know we have to wait until the Halloween party is over for the children before we can take you away?" Nolan growled in her ear as people started to step up to them to congratulate them.

She leaned over and whispered. "But think how magical tonight will be then to wait, just like our wedding. Plus, Halloween is better at midnight when all the goblins and ghosts come out," Storm said, brushing her hand down the front of both of her men's pants, getting a growl from them both.

"Storm, behave," Doc Lope said but smirking at both of

her men.

Oh, yea, her life was full as Alex came over and wrapped his arms around her, hugging her. "You're my momma now. She came to say goodbye to me last night, but she told me we would find my sister, that we would be that family."

Storm glanced up at Nolan then at Matty. Both of them placed their hands on Alex's shoulders. "We love you, Alex, and we are proud to have you in our family."

Yes, her men were her heart, magical just like her wedding.

About the Author

Trinity Blacio has been writing for the past ten years. She is married and has two children, living in Elyria, Ohio. Her favorite things to write and read are paranormal, ménage, science fiction, erotica, and fantasy.

Places to find me.
Website: *http://trinityblacio.com*
Twitter: *https://twitter.com/trinityblacio*
Facebook: *https://www.facebook.com/trinityblacio*
Goodreads: *https://www.goodreads.com/author/show/2856931.Trinity_Blacio*